STONY CREEK C

Stony Creek

Taylor Berke

EROTIC ROMANCE

Siren Publishing, Inc.
www.SirenPublishing.com

A SIREN PUBLISHING BOOK
IMPRINT: Erotic Romance

STONY CREEK COWBOY
Copyright © 2013 by Taylor Berke

ISBN: 978-1-62242-589-1

First Printing: February 2013

Cover design by Christine Kirchoff
All cover art and logo copyright © 2013 by Siren Publishing, Inc.

Printed in the U.S.A.

PUBLISHER
Siren Publishing, Inc.
www.SirenPublishing.com

DEDICATION

To my darling husband, my own cowboy, who reminds me daily that there are men willing to protect, cherish, and honor the woman that they love. I always believed that there was a man who would forever light my heart and soul on fire. You help me every day deal with the stresses of life while enveloping all that I ever dreamed that a man could be. I love you.

STONY CREEK COWBOY

Stony Creek

TAYLOR BERKE

Chapter One

"How the heck did I get here?" Billie wondered aloud.

Dr. Billie Rothman was driving herself across the country to a new life. The question was a thought that had rattled through her head a least ten times a day for the last two days. In the comfort of her Range Rover, she was halfway from New York to Wyoming. She felt awash with so many emotions, excitement, anxiety, fear, and hope. The dominating feeling, however, was confusion. Did she make the right decision? She was a doctor for Pete's sake. Doctors stayed in one place, had longtime patients who brought them cookies and asked about their children. Whatever had given her the courage to make this move had now deserted her momentarily and left her pondering her choice.

Ah, Matthew, what would he have thought about this moving business? Nuts, crazy, and irresponsible was probably what her husband would have thought. He would say, what was she thinking leaving a great job and practice behind? He was always the calm, responsible half of their marriage. He never got too excited and never got too upset. He had always been the voice of reason and was such a good, kind man and had been her friend since the first day of medical school. She had loved and respected him in so many ways, but her marriage had been based on the whims of immaturity and the hopefulness of youth, not on true love. Initially, it was his calmness that had made her feel as safe and secure on the inside as she had always wanted to be. It was that need combined with the hardheaded idea that she thought someone might want to finally love her forever.

Billie was a forever type of girl.

Her mom had passed away her junior year in college, followed by her dad in her second year in med school. "Just love me," she used to say over and over to Matthew. He was now her only family. He had tried, really he had, she mused. However, he just loved being a doctor and the power and privilege that came with it. He loved it so much that there was little room in his life or heart for his wife. He had, however, wanted both of them settled with all the respect and entitlements that come with medical success. She had tried to tell him of her dreams for happiness. She told him that she wanted to travel to see great spaces, practice medicine, and return to the secret pleasures of her youth, riding. He would just chuckle and figuratively pat her on the head as if assuming she was just daydreaming aloud. The need to follow her dreams only seemed to grow as time passed. The more that she tried to explain, the less he seemed to listen, immersed in his world of patients and patience. Then, without warning, he was gone. Taken by cancer so quickly, she still had to catch her breath and blink to believe it was real.

What am I going to do now? she had thought.

Billie shifted her mental gears and thought with the single-mindedness that she had always possessed. "I am going to be a success but on my terms, my way, and apparently, alone." Well, sort of, unless you counted the two huge dogs in the back of truck that could double as elephants. She wasn't about to leave Madison and Zeus behind.

She could always do this. In the face of fear, she had always pulled up her bootstraps, lifted her chin, cried quite a bit, and done what she had to. Laughingly, she realized that there was no longer anything in this world she had to do. She was now on her way to do what she *wanted* to do. Finally.

* * * *

"How did I get here?" mused Jackson while sitting on his horse, Lachlan.

Geez, he thought. Two years ago, he'd just figured it was time to settle down and finally act like a mature man. A rancher his whole life from a family of lifetime ranchers, there was nothing else in this world that even tempted his soul. He was the eldest of three brothers. All shared a love for the crisp, clean Wyoming air and the land on which they were raised. At a mere six feet six inches he was everything you would imagine a Wyoming rancher to be. He was big and brawny, the type of thickly muscled physique that came from a real day's labor and defined a rugged man. With sensuous green eyes and rich chocolate brown hair, he was definitely a man to make a woman stand up and take notice. Jackson bore the air of responsibility that only the oldest brother could wear. He had spent a lifetime of bailing his brothers out of scraps with other boys, schoolhouse pranks, and as they matured, some very irate female encounters. He had to laugh at that. The Powell boys sure did get into sticky female situations. He had had his fair share as a younger man, but now, at thirty-six, he was more mature and, as he thought, past his wild ways. Well, it had just been time.

He had married Gwen, a longtime Stony Creek girl who knew her way around the ranch, tough winters, and men. "Ah hell, that last part hadn't been so bad." Jackson laughed. She sure had tried to wear him out. She just hadn't touched him inside. "Damn, I am starting to act like a woman," he grumbled. He didn't need love, he needed understanding of his seriousness, he needed a woman to get that his job was his only true love. Not so sadly, she left him in a flurry of tears, drama, and runny mascara not more than a year ago.

"You have no idea how to love a woman," Gwen had spat out.

"Really? You seemed quite loved not two days ago," Jackson had said.

"Ugh, Jackson, you don't love me. You only need a body for pleasure and to keep the bed warm," she yelled. "You are a cold, unfeeling man. You have no joy in anything except those stupid cows and horses! I need a man who wants me around, wants to have some fun, ya know! Dinner, dancing, and shopping, Jackson. These are things women want! You are supposed to cherish me, adore me, and spoil me." Wow, Jackson had never thought of that, never wanted that...with her.

"I worked and slaved on your ranch for what? You never bought me a gift, never made me dinner, and I don't see any babies running around here, so what the heck do you need me for? Nothing. I am sorry, but Len Drexel—you know, the guy who hates your guts—has offered me something different, and I am going to try it on for size," Gwen had said finally. "It's over."

Suddenly, the sun had come out and as sure as he knew his name, relief poured out of him. "Sorry things didn't work out, Gwen. I know you wanted more," he said.

"Jackson, what I want is to be a woman, to have fun, and a life. You are too damn serious and domineering. Women just don't like that. Lighten up a little bit, will ya?" she griped. "I have already seen a lawyer and the papers should be delivered in a day or so. I would like to say that I am sorry, but I'm not."

Jackson couldn't help the huge smile that just burst across his face with genuine feeling. He was free. Free to try again. Free to be himself, not pretending to be in love or whatever he was "supposed" to feel. He needed a drink and some man time 'cause he was starting to feel giddy like a girl. Yep, some time with the guys would set everything back to rights.

The divorce was a year ago and now, sitting astride his horse, Lachlan, he wondered what the winter would bring.

* * * *

The six men sitting astride their mounts up on top of the ridge looked down at the new construction home below. The group of gorgeous related men started with William Powell, owner and boss of Rugged Hill Ranch with his beautiful wife, Lillian. His sons in order of appearance in the world were Jackson age thirty-six, Benjamin age thirty-three and lastly Troy, who was affectionately known as "Tiny," was the baby at twenty-nine. Bill's brother, Martin, who owned half the ranch with his wife, had tragically died in an accident eight years ago. His Florence and their two sons, Brody age thirty-four and Cole age thirty-two, lived in another beautiful ranch house on the other side of the property.

With its English cottage design and leaded insulated cut-glass windows, the new house was an architectural dream, particularly out in this part of Wyoming. There was a matching barn out back and an inground hot tub, all secluded behind a grove of evergreens near the back door. It needed landscaping, but it was the beginning of November, and that kind of work would have to wait until spring thaw. It was a soft sage-green-colored stucco with a slate roof. It was nice, really nice, if not quite the typical ranch-style house common to Stony Creek. It sat on one hundred acres that was west of the Powell Ranch.

"We kinda must look like a *Bonanza* episode," Troy said laughingly.

Jackson smirked at his youngest brother while Brody chimed in, "Yeah, but we are way hotter and can actually bale hay while roping calves!"

"Uncle Bill, you so know you want to sing it. Ba ba ba ba Bonanza!" sang Cole.

"Could you guys attempt to act your age?" said Ben, Jackson's other huge brother. "This New York guy is going to think he has jerkoff neighbors as it is. Building a home like that costs big-time. I wonder who he is and what the hell he is doing out here."

Bill filled in. "Sam and Phillip just said that he wanted the best and had very expensive taste when it came to the build. Apparently, it is state-of-the-art."

"Uncle, I say we send Mom and Aunt Florence over as the welcoming committee to see if he is friendly. They live for that stuff. Then we can just be neighborly and get a look at what he had built," said Troy. "I wonder why he didn't do any of the work himself," mused Jackson aloud.

"Maybe he doesn't know how, idiot," stated Brody. "Not everybody can be a superman like me."

"If you are such a superhero, how come I had to wake you up twice this past week alone to get out to the south fields to do the morning check?" inquired Bill smugly.

Cole snickered. "Uncle, he had some, uh, company, that wouldn't let him alone." That had all the men chuckling except for Bill.

"Perhaps this new neighbor will show you something about the rewards of success and hard work as opposed to trying to plow fields through all the young women of Stony Creek," Bill replied.

"Dad, man cannot live on beef alone. We must do our part to entertain the poor womenfolk of our town during the cold winter season. It is our inherent duty as men. Can we help it if they find us irresistible?" Troy piped in.

"They find you the least attractive, Tiny. I have that on good authority!" Ben shouted teasingly at his baby brother. At six feet two inches, Troy was the shortest on their branch of the Powell line.

"Don't be a dumbass. I am the one all the ladies look for on Friday night at The Pump!" Troy said confidently. "You are always so quiet, if it weren't for your good-looking brothers, they would never know you were there."

Bill looked at his boys. "Eh, I blame your mother. She is the looker. However, I seriously doubt that she will find it a compliment to know that you boys, and this goes for all of you, have not been treating the women with as much respect as you should be."

"She would want us to marry each one, Dad," groused Ben.

"No, she would only want you to be happy, son," he said, looking sadly at Jackson. "Enough dawdling boys, the herd isn't gonna feed itself, and I hear there is a new doctor moving in, too. I believe his name is Bill, perhaps it is him? It would be kinda nice having a doc for a neighbor. Very convenient." Bill laughed.

* * * *

The drive was beautiful. Already Billie felt her burdens lighten and soul soar. Once she entered Wyoming there was an endless parade of snowcapped mountains ringed with evergreens. She couldn't imagine what the wildflowers would look like come spring. I'm on my way, she thought. She had just gotten off the phone with Sam Tourgent, the contractor for her house as well as her office. She wasn't sure if she should be offended or laugh at his surprise that Billie turned out to be Dr. Billie Rothman and a lady at that. She chose laughing until the tears ran. He hasn't been able to stop sputtering that he thought "Billie" was a man. This should definitely be interesting.

She switched thoughts to her new home. Were there any sort of men around the area her age? It had been so long since she thought about that part of herself, but if she was going to be honest and start anew, she needed to acknowledge the part of herself that she couldn't with her husband. She craved the physical contact that only a lover who understood her could bring. She knew that men found her attractive but hadn't made her sexual side a priority, having primarily focused on her work. At five feet eight inches with green eyes, she had a generous chest and tiny waist. Her long, silky auburn hair wiped against her neck as she drove toward her future. Hopefully she wouldn't allow herself be caught under an avalanche of work once she got there. She was going to Wyoming to change her life and find herself.

Through the open window came a sudden gust of air, which swirled her skirt up over her thigh. She had on cotton tights with over-the-thigh boots but gave a shiver anyway. It wasn't from the wind as much as she was imagining her new lover sliding his hand over the newly exposed section of leg. She caught her breath and wondered how big his hands would be, the scent of his body and taste of his skin. She wanted…

"God, I have got to control myself. I haven't even gotten there and I am lusting over an imaginary muscled man. I wonder if any of the cowboys on the nearby ranches ever come in for physicals." She laughed. Her thong had taken on a decidedly damp description as her thoughts drifted. It was one of her secret passions. She loved her lingerie. It gave her such a silent thrill to be wearing nothing more than scraps of lace under either her dress clothes or scrubs. She had quite the collection even before Matthew had passed. He really didn't care one way or another. Sadly. However, she had. Since then, she definitely had shopped out of control. Just a bit.

"Well, perhaps this new imaginary man will appreciate my taste." She giggled.

As Billie drove down the long, winding drive that led to her new house, she couldn't help but feel excited. The house that came into view was exactly as she had dreamed. The contractor had followed the designs to the letter. It was enchanting. It was her own little hideaway. Sam waited on the front porch of the cottage with a smile.

"Dr. Rothman, I presume," he said with a sexy grin.

"How do you do? I am so thrilled with how the house looks! You have some serious skills, sir."

"Let me help you out, Doc, and I can show you around your new home. The moving van was here yesterday, but if anything is not where you want it, I would be happy to rearrange it."

His smile was sincere and welcoming as the beautiful day. She could feel herself blushing. He was a tall man with sparkling eyes. Billie wondered if he was an anomaly or if there were more men from Stony Creek like this specimen.

"Doc, I gotta tell you that you are nothing of what I expected."

Huh? What was he expecting? Insecurity ran its undercurrent through her as she wondered what it was he was thinking. "What is wrong?" she asked.

"Nothing at all, Doc, but I think you are gonna have a whole new clientele once word gets around you are a miss and not a mister. You are gonna have lots of 'visitors' once they get a look at you." Sam laughed.

"I assure you that I am quite capable of handling the patients that come into my office, Sam. There is very little that scares me unless you grow them differently out here," she said with a nervous laugh.

"Nope, Doc, you are gonna do just fine. It's just, well, you are pretty and all. I am not sure it is what people were thinking when they heard a new doc was coming on in. Doc Finnagan is just old. Old and cranky. Your smile is gonna have them lining up around the block."

A slow blush crept up her neck as she smiled. "Why don't we go in and you can dazzle me with your talents firsthand. I cannot wait to see the bathroom!"

"After you, Doc." He watched her walk past him and a wicked smirk formed on his face as he couldn't wait to share his newfound information with the rest of the "crew." He wondered what kind of havoc a woman like this was going to bring.

Billie was blown away from the moment she entered her front hallway. It was warm and welcoming with dark-brown wainscoting on the walls and rough-cut stone on the floors. A charming chandelier aged to resemble an old English candelabra hung above. To the left was a huge living room with the soft chocolate leather couches she had sent over, but it was her oversized chair near the fireplace that made her smile. She needed her cozy chair. It had to come with her.

The fireplace was beautiful with layers of stacked stone from floor to ceiling just waiting for its first fire. There was a nook for the stacked firewood outside the back door and beautiful picture windows lining the walls. The view was so breathtaking her chest hurt. She couldn't wait for the first snowfall to sit gazing out that window with a cup of tea.

She turned her gaze past the man with the perma-grin to her kitchen. It was a sight to behold. It was a cook's dream with rich wood cabinets, six-burner gas stove, double oven, and sub zero. A sigh escaped her mouth even before she could help it.

"So far so good, Doc?" Sam asked.

"Heaven, I have gone to heaven, Sam, and I refuse to allow you to wake me up." Billie laughed.

"Upstairs we go, then!"

The stairs were gorgeous with a carved banister and wainscoting up the wall. She was able to get a clear view of the open floor plan of the first floor and paused to appreciate the crown moldings from her vantage point. There were three bedrooms on the second floor. The two guest bedrooms were lovely with all the furniture placed perfectly as she had laid out in her drawings. It was the master bedroom that did her in. She had purchased a carved, dark English oak, king-size canopy bed. It stood in the center of the room amidst a gorgeous combination of caramel walls and white moldings. It gave her decidedly decadent thoughts.

She held herself together until they hit the master bath. Tears flowed down her face unchecked. Happy or sad tears, she had no idea. It was her dream home and it was time to stop dreaming and now start living.

"Doc? Are you okay?"

"Yes, it's just so much more than even I pictured it to be. I cannot thank you or Phillip enough. You have truly helped make me such an amazing home. Don't mind the tears. They happen from time to time. A girl thing."

"When you get settled in, give me a call and I would love to bring my girlfriend Victoria over. She has been dying to meet you since she found out it was a woman physician we were building for and not another loudmouth, arrogant man, as she put it," he said with a laugh.

She would definitely like that. A few new friends to go with a new house and life. Sounded good. "If this is what the house looks like, I cannot imagine how my office turned out. I am excited to see it, too, but will wait until I get myself situated here."

As she walked him out, thanking him again, she remembered to ask, "How many neighbors do I have, Sam, by the way? Are there any close by?"

"Yep, the Powell Ranch is just next door, so to speak. You are going to make quite an…impression"

"Why is that?"

"Like I said, Doc, look in the mirror."

Chapter Two

After refusing Sam's assistance with her luggage and things she didn't trust to the movers, she turned to her SUV and stared at it with disdain. Could she imagine the suitcases up into the bedroom? It was then she noticed a small piece of shiny metal at the corner of the gutter by the first-floor roof. Finding a ladder left behind by the construction men, she maneuvered it to the edge of the roof. See, I have skills, she thought to herself. *Only in Wyoming for a few hours and already I'm getting handier by the minute.*

Billie climbed the ladder to find that she was eight feet off the ground. Not afraid of heights, she tried to convince herself. As she reached up to inspect the shiny object, her foot gave way. She could hear her own screams pierce the quiet of the valley as she hung on for dear life.

"Oh my god! *Help!*" So much for her newfound skills.

* * * *

Riding along the fence line in the south pasture, Jackson read a cryptic text from Sam.

You have got to get a load of your new neighbor. I think you guys are going to be good friends. Very good friends. He is just your type.

"What the hell? I think he has had one too many shots to the head with a two-by-four. He has just earned the beat down he is going to get as soon as I see that idiot."

Jackson's curiosity was now piqued, though. Maybe he would ride over and introduce himself. It got really lonely out there and at least the guy could know he had nice neighbors nearby. As he got within sight of the new house, he saw a woman. Not just a woman but a gorgeous woman maneuvering a ladder against the roof. "What the hell is she doing?"

Who cared really? She had to be five foot eight and all curves. From this vantage point, he had a healthy view of her posterior and he was appreciating the sight. She wore a light, filmy skirt that fluttered gently in the wind. Why the hell would she be climbing a ladder dressed like that and who the hell was she? Thick auburn hair teased to mid-back and perfect hips teased his senses as she carefully climbed up. He edged Lachlan forward just as her foot slipped from the rung. Her scream carried on the wind and lunged him into action. She clung to the gutter with one hand as he got to her.

Oh no, Billie thought as she lost her hold on the gutter and began to hurdle down into...arms? Where the heck did they come from? And who owned the hard chest that she was plastered up against that smelled so darned good? All the questions could be answered in the moment she caught her breath. However, the task of lifting her skirt off her savior's face seemed like it ought to be first on the list.

Billie's heart was beating out of her chest, but now she was unsure of whether it was the fall itself or the handsome face staring amusingly down at her. Gorgeous green eyes smiled into her face and her breath caught again. Dear lord, he was delicious. He had tanned, strong features with a chiseled chin, and his mouth, wow, was there a medical description for the perfection of his lips? In the millisecond it took to observe her view, she began wondering what he could do with those lips. *Kiss, I hope he can really kiss with a set like those.*

"Are you all right, ma'am? Did you hurt yourself?"

She couldn't bring herself to answer. Her mouth felt like it was watering. He had caught her in such a fashion that one hand was on her left butt cheek and the right, dear lord, was cupped around the side of her breast. Her hands were resting on strongly muscled biceps, and she couldn't stop herself from gently squeezing her fingers, just to check if he were real. Perhaps she had hit her head and he was a hallucination? Her insides quivered as she processed that he was real, saved her life, and was holding her intimately. Somehow a potted plant to say thank you seemed inadequate, Billie thought, laughing silently to herself.

"Ma'am? Should I call the doctor?"

It was that comment that shook her out of her hormonal coma.

"No, no. I am just fine. Thank you, thank you so much, Mister, um, Mister…"

"Powell, Jackson Powell, ma'am, at your service." He chuckled. It was at that moment he realized where his hands lay. With almost a painful intensity, his groin tightened as he felt himself rapidly harden. He gently tried to shift his hands, but it was no use. When was the last time he had such an instantaneous reaction to a woman? Well, he was holding one of the most perfect breasts and asses to his knowledge, but it was her breathless gaze that was drinking him in. He felt himself start to lean down to caress her lips with his when he got some control back.

What the hell was he doing? He didn't even know who she was.

Her gentle laugh made his cock press against the zipper of his Wranglers with a painful intention. She wasn't afraid. She didn't look like the type of woman used to hard work, but instead, rather gentle in nature. She should have been the kind that would be shaken after a fall like that, but no. She just laughed. Intrigued, he had to ask, "Who are you, beautiful?"

"Oh, please excuse me. Mr. Powell, I am Billie Rothman. Your new neighbor. It is a pleasure to meet you." No kidding. If he didn't move those hands soon, there was going to be a seriously pleasurable way she could think of to say "thank you" and "hello" all in one.

Still having not adjusted his hold, Jackson tried to process that information. "I am sorry, but I thought our new neighbor was Bill."

With a smile, Billie answered, "It is. Billie, the girl version. Thank you for the offer of a doctor, but that's me, too!" She said that with such enthusiasm it was hard for Jackson not to smile back. Unconsciously, he stroked his thumb over the nipple jutting through her top. At her shudder, it was her turn to catch her breath as an electric bolt went straight through her body, ending in her clit.

Jackson's heated gaze met hers again. *Deep breaths, man, deep breaths.* He walked Lachlan over to her porch and swung her body so he held her up against his strong chest. As he slid from the horse, he gave her a gentle smile.

Her body was no longer her own. It couldn't and wouldn't stop reacting to this man.

Once on two feet, Jackson said, "Here we are. You okay to stand, Billie?"

Stand, why the hell would she want to ever stand on her own again? Nope, she wanted to stay right where was, if he was giving her the choice. However, somewhere she heard her voice say, "Yes, I think so." She slid down the front of his body, feeling every muscle and bulge. Holy Hannah was there a bulge. They sure didn't sell anything like that in New York, and in her profession, she should know.

Stepping away from Jackson, she tried to get herself together.

"Not the most dignified way of introducing myself but hardly regrettable," Billie said as she smiled up at him.

He felt his knees weaken. What the hell was wrong with him? He usually could control his lust, but this woman was different, definitely different.

Maybe he had caught more than just his neighbor, because he knew she was going to be his.

* * * *

"Come on in, Jackson. I am just getting used to walking in myself." She laughed. Her body, still heated from their contact, kept her aware of his presence. "So this is the inside. We watched the progress as Phillip and Sam built the place, but wow, this is incredible." He walked over to the kitchen and looked around admiringly.

"Do you cook, Jackson?"

"Well, I hardly think my grilled cheese would do this space justice," he said with a laugh. "My skills are severely limited, having what my brothers and I call bacheloritis. It is a serious disease affecting only the single males of a species."

"So there are more of you?" *Good god. How do the women around here function?* "How many?" she heard herself ask.

"Well, there is my middle brother, Benny, and my younger brother, Troy. You'll like them. They are always getting broken or hurt. They can pay your mortgage for months," he joked. "Rugged Hill Ranch is also home to my Aunt Florence and cousins Brody and Cole."

"So you all live with your folks, then? It would explain your lack of cooking skills."

"Hell no, they all have trailers around the property, except Brody and me. We both have small houses on the ranch. Our lack of ability is just a god-given gift. Please say you aren't one of those females who needs to prove that she can work like a man but has no need for other talents, like…"

"Like?" she questioned back.

Multiple salacious images quickly filtered through Jackson's mind, most of which involved her naked, seeing the soft skin he briefly got to hold. His cock yet again hardened at his thoughts, and he turned and shifted as he answered, hoping she hadn't noticed. He did want to be a gentleman, at first.

"Cooking, Billie, you are leading me on with this kitchen here. What can you do in this kitchen? I did save you and all."

"Well, I guess I am going to have to lose my virginity then."

He quickly turned with fire in his eyes. "What did you say?"

"My new kitchen. Steer me to the nearest market and let me cook you dinner. I would love the company and cannot think of a better way to spend my first evening here."

He rubbed his hand over his face as he fought to ignore his body's needs. "What time?" he managed to gruffly ask.

"Seven okay with you?"

"Seven it is." Jackson had a suspicion this was going to be a very interesting dinner.

Chapter Three

It had to be going without female companionship for too long. Yeah, that must be it, Jackson thought. On the ride back to the south pasture, he kept replaying the events of the last hour. The feel of her skin, the softness of her breast and the light, musky perfume Dr. Rothman wore. For the third time, he shifted in the saddle. His groin was hard and throbbing. It made for a difficult ride. He wanted another type of ride. His thoughts spiraled out of control with images of her riding him, sweaty thighs rubbing his hips, her head thrown back, eyes closed and uneven breathing... Enough. Jackson started counting the white pine trees, number of cows with white spots, and even the small wild thicket that grew along the paths. He would do anything to stop thinking of his new gorgeous neighbor. Inherently he knew he had affected her as she had clung to him. It was definitely going to be one of the most exciting first dates he had ever had. Hell, he reminded himself, it wasn't a date. It was just a neighborly dinner. He didn't need a woman in his life. He definitely wasn't good at relationships but couldn't deny his immediate need to take a taste. Maybe he should bring some of the boys over to keep him from touching her. Heck no. Then they would get a look at her and all hell would break loose. He never wanted to get in a scuffle with his brothers or cousin over a woman. This one may be worth it, though, he thought. Damn, she even made him salivate.

"Hello, earth to Jack. Are you drunk, asshole?" yelled a familiar voice. Jackson looked up to see Troy's best friend, Hunter Lane, riding up. Hunter owned the Green River Ranch, whose borders ran up the west side of their property. At thirty-two, he was a quiet but very good friend. Hunter was the kind of man who observed everything and figured out what was going on in a situation very quickly. It probably had to do with being a Navy Seal. Jackson remembered him being a slim, lanky kid but after he got injured and came home, he began to do some serious weightlifting as part of his rehab. The man in front of him bore little resemblance to the kid he once was. It was still Hunter on the inside as he was still a grouch.

"Did you get bigger since I last saw you? Shit, you are gonna have to buy some new shirts, man. You are starting to look like Fabio." With his blond hair and blue eyes boring a hole into Jackson, the start of a grin crossed his face.

"You think?" was all Hunter replied. He was always a man of few words and liked to communicate with the bare minimum, an occasional grunt. "You daydreaming or something?"

"Nah, just coming back from meeting the new neighbor."

"So?" Hunter looked bored with the conversation.

"So what?" There was no way in hell that Jackson was going to easily give up any info on the town doctor who made shivers race through his groin. Nope, that was going to be his secret for the moment. "Nice enough," he replied. "Gonna have dinner with them tonight so they get to know someone around here."

"Nice of you," was all the interest Hunter showed.

That's sure going to change when he gets a look at Billie, Jackson thought with a laugh. Damn, his brothers he could deal with, his cousins, he could slap around, but Hunter and the other men of Stony Creek. Ugh. Jackson could see lots of cold showers and sore fists in his future.

* * * *

An ease unfamiliar to Billie began to settle into her soul. When was the last time she felt this calm and excited all at once? The house was surreal, to put it mildly. It was just stunning and she felt immediately at home. Zeus and Madison had taken to it right away. They prowled around the rooms until settling in their usual fashion by sprawling all over the living room floor. Moving always unsettled Billie and this move was quite anxiety producing. She was all alone in the world and there was no one to provide the close loving comfort that she craved. She shook her head and reminded herself that she was strong and could do this. Besides, she thought, giggling to herself, she had a hot stud of a cowboy coming over for dinner. How the heck had that happened? It was as though someone from above had taken one of her dreams and fabricated a gorgeous man just for her.

As she momentarily reviewed her embarrassing introduction to Jackson, she could feel his hand on her breast. Her heart suddenly started beating faster and she swore a sweat was beginning. Darned hormones. He was her neighbor. There was no way she was going to respond to him like that. In the brief time they had talked, he had mentioned that he had two brothers and two cousins. Really? She needed a cold shower. If they looked anything like him, she would embarrass herself some more for sure in the next few days. She was looking forward to meeting his parents and aunt, though. Hopefully they would become good friends and a base of comfort in the new community. Speaking of comfort, she took a deep breath. Scents of heavenly cooking were filling her new home for the first time. Billie loved cooking, always had. It was a kind of outlet for her. After Jackson had ridden off, she had sat in her comfort chair and just listened to the peaceful quiet for a short time. Billie had grabbed her purse and followed the directions to McMurphy's Market for dinner ingredients. What a pleasure that had been. She was pleasantly surprised to find a tremendous gourmet section there with fine cuts of meat. Well, maybe not such a surprise, really. It was, after all, cattle country, she thought with a laugh.

"What does one wear for dinner with a new neighbor who makes you drool?" she asked the mastiffs. Not surprisingly, there was little response other than Madison lifting her head. As Billie wasn't offering any food items, Maddy plopped her head back down and joined her buddy in a snorefest.

Billie went upstairs and stared into her sumptuous new bedroom. She closed her eyes for a moment and imagined Jackson lying across the bed with only the sheet covering him to his waist. The tenting of the soft material gave little confusion as to his need. His need for her. Then he...

Ugh, knock it off, Billie! she thought to herself. She really needed a man. It had been far too long without sexual comfort that only a man could bring. Her need for pleasure had led to several burned out vibrators in the years since Matthew had passed. She would have to try to control herself better than this. Jackson probably had several women throwing themselves at him at a time. She knew that being new in Stony Creek and being its newest physician meant that a proper decorum was required. Damn, it was a hard image to uphold. Oh well. She would give it her best to try to be "friends" with her new neighbor.

She selected a soft, deep-red, knit V-neck top and paired it with khaki skinny pants that fit into brown riding boots. A silver necklace and bangles completed her hopefully casual but appropriate look.

After going back downstairs to check on the parts of dinner that weren't cooked fully yet, she noticed the time. The clock said six thirty. Thirty minutes. It felt like an eternity. Looking around at her dining room table, set beautifully with a tablecloth she managed to find in her boxes, Billie felt pleased. Although there were wrapped items and boxes everywhere, she managed to put enough antiques and personal items out so the room felt like it belonged to her.

Suddenly menacing growls erupted from the foyer. Crazed barking caused her to jump out of her reverie. Her babies were her built-in security system. Weighing in at two hundred and ten and one hundred and seventy pounds respectively, Zeus and Madison normally made her feel safe and comforted. However, at that moment, she jumped out of her skin. Billie rushed to the front window to see what had happened to cause the uproar amongst her normally very docile dogs.

Not expecting anything or anyone to be there, Billie gazed out with little reservation. Suddenly a chiseled face peered back at her through the glass. Billie stumbled backward in fright, tripping over two boxes and some large throw pillows.

"Shit!" came Jackson's response from outside on the porch. Jackson barged right through the front door in an attempt to see if she was hurt. Zeus and Madison apparently didn't care for this large, virile man entering without leave from their mistress. Combined with Billie crying out from her fall, the dogs turned their anger toward the man who had caused the distress. The menacing growls continued as they stood their ground, not allowing Jackson to move to help Billie up.

Shoot, she thought. *The only family I have left is going to run off the only friend I have out here.* They were very loyal and defensive dogs, but they seemed only to respond and listen to her.

"Sit. Now," were the words firmly spoken from the cowboy. Billie watched in fascination from her unladylike position on the floor as her two bodyguards, amazingly, listened obediently to Jackson. She also took note of her body's immediate response to the terse command. She would be lying to herself if she didn't admit how arousing his dominance and control was.

Billie's mouth hung open just gaping at the scene in front of her. "What are you doing down there?" joked Jackson with a gentle laugh.

"Well, I was following your orders!" she saucily replied right on cue. This cause a surprised look from Jackson that was followed by a devilish smile.

"So, if I just give you a command in the future, are you going to follow without question?" was his reply.

"I guess we will just have to see," she said with a smile.

Jackson extended his hand and gently helped her up. She lost her balance slightly and swayed into his side. He slid an arm around her waist, which caused light shivers through her breasts. "I am sorry. I keep falling around you. Maybe you have some sort of gravitational pull." She laughed. Billie felt silly and much like an immature girl for a moment. Good lord, he smelled delicious, like a mix of soap and spicy aftershave. She could feel her toes curl in her boots.

Control, she could maintain control. She smiled shyly and invited him in. Wearing a white pearl button-down shirt, with the cuffs rolled up, he looked like a model for a cowboy calendar. A pair of Wranglers never looked good in New York, but here…she felt faint.

"I didn't know what sort of wine you liked yet, so I brought you a merlot and a chardonnay." I intend to find out lots of interesting information about you tonight, Dr. Rothman, he thought. "Holy hell, Billie. Pardon me, I didn't mean to swear, but it smells like heaven in here. What are you going to pleasure my taste buds with this evening?"

Billie paused for a moment and decided to give the proper answer instead of the naughty images roaming freely through her head. They were the ones where Jackson suddenly leaned down to run his lips just below her ear and licked gently.

Bustling around, she took out two wineglasses and corkscrew. "I would rather show you than tell." She laughed. "Please sit on down and let me work. You can pour us some merlot in the meanwhile."

"My momma would take a switch to my backside if I didn't help you, Billie," he said with a devastating smile. "I was raised better than to let a lady, so kind to cook me a meal, do all the work."

A sad smile lifted the corners of Billie's lips. "Actually, Jackson, I would appreciate it if you would just sit and let me serve *you*. It has been so long since I have had an opportunity to do so, and it sort of makes me feel….normal again."

"What do you mean normal?"

"My husband, Matthew, passed away several years ago and he liked when, as he said, a woman acted like a woman. Truth is, I really enjoyed making him happy that way. It is sort of sexist but there it is. I am a sexist woman," she said almost proudly.

"How can you think you are sexist when you must work harder professionally than most men? He laughed out loud. "However, I don't think I would suffer any pain if it would make you smile to do this for me. Most men secretly get the hots for women who want to serve, Billie."

"I am all yours."

Trying to keep his thoughts clean was becoming difficult as she started shuttling the platters of marinated skirt steak, garlic mash potatoes, roasted Italian asparagus, and candied carrots to the table. He couldn't control his eyes caressing her amazing backside as she moved gracefully back to the counter by the kitchen. Her breasts sure looked decadent in the top and his hands sweated with the need to run his palms over their softness. Running them over his pant legs instead, he murmured, "To new neighbors," while raising his wineglass. Billie smiled back at Jackson and took a sip from her glass.

"This is delicious! Thank you. I completely forgot about wine with dinner."

"Cut yourself some slack," he said laughingly, his eyes twinkling. "You just moved in today. I cannot believe I let you cook me dinner when you probably haven't even unpacked your cooking pots."

"After what you did for me today, there is little I would ever deny you, Jackson," she said with an unintentional breathiness. "Okay, my hero, dig in."

Jackson tore his eyes away from her face and put the first bite in his mouth. "Good god, woman. I am so going to marry you!" he mumbled. With an ungentlemanly gusto, he started eating with enthusiasm. She was a woman who could really cook and with an ass that was just made to fuck. How would he maintain a proper distance? Gwen had never liked cooking, which was okay. He didn't marry her so she could slave for him, but there was just something about sitting down to a meal with a beautiful woman who enjoyed feeding him what he would enjoy. It made him want things again. Things he really didn't want to feel for another woman. Truth be told, he never felt strong feelings for her and from the way she cavorted around town now, he suspected she had never felt it either.

Shaking off the darker thoughts, he sat savoring the incredible skills of the woman sitting across from. "Where did you learn to cook like this? Most people do casseroles and the like around here. This is just heaven, Billie."

"Everyone has a hobby I guess," she said, unable to keep her pleasure at his compliment from showing. "I worked pretty hard during the week but on the weekends, I would practice my skills in the kitchen. It just gives me so much pleasure. Matthew worked so many weekends. I think it kept me from getting lonely."

That last statement had Jackson wondering what kind of fool man her husband was if he could ignore the beautiful woman across from him who cooked like an angel.

As they finished the meal, they shared stories of their past. Billie told him of how she always wanted to play doctor growing up, while Jackson told her of how he felt bonded with the land he worked. As they discussed the town's history and the funny and unique residents that resided there, she looked up at him. Not for the first time that evening her heart did a series of small flutters. His gaze ran warmly over her features as he said, "I meant what I said. That was one of the finest meals I have ever been privileged with. Thank you, Billie. I know you must be exhausted from the drive and settling in. I truly appreciate it."

"Well, then I suppose mentioning that I made my favorite dessert would be out of order?" she questioned him.

Like a starving man, he wished she would slowly undo the buttons on her shirt and delicately show him his dessert, but instead he heard himself say, "So, what would your favorite be, Billie?" Please say me, he thought, chuckling to himself.

She got up, and, with a small skip to the counter, brought over her offering. A warm, heavenly scent of apple and cinnamon wafted up to Jackson's nose. "Tell me that's not apple pie."

"Okay, it's not apple pie."

Jackson laughed heartily. "May I please have a big slice? I promise to help clean up this feast and even offer you a reward."

Billie had several ideas of what he could offer but was feeling so languid after the meal she decided to keep them to herself. "What sort of reward?" Instead of an answer, she was met with silence. She looked up at her cowboy, stunned to see him chewing with his eyes closed and a sexy smile of bliss across his face. It made her hot to see him in the midst of such enjoyment, even if it was only from her pie. "Jackson?"

"Oh sorry! This pie is really delicious. It needed to be savored with my eyes closed. You know, some things are just meant to be appreciated that way." Billie wondered what else Jackson enjoyed that way.

As they finished off their third glass of wine, Billie felt the warmth fan out from her belly to her limbs. Jackson helped her clear the last of the dishes to the sink and stood closely to her. She could feel his gaze on her backside as she loaded the dishwasher. Tingles began to run up her spine.

Jackson's heated gaze devoured the curves in front of him. She was built the way he thought a woman should be. Lush breasts that met the gentle curve of her waist made his hands itch to run his fingers lightly down her sides. His hands were halfway to cupping her ass when he turned to grab a dish towel on the counter. As he moved in closer, he reached around her, brushing her arm, reaching for a pot to dry. His mouth went dry and he felt momentarily light-headed as blood rushed to his groin. Shit, how was he going to hide his arousal? He tried to focus on the work at hand, but her sexy, sweet scent kept coming back to him.

Suddenly she turned around, not realizing how close he was. She placed her hands on his rock-hard chest for balance.

Jackson swiftly inhaled, feeling like he was being branded. Much like earlier in the day, he was bemused at his reaction. His breathing became slightly uneven and his dark gaze looked down into her sensual eyes.

"And now for your reward, my lady." Butterflies tingled over Billie's stomach as she heard the words that left his lips. He drew her by the hand to the couch. Jackson sat her down and gave her a wolfish grin. He pushed one dog in one direction on the floor and another in the opposite. What was that man up to, she wondered? As he set about making her first fire in the fireplace, she watched his muscles flex with pleasure in her gaze. It was proving very difficult not to look at Jackson like a man she was interested in. As though feeling her eyes, he turned and gave her a wide smile.

"To compliment the chef for such a prized meal goes a much coveted but rarely delivered massage from one Jackson Powell. I must warn you not to share the details of the experience as it may make a large percentage of the populace salivate with pleasure. I wouldn't want to have to defend you from other jealous females, Billie," he joked.

"That sure I will love it, are you?"

A very simple, "Yep," was all she heard. She lay facedown on the pillows he had arranged in front of the fire. "Do your best, Mr. Powell, and I may be convinced to cook for you again."

"I live to please," was his only reply.

Jackson couldn't believe that he had actually maneuvered his gorgeous prey into allowing him to touch her. *I will try to behave* was the mantra that he kept repeating over and over. His large, warm hands started to slowly knead her shoulders.

Billie imagined that she could see him as his hands splayed gently but firmly over her as they moved down her sides. She bit her lip as his fingers began a shivery trail down to the curve of her hip and then back up again. Wow, never did she ever have a man touch her with such confidence and strength. She felt his hands wander back and forth over her spine, soothing tired muscles from her drive, unpacking, and then cooking. She caught her breath as his fingers touched soft skin at the small gap between her shirt and her pants. Again and again she felt him return to that spot to run the tips of his fingers over the satin displayed.

Without thought, Jackson ran his hands up her sides again, stopping each time closer and closer to the sides of her breasts. He could hear her breathing deepen and increase. His own felt like it was starting to become labored and he itched to place his lips on her lower back. He wanted to trace the gap with the tip of his tongue. He felt so hard in his jeans and a small amount of pre-cum moistened his boxers. As his hands were just a breath away from stroking the gentle swell of her breasts, he heard her soft gasp. Regrettably, he changed direction and allowed his thumbs to swirl around her lower back while his fingers kneaded her hips. Desperately he wanted to continue downward to run his hands over her ass. He longed to gently squeeze those soft globes for the first time.

Her panties were soaking from this sensual interlude and he knew that she was suffering as well.

"Mmmmm, Jackson. I have to honestly tell you that no one has ever thanked me this well after only cooking a meal. Never. I hesitate to ask, but where did you learn to massage like that?"

"Funny, I could make up some immature guy response but the truth is that my mom gets lots of backaches. She claims that carrying three boys in there killed her back. Might be true, but anyway, she made us all rub her back when we lived at home. Ben and Troy probably can do it as well as I can, but I have never checked," he said with a laugh. He kept running his fingers under the edge of her shirt while he talked. *I am going to need her skills as a doctor after this.* I wonder what she charges for treating unrelieved arousal, he mused.

He extracted his hands from her skin as she slowly rolled over. He saw that she had a sleepy smile on her face as he offered her his hand. He couldn't stop himself from slipping his arm lightly around her waist and walking toward the door.

Two large, furry beasts lifted their heads to check on Billie. Satisfied that she was apparently in good hands, their heads thumped back on the floor. Jackson figured that she should take that as a good sign. "Billie, I cannot thank you enough for the meal, the pie, and the company. You are definitely not the Bill that I was expecting," he said with a chuckle. He wanted nothing more than to lower his head to her luscious mouth and kiss her passionately until they ended up in her bed. Instead, he wrapped her in his arms and gently kissed her forehead.

"Jackson, you are so welcome. Thank you for making me relax this evening. I really enjoyed spending it with you on my first night. Go get some sleep. I am going to go have a look at what Phillip and Sam did to my office tomorrow morning. Would you give me your cell number so I can catch up with you later in the week perhaps?"

He thought he would give her his bank account number by this time, he was so overwhelmed by her! After exchanging their numbers, he reluctantly bid her good night.

Neither of them would sleep well, he figured with a smile.

Chapter Four

Over the next several days, a tornado of activity seemed to dominate Billie's life. She was unpacking her entire life into the new house, settling into her office in town, and meeting her neighbors. Like a breath of fresh air, Florence and Lillian breezed right onto her doorstep the afternoon after dinner with Jackson. Bearing a delicious plate of cookies, they introduced themselves and the very handsome Brody and Cole. The men were only there to escort their mother and aunt, they said, and to be neighborly. Once the men took themselves off, Florence immediately laughed her head off, explaining that they were probably going right back to the main barn to let all the men in on the details of their gorgeous, new, intelligent, and available neighbor, Bill. Florence explained that after Jackson got off the phone last night with his mother and explained the mix-up in names and gender. She made sure she let as many individuals as she could in on the updated information. Lillian was quieter with a gentle air, insisting that Billie come over that Sunday for the big family dinner. Florence, on the other hand, was much more vivacious and quick with an easy laugh.

Billie was so pleased to be blessed with warm people so close to her home. After an hour, the ladies took themselves off to probably go gossip a bit with the other women in town at the Ladies Guild meeting. She had a sneaking suspicion that she and her single status measurements would be on the list of minutes. She laughed.

A few more days went by with an occasional text from Jackson. She always sent a message back telling him to have a good day but tried to keep it simple. She felt like she had been sucked into the

Jackson Powell vortex. He was all she thought about. How Jackson's eyes sparkled, how good his hands felt on her back, how deliciously masculine his scent was…

"Get ahold of yourself!" she scolded out loud. In the shower, bedroom, while cooking, walking the grounds, it was all she could think about. Just yesterday she had met with a lovely woman of about fifty for the position of receptionist and office manager. Julia Morgan was her name. It was hard to even focus then when Julia innocently brought up her intoxicating neighbor.

"Have you had time to meet with your new neighbors, the Powells, Dr. Rothman?" Julia asked.

Billie sputtered out some of the energy drink she was trying to consume. "What? Oh yes, I had the pleasure of meeting Jackson first." Billie left out the details of that embarrassing memory. "Then his mother, aunt, and cousins came by the other day." Damn. She was going to have to invest in drool cloths because now all she could do was imagine how Jackson's hand felt on her breast after he caught her. She shifted uncomfortably as fresh moisture soaked her thong. Ugh, why do I even bother getting dressed? she mused. That man was going to cause her to go insane or dehydrate. What a way to go, she thought.

Julia was going on and on about how Jackson was such a dear boy and how unfortunate it was he had married such an obviously immature and inappropriate woman. With a quick look, a sudden quiet filled the room.

"Did he make a good impression on you, Dr. Rothman? Now that I have stopped jabbering, I can see you are just a gorgeous little thing. Why, you might be just the thing to perk up that family and make that man really happy again. Yes! I can see it. I think I am going to have to call Lillian Powell and do some lunch!" Julia exclaimed.

"Um, Julia. A few misconceptions here. Firstly, please call me Billie, I know we are going to get along very well. Secondly, I am so not a little thing. I wish I was, but gave it up after I hit five feet eight inches. I am sure Jackson has a harem of women far more outgoing and exciting than me hanging around him. What the heck would he do with a woman who enjoys medical texts more than a beer garden? No, he was such a gentleman and I am sure we are going to be good friends."

A pang of regret filled her for a moment. She really had secretly hoped that Jackson was as interested in her as she had been with him after that first day, but alas, he hadn't asked for a date or dinner or anything since. Oh well, she really needed to focus on settling in more than dating right now. Dating? Who was she kidding? All she could think about was hot monkey sex with Jackson being the star attraction.

"Oh really?" was all Julia replied. Then, as though Billie hadn't said one word, Julia went off on a love-fueled speech on how she saw the future of Billie and Jackson. This was going to be a funny and much more low-key office environment than she had before. Billie felt pleased and knew she was going to like it.

"Ready to start on Monday? Do we even have any patients booked?" Billie laughed. Julia deftly flicked on the main computer and smiled.

"Seems people are coming either to figure out if you really went to med school or to run away from cranky Dr. Henry." Julia laughed.

"How many, then?"

"Try thirty-four, Dr. Rothman!"

"Holy cow! They just want to see if I am a vet or not. Maybe I am easier on the eyes than Dr. Henry, too." Billie laughed. "Please feel free to call me Billie."

"Well, dear, I think both you and they are going to have a very pleasant surprise! I cannot wait. This is going to be the most fun we have had around here in some time. They all think you are a man. Wait until they get a load of you, Dr. Rothman."

"Billie, please."

"Anything you say, Dr. Rothman."

* * * *

Things were going quite well, Billie thought to herself while sitting on the front porch swing. The sunset was a blaze of purples and oranges as she took it in. A cup of tea and a warm throw graced her legs as she took in the beauty on Saturday evening. Other than not knowing who to ask to help her choose two horses to buy, she felt content. A large cowboy had sauntered into her office yesterday while she and Julia were putting away the final supplies. Julia said a polite hello to the man, but Billie immediately picked up that Julia didn't care for that man.

"Howdy, ma'am. My name is Len Drexel. You must be new. What is a fine-looking woman going to do working with a crusty old doctor?" His leer slowly moved from her face to her breasts and downward. It made Billie very uneasy, but she put on her doctor face.

"Nice to meet you, Mr. Drexel. However, you are mistaken. I am Dr. Rothman and hardly qualify as crusty yet."

Len got a quick smile and leaned his hip on the papers scattered on the front desk. "Well, a woman with some brains. Now that makes me interested. How about some lunch and we can get to know each other a little more?"

Julia turned around sharply and gave a very leveled look at Len, one that Billie didn't miss. However, before she had a chance to politely decline this unnerving man, she heard a deep voice say, "Good afternoon. How are two of my favorite ladies doing? Sorry, Len, but the doc and Julia have already decided to grace me with their company for lunch."

Sweet relief flooded through Billie. Jackson's voice washed over her like a gentle caress.

Something about Len just made her skin crawl. She had learned over the years to trust her instincts, and they told her now not to be alone with that man. Her face awash with gratefulness and surprise, she turned to look at Jackson.

"Jackson, you are right on time. I assume you know Len." She conspiratorially looked at him.

The men eyed each other with a barely perceptible undercurrent of tension.

"Jackson," was all Len said with a nod. "Didn't know you had met the doc here. He then turned back to Billie and gave her another salacious look as though memorizing her body. It sent more shivers of unease down her spine. As he turned on his smile, he said, "Well, perhaps another time. I look forward to seeing you soon, Doc." With that, he narrowed his eyes and glared at Jackson as he left.

* * * *

Jackson had just pulled up to the curb by Barry's Feed store. His father had sent him into town on an "emergency" run for his mother. Apparently, she suddenly had to have an extra bag of high-protein grain for her flock of chickens that couldn't wait until her husband Bill had a moment off. Coincidentally, it just happened to be right across the street from their sexy new neighbor's office. He wondered if his mother was up to no good.

Sam and Phillip had done a really good job with the old building. An example of post-modern architecture, it had nice stonework decorating the front and roofline. Just as he was admiring the built-in flower boxes in front, he noticed an unwelcome visitor go through the front door. Jackson had never like Len Drexel. He treated his horses and women the same way, badly. Without thought, Jackson jumped out of his big black dually and walked across the street to follow Len in. He stood in the doorway listening with unabashed interest, quickly moving to controlled anger that Len was showing interest in his woman. His woman? Where did that shit come from? Why the heck was that thought becoming more and more appealing to him? He must need to get himself some. However, he decided to figure it out later and deal with the situation at hand, because one look at Billie told him that she was upset. He was going to kill someone. That someone had been Len. Instead, he had invited her out to lunch.

"I must say that I have never been so happy to be ignored in my entire life," Julia said with a smile. "Jackson, you are a naughty boy. Come over here and give me a kiss." Jackson dutifully walked across the room and graced her cheek with a peck.

"I will be right back. Just need to use the restroom and we can take Jackson up on his lovely offer of lunch, okay?"

"Yes, ma'am," replied the man smiling openly at Billie.

As soon as Julia left, Billie leaned back against the beautifully painted wall that Phillip and Sam had made. She found herself consumed with taking in the very tall and masculine man that was in front of her. He practically emanated sexual energy and power. How could she go from fear to lust in ten seconds? Looking at the handsome man before her, well, it obviously was possible. Her mouth suddenly feeling dry, she struggled for something to say.

"It seems that you are going to be forever saving me from situations. I haven't felt this well protected in, well, forever. A girl could get used to this, Jackson." She practically glowed at him.

"Just call me your masterful hero and we can call it a day!" he said suggestively.

"Funny, cowboy. No, really, thank you. I didn't care for him. He made me so nervous. I am not exactly a wimpy girl, but there was something in the way he looked at me that didn't feel so great."

"I hope you don't feel that way when I look at you," he said with a laugh.

"Heavens no! Not even speaking the same language, I feel so different."

Jackson turned his suddenly heated stare to capture her eyes. He walked over to her, and in a husky voice, he asked, "How do I make you feel, then, if not afraid, Billie?"

He leaned toward her and ran a finger along the side of her neck. The gentle rubbing of his roughened skin sent entirely different sort of shivers down her body. His gorgeous green eyes felt like they were caressing her soul, practically melting her to the floor where she stood.

Billie tried to concentrate on answering him, but it proved difficult. How could this man affect as no other man ever did? He had such a sense of confidence and control about him. She couldn't even play coy.

She answered him obediently. "Excited, very excited," she whispered back.

Jackson's right eyebrow just lifted slightly as he let his gaze roam over her body, as though erasing the previous man's possession and marking her with his own. This gaze was one that she didn't mind, actually felt she was starting to crave. He made her feel safe with this look of blatant ownership. It wasn't a feeling she was used to, but definitely getting to really like.

"Really. Now that's very interesting, baby." *Baby?* He called her baby? She had to confess to herself that she liked the sound of that. Getting personal must be a good thing. All thoughts of setting up the office, Julia, Len, and lunch simply faded away while she soaked up his endearment. How long had she just wanted a man to be affectionate like that? Just to want her, quirks and all. Forever, if she was to be truthful. She was under no misconception that Jackson was falling for her but she closed her eyes to indulge in the temporary fantasy of it all.

Just at that moment, Jackson leaned closer. His hand that had been playing havoc with her lustful thoughts went from stroking her neck to sliding around the back of it. With a gentle tug he pulled her away from the wall. All Billie could do was look in his eyes. The first touch of his lips sent her pulses soaring. A gentle taste was what he seemed to be doing, as though to see if she would protest. After a moment, he slid his mouth over hers again, this time with a gentle rub of his tongue along the seam of her lips. Billie felt the shivers turn to tremors as she fought to catch her breath.

Jackson had probably only meant to taste her. It was as if he was filled with determination that was born from the lust now slamming his body. Billie felt as he moved to deepen the kiss by rolling his lips over and over hers as she allowed his tongue to slide along his. She felt like he couldn't stop himself. Billie felt as his other hand slid up and around her back, pressing her breasts into his rock-hard chest.

Billie felt faint. She wanted to rip off her shirt and feel her skin melt into his. No man should be able to kiss like this. Did they put something in the water out here or what? She returned the passion now raging through her veins with the same intensity as he did. She heard him groan as she sucked his tongue into her mouth again.

A loud song about Bill Bailey suddenly filtered down the hallway, accompanied by a light laugh. Julia certainly wasn't being hired for her singing skills.

Jackson quickly lifted his head but did not release Billie. He wore a bemused expression that probably matched her own. He caressed her face one last time and on a sigh, let her go. Billie slumped to the wall, stupefied by what had just occurred. That man should be illegal. So, there are lots of men who look hot in jeans and ride around on a horse saving ladies, but to be able to kiss like that with such confidence, well, the stats had to be low.

Julia made lots more noise and comments as she moved down the hall. Probably dropping things purposefully, as though that sneaky woman knew more than a conversation was going on.

"Well, my dears, shall we have some lunch?" she chirped.

Lunch? Billie thought. Who the heck could care about eating now?

"After you, ladies!" Jackson said with a devilish grin. Offering both arms to the women, he proceeded to escort his dates down the street.

* * * *

Stupid bitch, Len thought to himself. He had looked his fill of her the other day while she had been unloading her SUV of medical books and equipment. He liked what he had seen. She was a hot piece of ass with perfect tits that he itched to get his hands on while he fucked her senseless. He was going to have her and now knowing that Jackson had definitely staked a claim, well, it made his choice that much sweeter. He would be rough. Rough enough to send her back to him with bruises, to show Mr. High-and-Mighty Powell that he could take what he wanted. Right now he wanted her but would have to settle for another one of Jackson's annoying little whores. He would bide his time and toy with his new one a little bit, but he knew his time would come.

Chapter Five

Lunch turned out to be a very enlightening affair. Having apparently much more difficulty shaking off the effects of "that kiss" than Jackson, Billie was a quiet observer for the first few minutes. The Stony Diner turned out to be a charming little nook. Not quite the menu of a typical New York diner, with their ten pages of offerings, this was a lovely mix of specials that varied day to day and meal to meal. The owner and obvious attraction was a beautiful woman, Lizzie Charmichael. A charming wit and sparkling eyes matched her obvious zest for life. Billie immediately warmed to her, seeing her as a definite future friend.

"Lizzie, isn't there some sort of IQ requirement to be blessed with a seat in your restaurant?" quizzed Jackson. Lizzie and Billie both look curiously at him like he had lost his mind. Well, Billie had already felt that he fried her brain, so perhaps his was toast, too.

"Shut up, you overgrown idiot, or I am going to tell Mom how you behave in the presence of the ladies in this town," Ben growled out at his brother.

Billie strained around Jackson on their side of the booth that they had taken to see the owner of the voice threatening Jackson.

"Do that and I promise to release certain information about what happened to Mom's fur muff when you were seventeen," was all Jackson replied. With a growl, Jackson's younger brother Benjamin turned around in his seat and tried to glare his brother into silence.

Benjamin was such a bear of a man. At six foot five, an inch shorter than his gigantic older brother, he was as sweet as he was broad but you would never know it by looking at him. It was only the warmth from his green eyes that betrayed he was in reality a gentle man. Billie knew that if she ever needed help, the Powell men definitely could double as body armor.

A small smile pasted on Lizzie's unusually quiet face gave the only hint of interest. It was the only indication that she was considering serving Ben more than just his food. Now, they would make for a very interesting couple, Billie thought.

"Come to think of it, you have been in here more and more often lately little bro and always by yourself. How come? Hmm, I wonder what succulent dish keeps bringing you back in for more?" Jackson teased.

A smack on his shoulder from across the table was delivered by Madame Julia. Billie mentally reminded herself that, in addition to not singing, she shouldn't tick Julia off in the office. Otherwise she might be bruised by the end of the work week.

"Boys, behave or else I might be persuaded to regale your gentle mother with the sordid details of both of your high school conquests of the dance squad after Jackson's senior year homecoming. Do I make myself clear?" an angelic Julia replied. The only responses were some controlled gulps and quietly stated, "Yes, ma'ams."

Billie had to laugh. She had never been in a town where everyone's lives and business seemed so interwoven. It was like a large family where there were all sorts of characters at play. She wondered where she would fit in and silently hoped this one time to be a joiner in the play.

A sudden, quiet hush fell over the diner as a very pretty and very provocatively dressed woman came in. Billie heard Jackson sigh and she followed everyone else's eye line to look at this newcomer. The woman, as though on a very specific search, spotted her prey. She walked, very slowly and with quite the show of swinging her hips, over to their booth. She gave her head a tilt and eyed Billie up and down, not hiding her interest or antagonism.

Instead of annoyance at being ogled for the second time today by a hostile person, Billie found this to be very amusing. Billie was quite comfortable with few things in her life. One was her medical training, which was her reason for being, and two was how she looked. A secret awareness of her attraction to the male sex had always given her a confidence rather than arrogance. She never used it in an inappropriate way but rather to bolster herself in intimidating situations, particularly when dealing with men.

A throat clearing snapped Billie away from her observation of the other woman's glare and then she heard, "Gwen, may I introduce you to our new brilliant physician, Dr. Rothman? Dr. Rothman, this is Gwen. She was married to Jackson for two years too long," Julia said with a smile. Both Jackson's and Billie's incredulous look at the introduction and explanations of this unpleasant woman made Julia cackle like a flock of geese.

Billie inwardly smiled at how enjoyable it was going to be working with this woman.

"Hello, Gwen. Please pardon Julia's remark. It is just her hypoglycemia setting in. It is very nice to meet you," Billie filled in. A loud snort and outright laugh were heard from behind Gwen. A very unashamed Ben and Lizzie were the owners of those sounds at Billie's remarks.

Gwen either ignored the scene going on around her or was oblivious to it all. "So you are a doctor? How nice," she said with an undisguised sarcasm. "I hope you don't get too comfortable here, though, with the way you look and all. Men like Jackson and Ben really aren't interested in brains and conversation. It bores them. Your hair and makeup need work, girl, and you might be interested in adjusting your wardrobe to fit in a bit better, too. That is, if you want to be any kind of successful. You stick out like a sore thumb. Too East Coast, ya know."

Jackson's arm went very tense at Gwen's insulting perusal of Billie's person. Before he could tell his ex-wife to stick it, Billie decided to take over.

"While I do appreciate your constructive criticism, I feel compelled to share a secret with you, Gwen. People go to doctors to get well, not see if they will be on the cover of the next issue of buckle bunnies magazine. I have every confidence that the people of this town will find me more than acceptable as a healer and may even grow to appreciate my lack of hairspray and cowboys boots. However, as for the personal front of holding a man's interest, if I so chose to do so, let's just say that you are right. Brains aren't the only thing I know how to use skillfully to entertain my chosen escort. By the way, if you feel the need to continue this false tension thing you have going on, I feel compelled to warn you. I come from New York and eat stupid cupcake women like you for breakfast."

Feeling both angry and surprisingly relieved at her ability to defend herself against the cattiness that was the woman before her, Billie unconsciously leaned in toward Jackson.

Just as Julia was revving up and about to take off in her own version of the Gettysburg Address toward Gwen, it was Jackson who spoke.

With a controlled angry glance he slowly unfolded himself from his seat. Surprisingly, Ben did the same. "Gwen, I will tell you this only once. You will behave in a polite and respectful manner toward the doctor here. Do I make myself clear?"

Gwen glanced from the scowl on one man's face to his brother's. A sharp nod followed by a sneering look was all the acknowledgment they were going to get.

The door slammed shut on the exiting drama queen and conversation again picked up amongst the diners. Billie watched as Jackson sat back down in his seat to feel the pat on his shoulder as Lizzie walked past. Without thinking, Billie took Jackson's hand under the table. She squeezed his fingers in hers, inwardly not only giggling to herself at the fission of desire she felt at the contact of skin but also that his oh-so-attractive and not-so-inner dominant man had made an appearance. She felt his intense gaze on her but was very confused as to his thoughts. She decided to try to lighten his mood with an observation.

"So, Jackson, did you pay for those or did they come with the floor model?" Billie asked with a straight face, referring to the other woman's prominently displayed assets.

A gleeful laugh from across the table drew both of their attention. "I knew that Dr. Rothman was just what this town needed to spice things up! She is going to have all the men doing some sort of booty dance and going to put all the women's panties in a twist!"

Both Billie and Jackson looked at Julia as though she had lost her mind. However, the only response they got was, "Okay, kids, eat your lunch before it gets cold!"

Chapter Six

Billie was sure she was going to have an anxiety attack. Sunday dinner with all the Powells and their friends had her pacing in her foyer. Flowers, check. Apple pie, check. Insecurities, check. Having never been in a family environment like the one she was blessed to live next door to, she found herself in unfamiliar waters. Would she look as awkward as she felt? Zeus gave a growl as he felt her tension. Billie gave him a reassuring pat on the head and spoke to soothe him.

"Don't fret, my baby boy. I am just hoping no one sees my new tattoo going across my forehead that reads *Hello, I want to fuck your son* or the one on my butt that follows with, *Jackson, if you are reading this, please try using this thing before it starts to sag.*" She laughed out loud. As much as her body seemed to have a mind of its own when it was anywhere within the vicinity of his, she also didn't want to be a onetime affair. Her heart couldn't stand it. He was starting to get to her in a way that no one else ever had. It was just like the way she had always dreamed a love should feel. She was sure that the pain of being a fling to Jackson would hurt too intensely, too intimately.

Her outfit had taken her an hour to narrow down. It occurred to her that perhaps Gwen's mean-spirited comments might have affected her more than she cared to admit. She did so want to fit in. She started to put together a simple look but noticing her direction, she stopped. Clad in a midnight-blue silk cowl-neck top with a tight, beautiful cream crepe skirt, she felt she was dressed appropriately. Four-inch cream heels finished the look. Her private little secret was what she had on under it. She did so love her lingerie. Wistfully, she hoped that

Jackson would someday be the recipient of the knowledge she kept quiet. A gold-layered set of necklaces and earrings added sparkle.

"It's just a meal. Just a meal with a man whose family I hope to make a great impression on. Yes, I am feeling very confident. Ugh. I am now talking to my dogs and lying to myself," she said.

The drive over to the ranch was uneventful but eye-opening. It said a lot about the family who owned it. The outer gates and landscaping when she first entered were meticulously kept. As it was November, the bushes were wrapped in their burlap to protect them from the heavy snows, and the beds were cleared of all their previous seasonal plantings. It spoke of love and pride in the land they owned. Billie smiled at that thought. It seemed exemplary of the warm, loving, and supportive family who resided here. The first house, as she was informed by Ben after lunch Friday, was their Aunt Florence's. How sad to lose the love of your life like that. Feeling a bit guilty for her thoughts, Billie sadly reflected that while she had loved Matthew, she had never considered him that. She took a left turn and followed the curve of the gravel road. She saw two small cabins, not far apart from each other, as well as a single shiny trailer far off in the distance. The land was so beautiful even as it prepared for its winter rest. She couldn't believe how huge a property they had here. She thought her hundred acres was large when she bought it. Now, she sort of felt naïve. And welcome back insecurities. She prayed they wouldn't be on display this evening.

Billie pulled up to the large farmhouse awash with lights ablaze inside. The faint scent of mouthwatering aromas began to tickle her nose. She went to open her door and a handsome face suddenly appeared in her window.

With a cutoff shriek of having been startled she yelled, "Troy! Back home, you might either have found yourself with a kick in your softer spots or punch in the gut for scaring a woman like that!"

"I am so sorry!" he said with a twinkle in his eyes that contradicted his sincerity. "Glad our beautiful new doctor was able to join us. May I have the honor of escorting you into the house?"

Winding her arm through his, Billie allowed him to steer her toward the action. The house was a delightful surprise. Antiques and comfort furniture were placed invitingly throughout the house. Delicious smells of home-cooked foods wafted as they walked from room to room saying hello. Billie felt the spinning of all the activity until she heard *him.*

"Welcome to our Sunday dinner, darlin'. May I take your coat?" asked a rich, deep voice that was a hairsbreadth away from her ear.

She turned while still hanging onto Troy's strong arm and glanced up at the owner of the masculine voice.

"Hello, Jackson."

As he gave her a very slow and very thorough inspection, she couldn't stop the slight tremble and excitement that she felt being under his gaze. When he used that tone, it seemed her body was already trained to follow his wishes.

Troy being Troy could never believe that a woman on his arm would have the slightest attraction to anyone else, particularly his big brother. "Are you cold, honey?" he asked her in concern.

"I got it from here, Tiny. Go help Mom, if you don't mind," Jackson said quietly.

As Troy gave a knowing look from one to the other, he made his decision and went off to the kitchen. As Billie turned around while Jackson was helping her off with her coat, she heard his swift intake of air.

"What's with calling him Tiny? In case you haven't noticed, none of you Powell men fit in the average height or basic development charts," Billie said with a laugh.

Jackson's visual study of her body continued as he commented, "It's just his nickname as he is the shortest." Her body felt like it was being heated as his eyes swept over how her breasts were framed by her shirt.

"You are just stunning, baby. Let me look at you."

And look at her he did, Billie noticed. It was as though his cock filled as he gazed at how the material of her skirt showed off the curves of her ass. He thought he was being inconspicuous as he leaned in slightly to view the small breast swells that were being exposed by the drape of the silken shirt. Billie met his eyes as he looked at her and smiled appreciatively.

Billie felt herself blush at his intimate perusal. After Jackson had hung up her jacket, she felt as he placed his hand on the small of her back and guided her into the den where his cousins Brody and Cole were arguing good-naturedly with Hunter. She heard as Hunter, being a man of few words, mostly grunted in reply to their teasing.

"You overgrown water buffalo, how are you going to find a woman who is going to put up with your shit, oops, pardon me, Doc, *stuff*, I mean, if you don't go out more? Don't you have, uh, needs?" pestered Cole with an apologetic glance at Billie.

Hunter swung his glance to the two blathering dummies that he considered family, apparently trying to decide to grace them with an answer. "First of all, there is a lady in the room in case you haven't noticed. Secondly, my love life is none of your business." It was simple, concise, and to the point, just like Hunter's personality. More ribbing about the reason Hunter took in so many sick or stray dogs was tossed about the room before Billie felt the need to join the conversation.

With a shy glance toward Hunter, she said, "Gentlemen, you all seem to require a lesson in anatomy. Firstly you think Troy is tiny and now Hunter is a large water animal. After his stint in the Navy SEALs, you would think the concept of rehabilitation and routine workouts would account for his size in your heads. Personally, I think his size is perfect and his taking in strays has less to do with his 'needs' and more with the size of his heart." Jackson had leaned back into the couch, obviously contented at her being so near his body. With her spoken support of the great, hulking man, however, he glanced a look at her large protectee, who looked stupefied. Hunter was definitely not accustomed to anyone coming to his defense.

Cole redirected everyone's thoughts from Hunter with his comment.

"I will take you up on that anatomy lesson soon, Dr. Rothman," he said with a devilish grin. Billie blushed at the blatant innuendo. It wasn't what he said but how he said it and that he said it in front of Jackson. After a lifted eyebrow and scowl from Jackson, Cole finished with, "Ummm, uh, perhaps not." A controlled series of male chuckles enveloped the room momentarily before polite conversation picked back up.

As they sat, Jackson was distracted by the feel of the silk and the warmth of her skin underneath. He could smell the light scent of her musky perfume and felt his arousal heighten. His mind knew he should get up and go somewhere else, anywhere else but here. Unfortunately, his legs apparently disagreed. What the hell was it about this woman? Maybe he should let Troy, Cole, or one of the others go after her as he knew they would. Just the thought of it, however, made him tense up with jealousy that anyone else should touch this woman. His woman. No, yes...*ugh*. He had to figure this out privately.

He removed his arm as they had sat on the couch, as she didn't belong to him yet. He didn't want to upset her with a mark of possession until he knew whether she wanted to be his. She damn well better want to, he thought.

"What's wrong, Jackson?" He heard the soft whisper. The urge to turn her face to his and kiss her until she begged him for her pleasure rushed through him at that moment.

"Nothing, darlin, why?"

"Your body tensed up is all. Would you rather go bond with your father and brothers, perhaps? I wouldn't mind. These guys are hysterical if a bit like a pack of Neanderthals." She laughed.

He looked into her eyes and leaned over to whisper in her ear. "Actually, there is no place I would rather be than here with you." He was momentarily shocked to realize that he actually believed it. After his divorce, he truly thought he would never find that kind of feeling. Maybe she slipped him some medical drug in his beer? Laughingly pushing that thought aside, he watched as his mother and aunt descended upon the room and swept her away with them to parts unknown within the ranch.

"So it's like that then, is it?" Cole asked.

"What the hell do you mean, dummy?" was Jackson's answer.

Hunter and Brody joined Cole with manly chuckles while nodding their heads in the direction of his groin. "You had better put that thing away before Mom or one of the ladies notices that huge hard-on you are sporting over there, Tex!" Cole taunted him.

"Shut your yap. She is just the doctor who is new in town who has a hot body and I just want to get to know better."

The normally quiet Hunter surprisingly inquired, "How much better, then?"

Jackson looked at Hunter and realized he didn't just mean sexually. "I am not yet sure, buddy. I am trying to feel my way through the situation. I'll let you know when I figure it out." Feel his way, yeah, that idea was sounding better and better.

"You had better figure it quicker than your slow-ass brain is going, my friend. I was listening in last night at The Gas Pump while having a few beers. There are several cowboys sniffing around the good doctor there, trying to find out if she knows more about mattress dancing than normal women."

With a sudden growl, he asked, "Who the fuck is talking about getting near her like that?"

"Well, that asshole Len, for one. He is just a pig. No respect. He sounded pretty pissed that you busted in there and took Doc out for lunch while he was trying to make points. I didn't care for the venom he was spewing about both getting even with you and about getting his hands on the doc. I let him know it."

"He wasn't trying to impress her," Jackson ground out. "He was trying to fuck her with his eyes and making both Doc and Julia nervous while doing it!" he practically spat out. "There was no way in hell I was going to leave her there with that asshole. He has always wanted whatever I had, since high school. He has some sort of screwed up competition with me going on in his head."

Hunter ignored his outburst and just continued with his observations. "Then there was Joe Saunders and his brothers. Well, Doc probably doesn't go for the whole sharing thing, though. Adam and Sean Taggart were also comparing notes about her figure and face, very respectfully, though. Hey, you asked!" he yelped as Jackson shoved him forcefully off his chair and onto the floor.

Frustration that had been climbing up Jackson's gut now had the added company of raw jealousy. He looked at her talking to his aunt while putting food on their trays. She was laughing uninhibitedly at something Donny had said. Donny O'Doyle was his Aunt Florence's "friend" and owner of The Gas Pump. Since his uncle had passed away, she had been a model of strength for his cousins. Women were so much tougher than men, he thought. His aunt and his Uncle Martin had been so in love all these years. His loss had been the most painful thing in his own life until that point. She made sure that her boys and nephews were loved and supported during that awful time while quietly dealing with her own devastation. She always put everyone else first and he loved her so much for that. In the last year, she began going out occasionally and seemed to frequent The Pump a bit more when his parents went out on the town. In fact, it was the place in town where everyone ended up on the weekends, regardless of their age. Donny owned and ran the honky-tonk and had an unabashed admiration for his aunt. He was quick with the jokes and probably easy on the eyes of the mature females, at fifty-nine years old. Donny had black hair streaked with silver and a quick wit. Donny made his aunt laugh again so it was okay by him. He heard his aunt blurt out that she thought that Billie was a much better companion for Jackson than his previous attempt with Gwen. *Ugh, this can't be good.* He tried to ignore the female twittering at that comment and how the ladies filled their new neighbor in on his "mistake."

He swung his attention back to Billie. He calmed a bit at how she seemed to seamlessly fit in. She exuded gentle warmth that he found so appealing to his battered heart. Would she run from him when he wasn't what she thought he would be? Jackson had a feeling that he was much harder and much more dominant than her husband had been. He wondered if she would follow his lead when they were in bed. Would she allow him to control her there? He had some intense appetites when it came to sex. Would she be able to handle it? With a shake of his head, he tried to redirect his thoughts. They certainly weren't convincing his dick to do anything other than memorize the number of buttons on the fly of his jeans.

Dinner was an exercise in torture as his mother had placed Billie next to him at the table. He "accidentally" brushed the side of her breast while holding the platter of roast beef for her. Trying to adjust for some space for his very aware penis, his leg brushed hers. It didn't help distract him from trying to imagine where it was on her body he wanted to shove his cock into first. In the background he heard snippets of conversation about this year's calving season, joy at having a full-time doctor in town, and an off-color joke unsurprisingly from Donny. Unfortunately, all that he could focus on was her. Surprise registered as the smoldering heat from his eyes was uninhibitedly reflected back as he gazed into hers. He had to clench his hands on his knees under the table.

He made it through dessert where everyone had devoured Billie's apple pie before he was able to get some. He noticed that she suddenly leaned over to him, having noticed his look of dismay at the empty pie plate.

"I saved a piece of my pie just for you. It's in my fridge, try not to frown so," Billie said quietly.

Awareness of the unintentional images flared. One thought led to another and he decided that he couldn't wait another second. As everyone rose to help with clearing the table, he firmly took her hand. He leaned toward his mom and told her that he was going to show Billie the horses as she was interested in getting some for herself.

Billie was very aware of the smiling and hopeful looks being passed from mother to father as she gracefully rose and followed Jackson outside.

Once outside, she felt as he shifted his hand from hers to her waist. Apparently, since she was in her sexy four-inch heels, he didn't want her to fall as they maneuvered their way through the darkness to the barn. The closer contact of their bodies forced liquid heat to pool in her pelvis.

His hand was firmly at her waist and she was tucked under his arm against his hulking height. Jackson effortlessly slid open the outer door and quickly pulled it shut so as to not allow too much cold air in the barn.

Once inside she found herself momentarily alone in a sea of blackness. She smelled the strong scent of horses and hay with a nervous smile.

"Jackson? Where are you? I know it is going to ruin your image of me being a tough city girl and all, but I am actually afraid of the dark."

She let out a squeal as strong muscular arms gently wrapped around her from behind. She certainly hadn't been freezing yet but was definitely getting cold. Now all she could do was sigh with the double pleasure that his arms afforded her. They were providing both warmth and stoking the fires of her simmering arousal. In this position she could feel his entire body dwarf her with his great height as he was plastered against her back. She leaned her head back to rest against his chest, trusting him enough to again close her eyes. She felt like he was burning into her and she didn't mind the flames one bit. His hands shifted and began a gentle inspection of her waist and hips. His hot fingers applied massaging pressure as she suspected he was inspecting her body. She moaned her approval while allowing her hands to slightly reach back of their own accord and rest on his rock-hard thighs. She felt her feminine parts flood with moisture as his hands lightly but confidently started to run down the front of hers as well. As his gentle exploration continued, she heard the change in his breathing. Hot rushes of air caressed her throat. He was leaning down, allowing his fingers to massage the lean muscle of her thighs while he ran his lips over the shell of her ear. She allowed herself to mimic his movements by running her hands over the raw power of his legs. It was all muscle and hardness beneath her questing fingertips, so much so she felt faint. She didn't have any experience with men built like Jackson was. Matthew has been her study partner, not this specimen of raw masculinity.

At the feel of his lips touching the pulse behind her left ear, she began to quiver. More moisture pooled at her core as she was sure her legs would give way. Her mouth was slightly parted as she began to pant while Jackson eased his hands upward over the silky shirt. He paused his hand's exploration for a moment to lave the base of her neck and bite.

"Jackson, what you do to me," she said wondrously as she continued to try to control her gasps of pleasure as he found her sensitive spots.

"Does it feel good to you, baby? Do you want me to continue? You don't have to answer, just nod your head yes."

Billie felt her head bob with permission as though it had a mind of its own. Her hands continued to rub his muscled thighs, gripping at the jean material every time he nipped and touched. Just then his hands began their quest anew. They slid up and down the sides of her waist reverently as if they had never touched silk over curves before. Suddenly her position was shifted slightly to the side as his left hand grasped her chin. His thumb caressed briefly over her full bottom lip before his own took possession of hers. This kiss was different than the one before. His tongue immediately thrust into her warmth as his hips started to mimic the rolling movements of their hips. She could feel his hard cock pressing and sliding against the space between her cheeks, fueling the fire in her body. She was actually momentarily distracted by the thought that she might have a moistened spot on her skirt from the cream running from her. As he feasted on her mouth, she could feel his hand firmly start to stroke the underside of her breast. Arousal as she had never encountered roared through her body.

For his part, Jackson felt like he was being gifted for his good deeds in this life. She felt like an angel. A sex angel sent here to tempt him into never leaving the world of sin if it meant she was in it. His cock was painfully erect in its position, rubbing the back of her succulently firm ass.

He continued to plunder her lips, twining his tongue with hers, over and over again. However, it was the feel of her body under his searching hands that put his blood to near boiling. Roughly now, he cupped her breast while moving his mouth to nip at her neck. She is perfection, he thought while stroking the lush globe in the palm of his hand, plucking at her nipple. He tried to be gentle but finally having her at his mercy to tease and explore left him unable to do more than knead her mercilessly while groaning his arousal. He had backed them up against the door to the nearest stall just as his hand delved under the opening in her blouse. He felt the lace of her bra as he momentarily gentled his touch to lightly stroke her nipples with his fingertips. She was perfection. He could hear her ragged breaths and scent her arousal in the air. He had to have her. Now. His hand plunged beneath the scrap of material covering her breast and felt the shock of burning pleasure from his groin to his legs. He was sure his boxer briefs were wet with his pre-cum, and he threaded his fingers in her hair while pulling her head back to expose the other side of her neck.

Billie felt his teeth against the base of the other side of her neck but couldn't protest as the air rushed from her lungs. *Please, dear lord, let him fuck me now.* She felt his hand that was roughly squeezing her breast as it alternated not only from side to side but from softness to rolling her nipples between his thumb and forefingers. She felt him move his other hand to the edge of her skirt. She felt him suddenly freeze, just as the hem of her skirt was slid upward so she could feel the cool air hit her wet slit. Voices outside indicated the approach of more than one man.

Billie knew that he felt her stiffen in fear and had quickly tucked her into his arms while lifting her. As though she weighed not a feather, he silently walked down past the last stall of horses and into the tack room. He fumbled for the doorknob that led to the outside and privacy the darkness afforded. She knew that he could see the tears form in her eyes as the moonlight emphasized her embarrassment at being caught.

"It's okay, baby," he whispered while gently kissing her forehead. "I have got you and won't let anything hurt you. Just trust me, Billie." Jackson was becoming less and less surprised at how true those words seemed to ring in his head.

As for Billie, she just cuddled into the safe warm embrace that Jackson had provided. Her arms tightened around his neck as they both fought to tamp down the raging desire flowing between them. Their ragged breathing could be seen in the mist from the cold night air as evidence of their aroused states.

"I know he wanted to show her Midnight. Jackson thought she was a gentle enough mare for her to try out next weekend," she heard Brody say. "Maybe they went for a walk instead."

The response they heard almost had her laughing when Troy chimed in with, "Idiot, she had on four-inch heels. Just how far do you think she could go in them?" That comment was followed by peals of laughter as it became obvious to Jackson that Brody thought with the way she looked in those shoes, any one of them would gladly help her see how far she could go. With that last brilliant commentary, they heard the barn door close and the sound of footsteps retreating.

With a sigh, he gave a quick prayer of thanks for not only the cold but the interruption of his brother and cousin. He couldn't believe he was a hairsbreadth away from fucking the life out of her against one of the stalls just after Sunday dinner. He had it bad and needed to get it under some semblance of control. A quick glance down at the precious being in his arms was no help. She had pinkish marks on both sides of her neck where he had either nibbled or outright bitten her in their passion. Her hair was slightly mused, lips swollen, and he couldn't stop staring at the blue lace covering up her gorgeous, abundant breasts that were still displayed before him. Taking a deep breath, he gently lowered her to the ground and helped her adjust her clothing as her hands had taken on a new shaking that wasn't there before he began mauling her. Without a word, he took her hand again and carefully led her back to side porch, where they could sit and regroup without fear of further interruptions. She said little and he said even less but both were acutely aware of the shift in their relationship. After he noticed her shivering from the cold, even while being enveloped in his arms, he declared it time to go in. Both took a deep breath and reentered the house. Quiet conversation and the sound of cheering for the game on TV were all the heard. Lillian and Florence looked up from their tea to smile at the returning couple.

"How was your introduction to the horses, Billie?" Lillian politely asked.

Horses? She realized that she didn't even see them with all the other activity going on.

"They were wonderful, Lillian. By the way, thank you so very much for inviting me to your family dinner. It was delicious and I cannot tell you how much I appreciated being included," Billie said while silently praying she didn't look like she was going to be the one to give this woman her first grandchild based on the way her clothing was wrinkled.

With a knowing but very kind smile, Lillian responded, "It was our pleasure. You are a delight and now that we are friends, we will expect you here with us every Sunday, no exceptions. Okay?"

A chortled addition came from Jackson's Aunt Florence. "Your apple pie alone was reason enough to have you back, but I think in time we will see other lamps becoming illuminated."

Jackson's expression revealed that he didn't think his aunt's wisdom was very funny. Billie simply continued her good-byes. She gave a stern look at Troy and Brody's knowing smirks and walked out with Jackson. He opened her car door and leaned across her to buckle her in. She felt her body light up again at the brief contact and his sensual grin.

"You drive home safely, now, and have a great first day on the job tomorrow, you hear?" Jackson murmured. With that, he gently took her hand and gazed into her eyes. He brought it up to his lips and lightly kissed her knuckles. The door closed and she found herself on autopilot driving home. She had to get her head together as tomorrow was the new start of her medical career. The whole night seemed surreal, and were it not for the state of her moist thighs, drenched thong, and swollen lips, she might think it the most real of erotic dreams.

Nah, no one would have noticed any of those things? Would they?

Chapter Seven

Billie used her keys to open the back door of the office. It was eight in the morning and she would have given anything to continue sleeping in her opulent bed with Madison and Zeus. Being the responsible woman she was, however, she got up at six and soaked in her tub. Unfortunately, the scented water didn't provide the anxiety relief that she was seeking. Her thoughts kept drifting back to chilly dark barns and tall, sensual Neanderthals. As she walked into her office, she heard a unique version of "Friends in Low Places" by Garth Brooks. Ah, she thought, Julia must also be in. Odd sounds met her ears. She must have lost some hearing from listening to Julia because she swore she heard the clink of glassware and the fizzle of champagne.

A glance around her private office yielded no clues, but a glass at the front reception area did. Julia stood with two glass filled with the bubbly and a smile. Billie moved to take a glass.

"To your success, Dr. Rothman!" she said with a smile.

"Thank you, Julia. I will just take a sip. I can't start seeing patients smelling like I've been at the honky-tonk, can I?"

"I wouldn't worry too much about that around here, doctor. It actually might improve business," she laughed.

With a start, they both turned at the sound of bells jingling, indicating someone had walked through the front door. They couldn't tell who it was because there was a *huge* delivery of sunflowers walking in. Billie always thought of sunflowers as beautiful and happy.

"Who are they from, Tommy?" Julia asked after the young man was revealed behind the greenery.

"Don't know, ma'am. Not my business to know, only to deliver. Hi, Doc. My ma says she has an appointment to see you at the end of the week and to start practicing not laughing when you see her," Tommy said to Billie's smile.

"Why would I laugh at your mother, Tommy? Did she hurt herself in a funny way?" Billie asked.

Tommy had a smirk on his face as though he thought the whole thing was a riot. "It will make sense when you see her, Doc. Good luck today! Bye, Ms. Julia."

Julia started to smell the beautiful flower arrangement that she placed on top of the reception counter. She handed Billie an envelope and told her to go into her office to read Jackson's note. Huh? How did she know that these were from him?

As though a mind reader, Julia filled in, "Who then, dear?"

Good point.

Billie sat in her office and closed the door. For a moment she just held the envelope as though touching the hands that had held it before. Damn, she had to be more careful with her feelings. She had little knowledge as to the depth of Jackson's feelings, if any at all. Perhaps they were as shallow as the puddle outside the back door. Nice to be positive, Billie, she groused in her head. *Just open the darned thing.*

Dear Billie,

Just wanted to wish you the best of luck on your first day of work. Many people are so glad you decided to move here and I am counted among their numbers. See you real soon.

Jackson

That's it? After practically needing a defibrillator from their time spent together last night, that's all he had to say? Ugh! The flowers were beautiful, and yes, he was a good man for observing that she must like them from some of the things in her house. However, she surely thought he must have some feelings for her, something, no? She became awash with insecurity as she pondered that perhaps she had misread the situation again. He wanted her. No doubts in that department. An erection like his does not lie, but perhaps she was being too much of a girl and getting swept away in the moments.

She decided to put the note and him out of her mind. Patients, charts, and abscesses. Yes, these were things she could handle with ease and made sense to her. With that, she went out to start her day.

"These are so much nicer than the dead bouquet that I found on the steps this morning!" Julia told Billie.

"You found dead flowers on the steps? Who the heck would do that?" Billie asked. It seemed like there were lots of weird things around here that she didn't quite get yet.

"I have no idea but I am sure someone just didn't make it over to the trash bin outside. No worries. Now, back to that gorgeous bouquet and that note." Julia smiled.

Billie looked at Julia and almost laughed at her expression. "What about it?"

"Did he tell you that he loves you yet?" quizzed Julia with a knowing look.

"Drink your darned champagne, Julia!" We are both going to need it! she thought.

* * * *

Cursing a blue streak, Jackson had the rapt attention of both of his brothers. He hated fixing the fences, but it was a very necessary job unless he felt like donating their cattle to the lucky dumbass rancher next door, Hunter. He felt unbalanced and confused. Those were two emotions that he didn't care to deal with and had little experience in handling successfully. I am a man, he thought. *What the hell do I need with all of this sensitivity crap?* So she got the flowers. So she politely thanked him. So what if she hadn't given him any subliminal messages on how she felt about the way he could make her lose her focus. He wondered if she sat there and had dreams like he did, for instance, his personal favorite, the one of him taking her succulent ass. It made him salivate with erotic images so intense, he could almost feel the tight heat of her taking his cock in. So what?

After his younger brothers watched him struggle with the same piece of fencing for what felt like the thirtieth time, Ben intervened.

"Got something on your mind that you would like to talk about, Jackson?" Ben asked gently.

The only response came in the form of a pair of work gloves Jackson had thrown, which went flying right by Ben's head. Well, that and then Jackson giving Ben a nasty look with his hands extended. He expected Ben to give him his gloves back.

"Hey Troy, do you want a new pair of really nice gloves? I apparently got a pair from our very generous *old* brother, who is acting like an idiot."

"Give me my gloves back, Ben, and I won't use your face as a hammer for these posts," Jackson grumbled a bit too loudly. "Troy, if you and Dear Abby over there are about done trying to dispense unwanted advice, do you think you can get your pampered asses over here to help?"

Jackson took note of the curious glances that went between the younger Powell men as they thoughtfully observed him acting unusually out of sorts. Jackson sighed and sat back down on a nearby rock.

"I sent her flowers. I, Jackson Elliot Powell, sent a woman flowers. Did she fall into my arms after receiving them? No, she didn't. Did she come over and kiss the daylights out of me to thank me? No, she didn't. Did she even call to acknowledge me? No, she didn't. She just sent me a text. A damned text! What the hell is that?"

With that out of his system, he then threw his pliers in one direction and wire cutters in the other. Troy and Ben watched the temper tantrum with unveiled amusement, much to Jackson's annoyance. He knew that they had never seen him so unhinged. Never. Not even with his divorce from Gwen. The whole family, including Jackson, had practically celebrated that event. This infrequently seen display definitely indicated stronger feelings on Jackson's part than he was willing to admit. He was sure that they couldn't wait to share this with the rest of the family.

Troy gave his cousin a look and said, "Um, Jackson. I don't really want to interrupt the fine floor show you are giving here and all, but perhaps you need a more objective view than your own. Maybe Doc is kinda inundated with patients today and that was all she could get out to you. Maybe she just started a new life here after her husband died. Mom and Aunt Florence said that she wasn't mourning him very hard, you know, so maybe she was disappointed or hurt from that relationship. Just maybe she is just as overwhelmed by her feelings as you are and is right now in her office throwing scalpels or vomit basins at poor Julia, too." And with that, thankfully, Troy ended his speech.

"Ben?" Troy looked at his older brother for his input.

"I think he needs to get his ass off that rock and pick up the tools." So much for Ben's input.

Jackson had to laugh, which proved contagious and ended up with the three of them wiping tears from their eyes. It was possible that he was overreacting to the text, but what was it about that woman? He hadn't needed a woman for more than sexual satisfaction for a while. He was sure that he had never cared if a woman was feeling pleased. He mentally corrected himself in that he always was a man who tried to please all women and if they weren't happy, then he was the guy to try to rectify it. However, what the hell was going on in his head? Why was it that all he could think about was her? He wondered if she had slept well, if she was wet while thinking of him, and if she needed help with her dogs. Crap like that. He was certain that he had never craved a woman's body like he craved hers, to dominate her with his presence until she couldn't remember another man except for him.

"This isn't what I want or need," Jackson replied angrily.

Ben swung around to look at Jackson with annoyance written all over his face. "What the hell is your problem, Jackson? A beautiful intelligent woman falls from the sky, literally, into your lap, and as it turns out, she finds you irresistible. She is obviously a kind, caring, unselfish woman who looks like she could double as a lingerie model. Give me your problems any day, dumbass."

Troy's gentler voice interrupted with a sober thought. "She's not Gwen, Jackson. I know I tease you plenty, but here it is. You were younger and made a mistake. Whatever your reasons were for marrying her, it doesn't matter. It's old news. This is your second chance. We all knew that Gwen was not for you, but you wouldn't listen. We all are pretty sure that Billie is damned amazing and if it takes all of us punching what little brain you have out of that stubborn dumbass head, then we will. You can't try to fuck this one and push her away. She is a lady and we are all in agreement that she was meant to be yours."

Jackson turned to look at Ben. "Yeah." It was Ben's simple word of support to Troy's speech.

"Well, I had no idea my brothers and cousins had joined the Ladies Guild and now gossiped better than Mom. I appreciate what you said, well, at least Troy's version, and will try to think about it but maybe I am not what any woman needs as her husband or boyfriend. Some men aren't. Gwen thought I didn't give her what she needed to stimulate her life. Fuck that. I really don't care what she thought, but Billie, well, I do care. I care more than I am willing to admit. I just don't want to go through all that mess again. Maybe all I have to give her is hot monkey sex," Jackson said to them.

She could get passion from anyone anywhere, looking like she did. The moment that thought rolled around in his head, he felt a violent surge of jealousy bubble up again.

"And there he goes throwing the needle nose now." Troy chuckled to no one in particular.

She was his. He didn't want anyone ever looking at her again, much less touching her. His eyes darkened as the thought. He was just going to have to deal with this situation like an unbroken horse. He was going to have to acclimate both of them to this idea of a relationship with each other. Slowly, he thought, very slowly.

"Uh, guys, help me find the tools, will you?"

Troy and Ben first looked at each other then turned away, walking toward their horses. "No fucking way!" they said in unison.

* * * *

The week flew by as Billie saw what had to qualify as a boatload of patients. She had decided ahead of time that she was only going to work three twelve-hour days. For the first week, at least, that point was mute. The business of her first work week here in Stony Creek kept her from thinking about Jackson. Well, during the day, at least. Once she closed the door to her Range Rover, however, the blessed quiet allowed all sorts of salacious thoughts to start running through her brain. She wondered what Jackson was doing. Did he think about her at all that day and was he naked while doing so? She would enter her house, play with her "puppies" and then perhaps go soak under the stars in her sunken outdoor hot tub. She fervently wished that she wasn't alone, but she wouldn't go running after that man. She didn't want to be anyone's friend with benefits. The feelings she had for Jackson seemed to be spiraling out of her control. She could practically taste him on her tongue while trying to forget how his hands sent electrical sparks throughout her body as he touched and caressed her breasts. His leveled, intensely dark look that he gave when he was about to kiss her was burned in her memory. She never wanted him to look that way at anyone else again.

Slow tears began to roll down her cheek, now that they were free to do so driving home. She moved out here to start a new life not to get mired down in a heartbreaking romance that hadn't even really started yet. Tomorrow was a new day. She would sleep in and decided to get her dreams back on track. Maybe Mr. Powell, as the wise head of the family would be able to help her choose some quality horses and slap some sense into his eldest son. She was looking forward to getting her horses and checking another wonderful goal off her bucket list of reasons for coming out west. She secretly could ride like the wind but knew next to nothing about recognizing a good horse from a bad one, apparently kind of like her ability to judge men.

* * * *

Lizzie felt a trickle of fear run into her belly as she looked in to the cold eyes of Mr. Theodore Davis, the new banker at Wyoming Mutual. She was in desperate need of funds to float the café and her house, but not that desperate. The death of her father had left her with an unforeseen mountain of debts from seemingly everywhere she turned. She was struggling to try to protect her good name while slowly paying off what he had owed, but it left her with little money for the monthly bills. She was all alone with no one to ask for help, but she sure as hell wasn't going to stoop that low. Having him in her café made her very nervous.

"Well, Mr. Davis, I sure do need that loan, but, as tempting as your offer is, I am going to have to decline," Lizzie answered Mr. Davis with a barely concealed shudder. He had offered her a loan, at a ridiculous interest level, in return for some personal company. By personal, he meant intimate. Just the idea of having any sort of physical contact with this man left Lizzie nauseous and sick to her stomach. No matter how scared she was at the prospect of losing her café, she wouldn't touch his offer for any amount of money. She would have to look elsewhere. Her eyes welled up with unshed tears at her frustration and anxiety. Lizzie quickly turned around so that horrible man wouldn't see her distress only to confront the most beautiful green eyes from a very huge man. The kindness and concern that radiated back to her from them was her undoing. Fat tears began to spill down her face as he reached over to her to gently wipe them away with his meaty thumb.

Ben. Even his name was solid like the hulking man that he was. Lately it seemed that every time she turned around, he was comfortingly just there. She couldn't even muster up the emotions to get upset with him that he had apparently eavesdropped on a very personal and embarrassing conversation.

"Mr. Davis, I believe the lady declined your offer and you may leave now. In fact, I strongly recommend it," Ben said very quietly with an unnerving calmness.

Lizzie watched as Mr. Davis snatched up his briefcase, gave both Lizzie and Ben a nasty look, promising that this wasn't the end of the conversation, and left the restaurant. Lizzie returned her gaze to Ben.

"Lizzie, what was that all—" It was all that Ben managed to get out before Lizzie cut him off with a wave of her hand.

"It was a mistake, Ben, just a stupid mistake," she said very softly, her sadness apparent even to his ignorant male ears.

"Can I help you?" he asked.

With a sigh, Lizzie looked up into his gorgeous face. "If only, Ben, if only."

* * * *

I will not think about that woman. Nope, I am not gonna think about Billie. I am going to enjoy my beer, vintage Bon Jovi tunes and repair this water pump. Not gonna think about who she is with or what she is doing. Not gonna think about how she was able to hold her own against Gwen without acting as classless as my ex. That thought made him hot. She was a woman who was able to be strong outside the house but a soft submissive in the bedroom. She was perfect. Intelligent, beautiful, funny, independent, and she knew how to really cook. He knew that was part of the problem.

His mother had told him that Billie was the talk of every knitting circle in town. Apparently, they couldn't get over what a lovely young lady she was, such a smart professional physician and so refined. He couldn't agree more, but he had a more intimate opinion of the lady. He was tortured by the memory of the taste of her on his tongue and how sweetly she had responded to his rough caresses in the barn. His poor suffering cock rose up yet again against the restrictive material of his jeans.

He was going to need medical attention if he didn't get some relief before long. He would have to go see the fine-looking doctor to see what medical treatment she would recommend. He imagined her unzipping his fly slowly, so as to not further injure his swollen perma-erection. Jackson could see the concern in her eyes as she observed its stiffened condition. With a graceful movement, Dr. Rothman would have descended to her knees and looked up into his gaze. "Don't worry, Jackson. I know exactly how to make this better." On her next breath, he watched her gently lick her lips and softly kiss the tip of his staff. A small bead of pre-cum appeared on its end. She deftly used her tongue to lick away the small amount of moisture there. He heard his own hiss as her mouth took his hard length completely to the back of her throat. She hollowed her cheeks and she sucked him in. He threaded his hands in her hair and with controlled strength started to fuck into her mouth. His eyes never left her face, fascinated by watching her take his cock into her warm, wet mouth. She would be heaven. He needed this woman and the way she made him feel. Jackson could practically feel her tongue start to lick around and around the tip and she struggled to pull him back into her throat. He felt pricks of electricity start to pool at the base of his spine and leaned his head back. With his eyes clenched, he shot streams of cum to the back of her throat, thrusting until not a drop remained. She looked up at him with her half-lidded eyes, looking with pleasure upon his body. She had swallowed every drop as he directed. "I believe that should cure the problem, Mr. Powell. If you have any reoccurrences, please feel free to come again."

Jackson regained some semblance of consciousness. He was lying on his leather couch, pants unzipped, and had a rock-hard cock in hand. "Fuck me!" he shouted out in frustration. So caught up in the fantasy, he didn't realize it was he and not Billie that was bringing him to pleasure. He looked with disgust at his seed all over his hand. If he wasn't such a stubborn piece of chicken shit, he would drive over to her house right now. His thoughts were interrupted by the grating sound of his phone ringing. Caller ID indicated it was his father on the line.

"Dad, what's the matter?"

"Evening, Jackson. Does something have to be the matter for a father to call his son?"

"No, but it isn't your habit to call after ten in the evening, Dad. So, what's on your mind?"

"Well, I won't beat around the bush, then. I just got off the phone with Doc and she needs some help. I would be happy to help her but I have plans and I can't change them easily," his Dad said.

"Is something wrong? Does she need help right now?" he asked almost anxiously.

Jackson heard his father give a quick snort. The whole reason for this phone call was probably that his parents felt that both their idiot son and Billie needed help, and the only way they could get it was with a little push from concerned loved ones. "No, nothing is wrong," Jackson heard his father say. "I just promised I would help her go look over some horseflesh tomorrow and realized just now that I am, um, busy. Do you think you could take her out to the Saunderses' ranch tomorrow and help her out?"

Jackson inwardly groaned. How was he to resist her sweet self if he was locked in the cab of his dually with her for an hour in each direction? Did his father not know what damage he could do in five minutes, much less two hours? However, he realized that if he did want to further his acclimation plan, he couldn't do that if he wasn't alone with her at some point. It was a way to aid in making her more comfortable with him and for him to decide if he really wanted to do more than fuck her senseless.

"I might be able to squeeze her in after eleven. What are you doing that you can't get out of, Dad?" he asked suspiciously.

"I, uh, have to help your mother and aunt reorganize the Ladies Guild supply closet. Listen, I really like Doc but I respect your mother and her temper more. Troy and Ben will gladly take over the evening cattle check. I know they won't mind if you are helping Doc."

Jackson snorted to himself. Yeah, he was sure his brothers were *happy* to volunteer for more chores. If Jackson had to guess, he ventured that his mother had somehow threatened not only his brothers but his father for their cooperation in operation "good daughter-in-law."

"Broke out the big guns with that one, huh, Dad?"

"What does that mean?" his father quizzed.

"No worries. Just tell her I will pick her up at eleven thirty tomorrow." He heard his father mumble his thanks as he hung up. There was no way Jackson was ever going to be so in love with a woman that he pulled that kind of crap on his son.

He knew he should seek professional help after he hung up the phone and realized that he still had to find a towel to clean himself up.

As Jackson made his way up to Billie's front door, he heard the seemingly menacing growls that Madison and Zeus made. He was glad to hear it, because it meant that very few things would be able to sneak up to her house without her knowing. At the sound of male voices within, he twisted his head to the side to listen. Just then the door swung open, revealing a beaming smile that she bestowed upon him. Damn, that just made him feel so good. He figured that dogs had announced his arrival and the departure of two men he wasn't expecting to see.

"Morning, all. What brings god's gift to cow paddies out this way?" Jackson innocently asked with a smile.

With a devilish smirk and a shy glance in Billie's direction, Adam Taggart sheepishly answered, "Why just asking Doc if she would like to come over to our spread for a late afternoon ride and some dinner is all." If Jackson wasn't sure of his two friends' intentions by that comment, he was positive of them after seeing the look on Sean's face as he gazed at Billie. Shit. These brothers were good guys and in only the two minutes he had been in her house with them, he was ready to rip their heads off for breathing in the same air as she did.

Billie had an odd look on her face as she spoke on her phone to Sam, apparently about a broken window. Jackson figured he could ask her about that later. He turned his direction back to his misguided friends.

"Tough luck, boys," he heard himself say. "My dad would have my hide if I didn't assist the doc here in choosing some horseflesh for her barn."

Without blinking an eye, Sean turned to watch Billie gather her things across the room. "You know, Jackson. We know you have so much work to do on that monster ranch of yours. Adam, why don't we let him do his chores while we squire the doc over to the Saunderses'?" He turned his far too good-looking face in Jackson's direction as though to bait his friend further.

Like hell they would. He had been looking forward to figuratively and literally feeling his way through the situation he was in with Billie. "Thanks for the offer, boys, but I have it covered. While I appreciate the help, Doc here needs some 'experienced' assistance."

The men gave several chuckles as they watched Billie gracefully walk back into the room with her purse. She looked radiant.

"Can you guys believe that some kid shot a hole through my front window at the office already? I haven't even been here that long and I have to replace it already!" Billie lamented to her group of men.

"That happens from time to time when the kids get bored, Doc. Don't worry, Sam will get it all squared away for you. If you have any problems, though, feel free to call Adam or me anytime." Jackson gave Billie a look that left her with little confusion as to Sean and Adam's interest in her.

Jackson was momentarily distracted by the way her breasts sensually bobbed slightly with her walk when he heard her say, "I will, and thank you so much for coming over and giving me the opportunity to get to know you both better. I would love to take you up on that ride really soon. Let me get squared away with my own horse or two and I promise we can make some plans. Jackson here was kind enough to take time out to assist me in my purchases."

With a huge grin, Jackson took note of the dirty looks that Adam and Sean gave. He felt that they had little remorse as they smacked him in the side of his head as they said their good-byes. Jackson knew that his friends were well aware that he was rarely interested in more than a quick fuck when it came to all women. It had to be obvious to both Taggart brothers that this woman was of more than a casual interest to him. Jackson appreciated their gracious retreat from their prey by acknowledging his unspoken claim on Billie.

After he watched them drive away, he turned to Billie and placed his hand on her lower back. With a gentle nudge, he ushered her through the front door to the passenger seat of his truck. After opening the passenger-side door and lifting her inside, he looked into her questioning expression.

"Don't the men in New York assist the women into the car?"

"Yes, of course they do, but I never saw a man lift a woman into their truck nor a man who was strong enough to be able to do so." Billie's hands still burned from having touched Jackson's huge biceps as he had effortlessly lifted her up and into the truck. What the heck kind of supplements did these men take in Wyoming? She figured she could bottle it and make a fortune.

The drive to the Saunderses' horse ranch was a quiet one. Billie tried to focus on the rolling hills, evergreens, and Wyoming Mountains that rose majestically off in the distance. It was a losing battle in her mind. She was confused and felt off-balance. The man was making her so crazy that she was sure she couldn't trust herself for making any decisions today. Just his masculine scent, a mix of the outdoors and his cologne, that filled the cab of his truck send her pulses racing. Was she actually starting to sweat? It was mid-November, for Pete's sake. What did he want from her? One moment he was tender and possessive. They kept having stolen moments of what had to be foreplay that was so hot she was sure her boots were singed. Then usually the next day, after the man probably had time to digest his actions, he would pull away and be just a polite neighbor. He would give her warm smiles then place two feet of walking distance between them. Even right now he was sitting on the driver's side, looking more delicious than any man had a legal right to, with an ocean of unspoken thoughts between them. She let out a sigh and decided to put Jackson on the shelf of good neighbor and friend. She wasn't going to sit around waiting for anyone anymore. Her heart felt leaded and her eyes blurred at the thought that he might even bestow his passion on another lucky woman in the near future. Could she bear to watch? No, she would try to enjoy the company and laughter of some of the other fine specimens of Stony Creek. While she desperately wanted to sit on Jackson's lap and suck all his thoughts of previous or future women away, she knew for her own sanity, she had to accept that those women may be a reality, ugh. How did she get to this pathetic lovelorn place in such a small amount of time? It almost felt cosmic between them, destined. She had been wrong before, though, and turned back to watching the landscape roll by.

Jackson heard her sigh and chanced a look in her direction. She looked so forlorn and sad. Had he done that? He suspected it to be true, but because he had taken to acting like a coward where she was concerned, he said nothing. How could he get her used to the idea that she could belong to only him while he struggled to figure out his own feelings? Why did her sadness make him want to envelope her in his arms and kiss her until she smiled? What was it about her? Maybe it was that she was new and from the East coast, a novelty perhaps. Or maybe it was because she had a smile and time to care about everyone and everything around her. He smiled to himself as he recalled watching her through the front window of her office as she greeted Daniel McGuire last week. He had fallen and ripped up his knee pretty decently. She had knelt down right in the waiting room and fed him chocolate cookies until he smiled and hugged her senseless. Would she be tender like that with their children? It was thoughts like that, Jackson realized, that were getting him into trouble in the first place. Sure he wanted her. He wanted her with an intensity that almost rattled him because there was more than just passion interlaced with his need for her but another emotion, too. A possessiveness and need to have her near him as often as possible. He hoped he would figure it out, as his balls were of a fine shade of blue and probably about to fall off if he didn't get to have her soon. He smirked when he remembered how he luckily ended up being the one to come to her aid today. His family was a riot. After a moment of thinking of an appropriate retribution for them all, except his mother, she had his permission to meddle, he came to a startling conclusion. Maybe they did know something he didn't know. The Gwen disaster really made him question his perspective in starting new relationships. Perhaps he should change tactics and start to trust the opinion of the ones that he loved. He decided to give it a shot.

"We're here," Jackson announced as they pulled up to a beautiful ranch spread.

Billie was amazed to see that the corrals and barns were spaced apart with what seemed like a tremendous amount of horseflesh. What the heck did she know, though?

"Thank you for that public service announcement, Mr. Powell. I would never have figured that out on my own." The sarcastic comment, very unlike her, just tumbled from her lips without thought.

Jackson's only response was to raise an eyebrow at her. "Hey guys! Doc, welcome to Wild Mustang Ranch. I knew we would get you out here, and thank god it wasn't a moment too late!" Beth Saunders hollered out enthusiastically.

Beth was around thirty-three and just about as cute as a button. She and her brother Gabe had brought their very cantankerous father in this week to have a check on his cough. Beth had a *joie de vivre* that was simply contagious and Billie liked her immensely.

"We totally need some girl time, Doc!

"Well, miss thing, it would grease the wheels rather quickly if you would stop being stubborn and call me Billie already. I sometimes forget my name out here. Everyone calls me Doc, Dr. Rothman, or darlin'!" She laughed.

"I agree with Beth. We so need to get our nails done and talk about the evils of men," Jackson said with a hearty laugh.

Jackson kept on laughing for the moment until he realized he was the only one participating in his hilarity. He watched as two unimpressed female expressions were trying to stare him down and looked downright hostile.

"I guess, I, um, will go see what the guys are up to. Excuse me for a moment, ladies," Jackson blurted out as he made a beeline for the nearest barn.

"Go help Preston and Gabe muck out the stalls, will ya?" Beth yelled at the swiftly retreating back. The women were quiet for a moment then gave a snort of laughter.

Beth looked interestedly at Billie for a moment. "I don't know how you stay calm around that man. He looks as good coming as he does going. Women have been throwing themselves at him since he got divorced, but you are the only spark of real interest since then. Lucky girl! You must give off some sort of man aphrodisiac because you got a serious harem of men just waiting for that man over there to mess up, and they are all sure that he will!"

"You've got it all wrong, Beth. We don't have anything between us. Well, I thought we might have, seemed like it was going there, but now, well, there appears to be nothing! Ugh! Men make me crazy!"

"Me, too, but you are wrong on the Jackson thing. That man gives you some seriously burning looks when you are too busy to notice. I am surprised he doesn't have a drool cloth."

The image of Jackson drooling over her made her stomach get butterflies again. She had to tamp them down immediately.

"Where are your brothers and parents, Beth? I want to say hi and check on your dad. By the way, did I see you giving Hunter the once-over when we were talking by the bank?"

"You cannot give a man like Hunter the once-over. You need to do it at least twice, maybe even three times! He is too darned big." Beth laughed. "He has a whole rough, rugged mountain man thing going on with a side of cranky. Still, I wouldn't mind if he asked me to help him check under the hood!"

"Beth Saunders, you are a nut, but I think I love you. Jackson said you all have the best horses so let's get at it. I want a boy horse and a girl horse, please," Billie announced.

"For a woman, who I happen to know is brilliant, is that the best you can do for vocabulary? Boy and girl horses? How about a stallion and a mare?" Beth erupted in giggles again.

Just at that moment, the men walked around the side of the first barn, kicking up some dust. The drool they had been just teasing about in reference to Jackson seemed to just appear in her mouth. Gabe, Jackson, and Preston created quite an image of male perfection in their Wranglers, boots, and cowboy hats. It seemed a shame to have shirts on those bodies. Maybe a stiff gust of wind would blow them off?

"See anything you like?" teased Beth into her ear.

"Hey, Doc! We are so pleased you decided to come out here today for your horses. Let's go and get started, beautiful lady," announced Preston. With one Saunders male on one arm and another fine specimen of Saunders men on the other, they deftly steered her into the gloom of the first barn.

Jackson attempted to give the trio a look of disgust and kicked at some small rocks. Giving Beth a sideways glance, he offered her his arm. Friends since they were kids, there was no tension to be found when Beth found her voice. "Um, Jackson, when are you going to let Billie in on your feelings for her? She has been the topic of discussion around the dinner table and in the barn since the moment she moved into town. My brothers are interested, very interested."

With a gentle voice that did not betray his frustration at the situation, he said. "What feelings would you be referring to, Beth? How can you be sure something exists that even I have no personal assurances of?"

"Then you are a blind ass and deserve it if the boys steal her out from under your nose. Men truly are idiots, you know! Thank you for proving it yet again! That woman is as crazy for you as you are for her. I know it is none of my business, but she isn't Gwen, you know," she practically yelled at him.

"I am hearing a lot of that lately."

"Well, maybe you should have your hearing checked or better yet, a brain scan, because you sure aren't showing signs of life over there. Maybe she would be better off with the three amigos. Then she would be my sister-in-law and never leave the ranch. You know what? This is starting to sound better and better..." Beth crowed.

"Okay, little girl, I heard you. As soon as I figure things out, you will be the second to know," Jackson said with a warm smile.

As they walked into the dim light of the barn, they heard soft male voices peppered with the occasional gentle female laugh that stirred Jackson's blood into fire. Just as his eyes adjusted, he saw Billie in what had to be their version of a Saunders triple-decker sandwich.

Three large cowboys practically squishing into his woman! *That's it!* He had had enough of this crap! Beth tried to pull on his arm to keep him from going over there and getting himself flattened by her brothers. Jackson knew that he was a huge, strong beast, but even though the three of them were a couple inches shorter, he could do the math. Three against one weren't fair odds. "Billie, did you go on that date with Sean and Adam Taggart yet?" Beth asked innocently. All four sets of male eyes suddenly swung in her direction and then back to Billie.

Billie couldn't keep the smile out of her voice. Beth was a quick thinker.

"Um, no. They only asked this morning. Thank you so very much for bringing that up right about now, Beth." Jackson firmly extended his hand in her direction, daring her with his eyes not to accept it. Cool, soft fingers slid almost of their own volition into his hand. With a firm clasp, he whispered roughly into her ear for her alone. "And there won't ever be a date with them, baby. Not with them or the Saunders idiots or anyone else. You. Are. Mine."

She paused at the heat and firm set of his voice but stopped as a surge of anger bubbled to the surface. She leaned into him, deliberately pressing the breasts that he had been admiring this morning into his arm. Her confidence was bolstered by her suggestive motion when she felt him shudder as if in pain. "If I truly was yours, Jackson, then there would never even be a question. However, since you have no idea as to what you want, then I will continue to do as I choose. You are not the boss of me."

Jackson's smile made her nervous as he murmured back, "Ah, darlin'. I will be."

The rest of the day was punctuated by lots of good-natured ribbing between Beth and her brothers and the brothers toward Jackson. Billie, under Jackson's surprisingly gentle guidance, chose a dark-brown stallion that she promptly named Danny and a sweet white mare with a black speckled muzzle who she named Sheeza. Joe promised to deliver them over to her place in a day or two.

Billie turned toward Jackson's truck when she heard Beth call out to her. "I can't wait for Friday night, Billie! Lizzie and I cannot wait to see if they teach East Coast girls how to shake their ba donka donk in medical school!" Everyone except Jackson laughed at that.

"What the hell is going to happen on Friday?" Jackson pointedly asked Beth.

Beth chanced a look at Billie and answered Jackson. "Doc here is going out on the town with Lizzie and me. We are taking this greenhorn girl dancing with the girls at The Gas Pump."

Jackson looked from Beth to Billie, who nodded her affirmation at the comment. Billie thought Jackson looked like he was going to explode while attempting to try to control his temper. She figured he couldn't think of how to tell her that she couldn't go unless she was with him. Hah! He was just going to have to deal with it. If he didn't want to date her seriously, the only way she knew how to date, then he would just have to get used to seeing her talk, dance, and socialize with other men!

While Beth cornered Jackson, the Saunders men were able to talk to Billie alone for a moment. "Doc, we just wanted you to know how much we enjoyed spending the afternoon with you. We also appreciate you taking care of our father. No matter what happens,"— Gabe inclined his head in Jackson's direction—"if you ever need us or some help with *anything*, we are here for you. Okay?"

"Thank you guys so much. I had a wonderful afternoon. I will keep in mind what you said. The woman who gets to claim all of you is a lucky one indeed. However, right now I kind of have my hands full," she said, it was not without a blush that ran across her neck down to her breasts. The men made no attempt at hiding either their gaze or their pleasure in it as it followed the path of her increased coloring.

"Doc, it would be our pleasure. Truly," Joe finished with a confident grin.

Billie heard a growl and looked up to see that Jackson had just approached the group and didn't seem too happy about the way the Saunders men were eyeing her breasts. After a quick farewell, Billie and Jackson walked back to the truck, where he lifted her up into her seat and began the drive home.

Chapter Eight

"So, what do you think, Doc? A little noisy, but I know the East Coast clubs can't hold a candle to excitement going on here in The Pump!" Lizzie exclaimed enthusiastically. They stood off to the right of the main bar. There were tables for ordering the heavenly scented pub food that was coming out of the kitchen. Then there were more booths and many tables set to the sides of the main dance floor. The floor was huge and good thing it was! So many people were twirling and dancing away to the smooth two-step tune that was currently playing. Billie felt pangs of sadness and disappointment looking at all the couples. She glanced over toward where Jackson sat with his friends and younger male family while he was nursing a beer. She wondered if he even noticed that she came in. Why would he? There were so many beautiful younger women here in tight busting open shirts and skirts that barely covered their perfect assets. It seemed cowboy boots and hats were a dress code that made Billie feel ridiculously conspicuous. She had come right from work after finishing up and was wearing a white silk V-necked shirt with a high-waist black pencil skirt. Her four-inch black heels made her legs look sexier than all heck, but there was only one man that she wanted to notice. It was hard to see if Jackson glanced over with his hat pulled low on his eyes. Billie pursed her lips and tried to look like she was happy to be here.

"Does everyone come here on Fridays voluntarily or it is in the town constitution or something?" Wow, Julia and her husband Thomas, all the Saunders including the parents, Hunter and all Powell's men and women were in attendance. Even the mayor Elijah

Carson and his wife Thea, even the feed and seed's owners, Gus and Millie Braxton were all here.

"I think they are all here to watch the show," laughed Beth. "I know I am!"

"I think I need to get you some meds. What are you talking about? What show?" Billie asked Beth, confused. She had a sneaking suspicion that she was somehow the star attraction and her worry began to grow.

"I don't think you are going to have to worry about that, Dr. Rothman. Just prepare yourself for the fireworks that I am sure will show up later," a voice belonging to Lizzie said a bit too loudly. Billie looked behind her at Lizzie but got no further comment. Lizzie was lost in a dreamy gaze at another huge bear of a Powell that was making its way toward the bar. At six foot five, Ben was looking extra handsome tonight with his shirt sleeves rolled up, showing off his muscular arms. A curl of thick hair hung onto his forehead in the most charming way as he ambled his way on over to the girls.

"Evening, ladies. Doc, I sure am glad to see that you finally were able to join us for a night out. You know how to dance to something other than New York rap?" Ben asked with a sweet smile, but instead of looking at Billie, he was looking down into someone else's eyes. Lizzie had her head tilted all the way back as she tried to return Ben's gaze. Billie inwardly laughed as she imagined Lizzie falling on her tush in her current position. With another pang of regret, Billie wished momentarily that it was the eldest Powell son who was asking her to dance.

"I sure can, Ben. Lead the way, O great cowboy whisperer and dance king. I am ever your loyal servant, however, don't you want to dance with someone else first, perhaps?" she fired back at the huge man.

"Nope, that little woman can just wait her turn. You are new to both Stony Creek and The Pump. I would be irresponsible in doing my civic duty if I left you here not having your first dance with a trustworthy neighbor."

"Okay, but you will try to keep up, won't you, Ben?" Billie laughed. The tension that had been knotted in her chest began to ease. Maybe this wouldn't be so bad. Ben was a good-looking man and could always make her laugh. This might be fun. Unfortunately, her body didn't respond to being held by Ben like it did with Jackson. There was also the fact that it was quite apparent to her that the middle Powell male had a more than passing interest in a certain lovely café owner, apparent even if neither of them had come clean yet.

Ben laughed and started toward the dance floor. In no time, Billie was laughing her head off at Ben's outrageous observations of the people in the bar. He told her of who was sleeping with who, who had already slept with who and wanted to be sleeping with who. It was very enlightening. He obviously skipped over some of the men in his family and Billie was glad for it. She didn't think she could stand to hear of Jackson with another woman.

She felt an icy chill just then as she noticed an intense leer from a very unwelcome source. Len was staring at her with a bunch of other men that she didn't recognize. It made her uneasy. As if he felt her feelings, Ben suddenly turned and blocked her from view. "Don't you worry about anything, Doc, we got you covered," he whispered. Before she could ask what he meant by that, she was twirled out of his arms and into Cole's.

"Well, hello, gorgeous doctor! Fancy meeting you here. If I may say so, you are looking very fine this evening. If this is how you dress for work every day, I just may have to get sick more often," he quipped. Cole was a very good dancer, but there was something about the way he was holding her that made her look up at him with a questioning look. "Just lean on me, Doc. Play along. We got it all under control. Cowboys know how to deal with stubborn animals."

"Are you cracking up, Cole? Are you calling me a stubborn animal? Because if you are, my heel is going right into your foot."

"How could you be so smart, so beautiful, and so wrong at the same time?" he asked. Just as he said that, Billie felt him pull her a little closer. He gently ran his hand down her back into an intimate area, his finger lightly grazing over the top of her ass.

"What are you doing, Cole?" she asked with annoyance.

He laughed quietly, like a rumble, and whispered in her ear. She was sure it must look very intimate to anyone watching. She got her answer as to whom specifically when he told her to glance over at Jackson. She did as he asked and noticed Jackson was now sitting up with his elbows on the table with his gaze concentrated on the dancing couple. A huge gush of moisture flooded her feminine parts as she closed her eyes to his glare. The man could turn her on with a look. She thought she heard Cole whisper to her the word *jackpot*!

It hit Billie like a ton of bricks. This was a group effort at pushing Jackson in the right direction, which they all seemed to believe was toward Billie.

"Cole, I don't think this is a very good idea. Whatever you are thinking, I appreciate, it but I would rather know that a man wanted to be with me for me, not because he is jealous," Billie said sadly.

"The big idiot is crazy about you, Doc. He was just badly burned and needs some gentle encouragement. Pardon me for the language, but he can get laid any day, but to fall for the most beautiful, perfect lady…well, that isn't something that is easy to come by. We all know it, including him, but he just doesn't trust himself when it comes to women. We are just giving him a nudge," he said with a smirk. He took her hand in his and led her over to the bar.

"Donny, may I have a melon ball, please?" she asked with a smile. Donny looked at her like she was crazy then started singing an Irish tune. "What?" she asked when she realized everyone was looking at her. "I like green drinks. What's the problem, people? If you are all so determined to meddle in my life, then I am going to help you, but I require green fortification first." She heard laughter all around her and she took some very long swallows of her beverage after Donny gave it to her, shaking his head. The alcohol hit her empty stomach with welcoming warmth. She felt calmer about their plan but still was not going to encourage them. With a devilish grin, Cole slipped his arm around her slim waist.

"This ought to fire him up. Is he looking?" Cole murmured to the group. There were several nods of affirmation and soft bursts of laughter from varying points close by. So, they really were center stage for tonight's entertainment. This should be interesting.

Billie took another long swallow and felt another hand curl around her waist from the other side. "Mom, we don't want him thinking that you are interested in her, too!" Cole laughed. Florence Powell smacked her son in a place that was out of view and gave Billie a hug while whispering, "Don'tcha worry none, sweetheart. Jackson is going to hate this. He doesn't like it when we interfere."

"Then what do you call all of this then?" Billie laughed.

"Hugging, dear, just a huge helping of Powell hugs."

* * * *

Jackson watched from his darkened vantage point across the room. When she had walked in earlier, his entire body reacted and his heart jumped. How the hell was he going to control himself all night? He had tried to convince himself he was just coming here tonight to keep an eye on her. Sometimes some of the cowboys got themselves so liquored up that they made some bad choices. Yep, that was it. He wanted to make sure she was safe. She stood out like an aphrodisiac in a sea of denim. Her silk blouse fluttered with every step she took. It was V-necked and showed the tops of her creamy breasts as she moved. Her ass was showcased to perfection in her tight black skirt. At least the damn thing went to just above her knees, but then there was the slit to worry about. Jackson had tightened his hands into sweaty fists as he watched her shimmy and roll her gorgeous ass first with his big oaf of a brother and then again with Cole. He didn't start to lose it until he saw Cole's hand run over the top of her ass crack. What the fuck was that? She let him! Whether he was hard from wanting to run over there and fuck her senseless or from tension he didn't know. He gulped the rest of his beer and motioned the waitress for another. It was going to be a long night.

Chapter Nine

Billie was a little more than tipsy when she felt her dance partner change yet again. Donny had made her another one of her green thingies and she was starting to love that man! Aunt Florence, as she was starting to think of the woman, was lucky indeed to have such a funny and kind "friend." She was almost dizzy as she looked up into her new partner's arms. Ah, so it was Troy's turn. While he was also a delicious-looking specimen, he wasn't her Jackson. It was an excellent diversion! she figured tipsily. Suddenly she was swept up into a graceful turn that took her breath away.

"Wow, Troy! And I thought Ben was a good dancer. What other talents do you have hidden?" Billie giggled up at him.

"Ah, my fair maiden, I will have to leave it to my big, dumb brother to show you where the Powells' real talent lies! My lug of a brother looks like he is going to make a move. You have got that man tied up in knots so tight it has cut off circulation to his brain and possibly some more interesting places. Promise me that you will untie them tonight if given the chance," Troy crooned to her.

"Troy, I don't know where you get your ideas, but you are adorable! Now, please escort me to the nearest ladies' room! I have had too many green drinks," she asked pleadingly.

Troy walked her over the ladies' restroom and kissed her hand. A moment of privacy allowed Billie to stop the swirling thoughts in her head. It was Jackson's hands she wanted on her body and his body she wanted to be pressed against. She heard a loud clearing of a throat and with dread turned to see Gwen.

Ugh, please make it go away! "Hello, Gwen," she politely responded.

"I see you have moved on to other Powells unplowed, Madame Doctor. I wouldn't have pegged you for a slut, but if the shoe fits," Gwen said with a malicious grin.

Billie couldn't believe the malevolence of the woman and decided to try to ignore her. "Gwen, if I close my eyes, will you just disappear?" She didn't want to be as rude as she was being, but there was that sneaky feeling that there was more to this verbal attack than met the eye.

"Nope, in fact, I intend to remind you quite clearly that I was a Powell long before you and will still carry the name long after you leave Stony Creek," Gwen spat out.

"Um, my mistake. I thought you had divorced Jackson. Pardon my error." With that, Billie sauntered out of the restroom. Phew, she was glad that was over. It was dark in the hallway and she didn't see the wall she had walked into. *Ouch!* Hot hands reached out and slid over her shoulders while gently enfolding her. Heat seemed to emanate from her wall, but oddly it smelled heavenly, like Jackson. She sighed against the heat of the bricks only to hear it speak.

"Baby, what are you doing to me? You are killing me dancing with every available man here, and what the hell kind of blouse are you wearing? I should rip that thing off of you. Your luscious breasts are on display for all your dance partners, and I am going to have to beat the crap out of each and every one of them for noticing," Jackson growled out with his lips near her ear. She felt as his hands shifted from her waist to the sculpted abundance of her ass, his fingers digging in slightly. She could practically feel as pleasure roared through his body at the contact and the ability to control hers.

Billie felt his cock harden and pulse against her stomach, bringing a fresh flood of cream to her thighs.

His lips nipped at her sensitive place on her neck just under her ear. Billie couldn't contain her moan as he pulled her flush against his arousal. Just as his lips were descending to hers, they heard a loud throat clearing.

"Jackson, I am so sorry. When you asked me to meet you here, I figured that you would be alone. I mean really, I think you can do better than this." As Gwen continued on her tirade, Billie eased herself off of Jackson and stepped back. She heard Jackson's angry growl in answer to her nemesis's poisonous speech and continued down the hall. Relieved to be away from Gwen's negative energy, she scanned the room for Lizzie or Beth. She had to inform them that she was now apparently a slut. Billie felt a hand grasp hers in a less than gentle grip. She felt herself tugged against another wall of muscle, but this one was scented with beer and sweat. She looked for Jackson, but he had his angry attention directed on his ex-wife.

"You danced with everyone else, teasing me into a frenzy tonight, Doc, so I figure it's my turn." Much to her dismay, the unpleasant odor was attached to Len. She struggled to get him to release her, but he had gotten the upper hand with his surprise attack and strength.

"Len, let me go this instant! I will dance with whomever I choose, and I do not enjoy being manhandled!" Billie spoke firmly, but it seemed to fall on deaf ears. Her nervousness ratcheted up another notch when he looked at her leeringly as his hand snaked around her waist. She felt her panic start to rise as she began to struggle against his stronghold. Just then, she felt Len startle from a slap on his shoulder. She looked up, pleased to see that Jackson had seen what had occurred and was putting a stop to it, only it wasn't Jackson with his hand on Len's shoulder where it had been firmly placed.

"Sorry, Len, but I believe that Doc here promised this dance to me. My Lillian abandoned me to dance with one of her nephews, Brody, I think, so I need you to hand this lady over to me. Now." The firmness and cold control emanating from her new savior's eyes made Billie understand how DNA worked. Bill Powell stood there like a pillar of calm strength and confidence, waiting patiently for his request to be met, and it looked like it would be unwise for Len to disagree.

"I don't want to fight with you, Bill. You are getting older and just might get yourself hurt," Len had the audacity to say without a bit of humility.

"Well, then there is more reason for you to hand the doc over to me as she could fix me right up, but I can assure you that I am not that old yet. Either way, you are going to get in a heap of trouble, so make a choice, son. I am waiting." The air became very still and very chilled with that last comment. Billie felt her knees weaken with relief when Bill enfolded her in an embrace and turned her out on the dance floor.

"Thank you, Mr. Powell. I was actually a bit scared there. I don't think I like that man very much." Billie laughed nervously.

With a loving gesture that touched Billie, Mr. Powell gently pushed her head onto his shoulder and lightly rubbed her upper back. "Don't you worry none, Doc. We take care of our own. There isn't one of us who would let anything happen to you. Especially my eldest. Do this dad a favor and have patience with Jackson. He had his heart broken by making a really poor choice, and although he would never admit to it, he is insecure with his feelings around the gentler sex. Well, with matters of the heart, anyway." Mr. Powell had a naughty grin on his face. It was nice to know that all the Powells loved Jackson so much that they were united in trying to help him by being honest and aware of his weaknesses.

Suddenly, they heard a slight scuffle going on toward the rear of the bar and some shattering glass.

"What is going on back there? Maybe I should go look at the casualties?" Billie inquired with a laugh.

"Nope, just proper manners being taught. We don't quite handle things by the book out here, Doc. Men need to act like men, respectfully." With that, he ended the conversation. A sudden tap on Mr. Powell's shoulder had both their attention immediately.

Billie breath caught as she saw Jackson's gorgeous face towering over his father's shoulder. He wore a hard, possessive look, and she could feel the tension that radiated from his body. Billie was barely aware of the soft kiss that was pressed onto her cheek by Mr. Powell. She was smoothly transferred without preamble into Jackson's waiting arms. There was nothing polite about the way he hooked his right arm all the way around her back, pulling her into his embrace in one swift move, flush against his rock-hard body. He felt all male as he was tense and aroused. She could smell his cologne teasing at her senses, making her knees weak. His hot, light breath skimmed over her skin, causing her to practically puddle in relief at his feet. She felt his mouth on the sensitive spot on her neck as he bent near.

"Are you okay, baby?" Jackson softly inquired, letting his lips rub on the outer shell of her ear. Streaks of hot electricity ran down to her core as she caught her breath. "You are safe. I saw what happened and took care of it. He left for the evening and won't be back tonight. My family and I will never let anything happen to you."

Billie just gazed up into Jackson's gorgeous green eyes that seemed to be getting darker as the moments passed. With his body erotically rubbing up against hers under the guise of the sway of the dance, both Jackson and Billie could hear and feel the increased sounds of breathing from each other. His rock-hard erection was molding into her stomach. She shifted her body over the thick, hard ridge once, then twice with a light twist of her hips. She heard his deep groan. He pulled her tighter, his hands kneaded into the top of her buttocks with his index finger running the crack between them. Billie moaned into his chest at the sensual caress. She would be lying if she didn't admit to herself that Jackson's handling of Len and possessive hold didn't fire her blood to even higher levels of arousal.

"Jackson, what are you doing to me?" Billie moaned breathlessly. "I thought you cared about me. I thought you were my friend. You are killing me." She knew she must look as desperate as she felt. She felt like she couldn't take another round of feverish kissing and then…nothing. Her arousal had her rubbing her thighs at feeling her juices running out of her swollen, drenched pussy.

Jackson gave her a scorching look that was determined to win its prize. "Baby, I don't want to be just your friend anymore. I am going to make love to you. Tonight. Now. If you have any reservations, now would be the time to tell me, where I have the pressure of an audience to stop myself. If not, then we are going to wave our good-byes and leave. They are all waiting for it anyway," he said with a laugh that almost hurt from the steel in his painfully thick erection. "Say yes, Billie, and we can go." She was his and he damn well was tired of fighting himself and his past.

Billie never even had a moment's hesitation. She was lost to her desire for the man who held her so possessively in his arms. She felt his fingers sliding lightly now over the softness of the material of her shirt, tracing the line of her bra in the back. Every few seconds, she felt his fingertips slide to her sides, secretly caressing the sides of her breasts through the satin of her bra while forcing her breasts harder into his chest. Her breathing was starting to now become erratic as he inserted his thigh slightly between her legs. The motion forced one of her thighs into view from the slit as it was being shifted open.

Jackson leaned further down to admire the view and murmur into her ear.

"I bet if I slide my hand under your thigh and lift it to wrap around my waist, my fingers would find you very, very wet, baby, no? What happens when I do this?" With that, he let his lips slide over to the pulse point behind her ear while using one hand to roughly grasp and squeeze her ass cheek. He expertly rolled his hips to push his hard cock into her as he applied counterpressure from his hold on her ass.

She moaned in pleasure, trying to move her hands from his neck to touch him, anywhere, but his steely strength and height prevented her movement. She was captive while being pinned against his body and his erection, both of which were waiting for her answer. She shivered at his control in this position.

"Please, Jackson, take me. I cannot bear it anymore. I want you to take me, please. I beg you," Billie almost cried out.

Jackson gentled his touch to a loving stroke along her upper back and turned with her in his arms. "Do not beg, my love, I will take you. Now. We are going. Do not stop or talk unless I tell you to. Do you understand?"

"Yes. Anything, Jackson, but *please* hurry," she said desperately.

Jackson used his huge body to make a path through the enormous crowd on the floor as well by the bar. Many people called out to them as he gently eased them through the sea of people. Billie turned in Jackson's arms as she felt another woman's soft hand placing her purse into her hands as they made their way. She saw it was Lillian Powell with arms linked with Florence. They both had soft, approving smiles on their faces. Billie tried to smile back but was distracted by her pussy clenching in anticipation as Jackson ground his erection against her backside where it was hidden by the crowd. He stopped momentarily to listen as his father said something to him. She heard some clapping and bursts of laughter as he pulled them away from the crowd. Jackson then began maneuvering them toward the door and out into the cool night.

She turned to him once outside but he took her hand and set a brisk pace to his giant dually. She moved toward the passenger side to suddenly feel him gently push her up against the door with his body. He lifted her skirt slightly and ran his fingers up the backs of her knees encased in her silken stockings. Hot lips traveled down from the back of her neck with soft nips to the side. His strong hands were now free to wander in the shadows by his truck. She felt them run from her waist up to the sides of her breasts. He paused for a moment, as he took a deep breath, as though inhaling her scent, and ran his hands determinedly around to knead both breasts at the same time.

"Oh god, you feel fucking amazing, baby. I want you so badly I feel like I could come right here by grinding my cock into your ass. Give me your lips, darlin'. I cannot wait another second or I will rip this scrap of silk off you to get at these breasts," Jackson said, panting like he was on the verge of losing control. Billie felt herself tremble slightly at his words. Her nipples were so erect against the overwhelming pleasure she felt on having his hands cupping and massaging her breasts one at a time, then together pushed up to her neckline. It was ecstasy. She half turned, while still pressing backward and grinding her ass back into his groin, reveling in the feel of his cock pulsing against her.

He took possession of her mouth in that moment. Hot lips met hers, strong and masculine in texture. He ran his tongue lightly over each lip, almost in reverence. The second he heard her sigh in pleasure, he deepened the kiss almost savagely, thrusting his tongue into the caverns of her mouth.

She cried out in the unbelievable passion that ripped through her as she tangled her tongue with his. His mouth slashed over and over hers as though trying to consume her in a way completely different from any kiss he had given her yet. She could feel his possessive need rolling off of him and she liked it. Billie felt her knees buckle as she sagged backward against him.

With seemingly no effort, he ripped open her shirt in search of his prize. The top button flew off as she felt him slide his callused right hand onto her left breast. It was as though he was desperate to touch her silken skin, by the way she felt him thrust his fingers along the edge of the satin cup.

Gushes of moisture ran from her as she felt his fingertips erotically running back and forth across her sensitive upper swell. She shivered in his embrace as he found her erect nipple and stroked over it with reverence.

Jackson could no longer control himself as he started to grind harder into her ass as he ran his other hand over her partially exposed thigh, lightly squeezing. He shuddered with the sensual feel of her firm, muscled leg and nipple within his hands finally. She was his and he was never going to let her go. Jackson's head swam as his lips returned to tasting the sweat on the side of her neck, alternating between sucking and licking her as his own pleasure soared. His cock wept pre-cum as he practically cried out in need to be inside of her. With a savage intent, he switched from stroking her nipple to finally enveloping the entire succulent globe into his hand. He growled in his pleasure, causing her to cry out.

"Jackson," she panted out, her breathing violently erratic against his chest. "Take me, take me here. I cannot stand it another second. Fuck me please, baby."

It was her words that sobered him for the split second he needed. He took a momentary stock of their surroundings and how chilly it was. Shit, he was so overwhelmed by his need for her that he didn't even realize that she might be cold. He was going to fuck her and fuck her hard, but not out here with the potential for anyone to interrupt them. She was the town doctor and she was also his! No one was going see her like this. Jackson took several deep breaths as he smirked in anticipation of taking her in a more secluded environment as he picked her up and cradled her into his arms. Billie wore a bemused expression with her eyes glazed with her passion. Her lips were swollen and her hair was seductively mused around her face. He placed her gently on the seat and he buckled her in. Jackson, however, stopped to place his lips right over where her skirt covered her mound. He fastened his wet, hot mouth directly over her hot, wet inferno. She cried out at the unexpected sensations that threatened to take her over. Instead of a quick kiss, he sucked and licked through the material hiding his desired target, thus further arousing her to a crazed state. He then stood, shut the door, and walked quickly to his side of the truck. Once in, he looked at her heatedly, passion making his features taut.

"Remember, no talking until I give you permission." His breathing was as labored as hers. It was comforting to know he was on the same precipice that she was.

Jackson pulled out and sped toward her home. Needing to touch her, he reached out with his right hand and ran the backs of his fingers over her cheek.

Billie's anticipation made her unable to sit passively and turned her face to kiss his palm. Her tongue swirled into his palm and then unexpectedly sucked one of his fingers into her wet mouth. She heard as Jackson growled out either in pleasure or arousal, Billie knew not which it was, at the action.

He pulled his hand away and ran it down her neck, to her shoulder, and finally onto her exposed breast. He never took his eyes from the road, but she knew he was on edge by his shallow, erratic breathing, which was now mimicking hers. He squeezed her breast determinedly.

"Baby, if I knew that these were so going to feel so amazing, I would have started worshiping them from the first moment I caught you and never stopped," Jackson ground out. He tried to focus on the road as his mouth watered at the thought of sucking her nipples until she screamed in pleasure. He shifted in pain as his cock strained against its restraints at the image.

"You did touch me then. Don't you remember? It was the most scary, embarrassing, and erotic moment I had had in my life up until then," Billie softly reminded him.

Jackson responded by using his thumb to rub deliciously over her pebbled nipple, causing her breath to hitch further. He rubbed the nub between his thumb and forefinger, causing her to moan in pleasure. He had some mercy on her and slid his hand further down, while keeping the other hand on the wheel. It ran over her hip with the thumb on the outside and his fingers grazing over her mound again.

Billie shuddered and knew she was dripping her arousal. Could he scent it in the confines of the cab? She was sure there would be a wet mark on his leather seat and didn't care. It was her mark on her seat for her man. If he kept stroking, she was sure she would come right there. Just as the tingling started up her backside, he shifted his hand lower. She groaned out her frustration and almost pulled his hand back. Jackson turned slightly to admire her legs encased in her soft stockings.

"Silk, baby?" he questioned, running his hands unwaveringly over thighs again and again.

"Yes," was all she said, as he had told her not to talk.

Just then, the dually pulled onto the road leading to her home. If anything, he seemed to press the gas pedal even harder in his determination to get her there. As he pulled in front of her house, he shut off the truck and turned to her. He seemed to be trying to get his respirations under some sort of control.

With a very serious, no-nonsense look, he gave her one last chance. "Darlin', this is it. If you want me to stop here, I will. It won't be easy, but I will. However, once you agree again, you are mine. Period. I intend to fuck you senseless and until we both cannot stand."

Billie looked at Jackson and couldn't even speak anymore. She unbuckled her seatbelt and slid over to him on the seat. She mashed her body up against him and lifted her face. She met his heated gaze with her own and nodded firmly.

Chapter Ten

It was all Jackson needed. "Baby, I haven't had sex in a while and was given the clean and clear by old Dr. Cranky. However, if you want me to use a condom, I will, darlin'."

"I am on the pill, Jackson. I want to feel you hot and raw. Please. I cannot wait anymore. Hurry up and please take me."

He opened his door and pulled her body with his out of the cab. He kicked the door shut with his foot as he again lifted her up into his arms. His mouth met hers in a carnal kiss that reignited the embers that were simmering in the truck. She wound her arms around his neck and opened herself to his scorching kiss. He shifted his position as he slanted his mouth over hers, trying to drown her under a wave of intense arousal so her pussy would feel like it was on fire to be filled by him. He used her key to open her door and place her down just inside. There was a soft, small light on in the foyer, giving it a cozy, romantic feel. Without hesitation, Jackson slammed the door shut and shoved her against it with his barely controlled passion. He thrust his chest and hips into hers, grinding desperately through their clothing. His hands ran down her legs to her thighs as he leaned over. One questing hand ran up the left thigh slit and stopped abruptly.

"What the hell, baby?" Jackson questioned. He fell to his knees and shoved her skirt just up to her waist but still covering her. "Oh fucking hell, Billie. You are full of hot surprises, aren't you?"

He couldn't stop staring at and touching the lacy tops of her thigh-high stockings encasing her shapely legs. He leaned in, running his tongue over the edges from the outside to her inner sensitive skin. He heard her swift intake of breath as he lapped his tongue nearer to her molten core. He could taste her cream as her thighs were covered in it. He groaned in heavenly pleasure, thanking god for dropping this woman on him. He began to lick his way up toward her wet, clenching pussy as he kept her in place with his hands firmly clenching her ass cheeks. He kept taking deep breaths, unable to stop himself from drinking in the scent of her arousal. His woman's arousal…for him.

Again he stopped suddenly when he pushed her skirt up that last inch. She smiled down at him knowingly at what he had found this time. "Fucking hell, you are gonna kill me, woman. No panties either? Fuck," he roughly ground out.

Jackson's pleasure burst into an unquenchable fire at his first sight of her bare mound. With a deft stroke he leaned in and ran his thick, hot tongue from her slit up to her clit, desperate to taste her.

"You are the most fucking desirable thing I have ever seen. I am going to eat you raw later but I have to fuck you. Now!" He violently stood and again took possession of her mouth. He quickly lifted her one leg and then the other up and around his waist. Sounds of moans, feverish kisses, and wet sounds were all that could be heard as he ran his fingers through her cream over and over again.

Billie felt her pussy clench as her body screamed its impatience, waiting to be filled by his cock. She could already feel the electric tingles from his hands running through her dripping lips.

Jackson shifted his hand and managed to undo his belt and jeans. He shoved them with the top of his boxers off his huge pulsing erection, and he bumped her back into the door as he bent his knees slightly and positioned himself quickly.

She thought he would pass out from pleasure as she felt the head of his cock slip against the scalding juices that were flooding her pussy and running down her thighs. She knew he could smell her arousal and she thought she was going to die if he didn't get inside of her that second. "You are mine, baby. Mine. Understand that after this, I am never gonna let you go." With no further comment he plunged into her silken heat roughly to fill her to the hilt in one hard thrust.

Billie felt so full, so heavenly full, she thought she might faint. His thick cock filling her sent unbelievable waves of pleasure rolling through her. He was so long that he pressed against her womb while he impaled her on him. She clung to his shoulders and silently begged him to thrust and fuck her.

Suddenly, Jackson began thrusting up while clenching her ass tightly in his grip. He groaned his pleasure as he pumped his cock into her ferociously. Her cream was bathing him inside of her and he felt the erotic wetness on the cool air every time he pulled out to only leave his thick head just inside of her. He heard her feminine whimpers of pleasure mix sensually with his own masculine groans. They were banging against the door over and over in a violent ritual of erotic thrusting. He felt her start to clench tightly on his cock as she began to scream over and over again with what must be incredible bursts of orgasmic pleasure. Her head was thrown back and her nails were digging into his shoulders, trying to hold her purchase onto her lover.

Jackson watched as Billie couldn't breathe from such an incredible orgasm exploding violently from her.

Jackson increased the aggression and pace of his thrusting while trying to protect her back from their animalistic movements. He was helpless as he felt the electrical pulses start and the drawing up of his sac. He drew his head back and released uncontrollably what seemed to be endless streams of hot cum inside of his woman. He roared his pleasure so loudly, it seemed like the house shook. When his cock finally stopped pulsing, he leaned his head against her shoulder as she limply clung to him. He sunk down onto his knees holding her to his body protectively. Their harsh, uneven breathing finally began to settle. His woman, finally. He felt momentarily disoriented from what had to be the best fuck of his life. He was able to refocus as he felt her hands lightly run over his shoulders and sensed her lips tasting the salty sweat on his neck with her soft kisses. Jackson leaned his head back to look into her eyes. He saw satiated warmth emanating from his woman. He leaned forward and softly kissed each eyelid, then her nose, and finally her lips. He couldn't bear to separate from her yet, so, with his cock still hard inside of her, he rocked on his heels and forced himself back to standing while still holding her ass in both hands.

"Baby? Where is your bedroom?"

Zeus and Madison were hovering around them in circles, trying to figure out what he had just done to their mistress. They weren't whimpering, just trying to assess the situation.

Jackson took one hand and petted both on their heads to momentarily give them comfort.

She seemed to be so overcome by the electrifying pleasure they just had, it was as though she was having trouble formulating a thought. Jackson smiled to himself.

He barely heard her whispered answer. "Upstairs, Jackson."

He took the stairs two at a time while cradling her against his rock-hard body. He felt bemused as he realized that he was still hard as a rock inside of her, their rough initial mating doing little to quench his desire for her. At her bedroom door, he hesitated as he found the light.

Her bedroom was quite a surprise to Jackson. It looked like it was designed for pleasure and he told her so. He looked at her sideways, wondering if she had designed it with that hope in mind. There was an antique Elizabethan carved canopy bed with a sumptuous deep-red and gold silken bedspread on it. The additional pieces of furniture, dressers, night tables, and lounge, matched the carved scrollwork of the bed.

She looked sheepish as they took in the deep-rose-colored walls and silky draperies covering the windows. "Perhaps I had something in mind but never did I imagine in all of my planning that it would feel like that, Jackson. That was indescribable. You were beyond my wildest dreams."

At her mention of their downstairs activities, he was immediately concerned. "Baby, did I hurt you?" he asked, looking for some sign that he was too rough with her.

"If you did anything, Jackson, it was a mark of the incredible pleasure you just gave me. Is it always like that for you?" she shyly questioned. He felt completely sated and couldn't help but grin with masculine arrogance over her obvious extreme satisfaction.

"No, baby. I have never felt like that. You brought me to my knees," he murmured, realizing the truth to his words. It had never felt like that before. "Now, I want to look at you. We are going to take this slowly as we waited too long to do this. I am going to worship this body all night, darlin'."

Jackson gently placed her lying across the huge bed. To him she looked like a very satisfied, sensual goddess with her long, gorgeous hair spread around her. He took in her torn silk shirt where her white, lacey bra was displaying her succulent breasts for his gaze. He laid himself down next to her and ran his hand gently to the side of her face. He felt her eagerly meet his kiss, which brushed across her lips in a loving caress. She was even more amazing than he thought she would be. He felt like a starving man at a feast and feared that he would never get enough of her.

Billie wanted to deepen the kiss, but Jackson continued to love her by sliding his lips along her jawline to her ear.

Jackson lightly traced the shell of her ear, causing her to shiver in delight and then moan as he sucked on her neck right below it.

Her hand started to wander over his chest, delighting in the hard planes around his pectorals. She slipped button after button free while slowly unwrapping her gift. His skin was still lightly bronzed after a summer of exposure with a light mat of soft curls. He was all man and she couldn't believe she was here, touching him.

Wanting to explore more, Billie eased herself up and smiled sensually at Jackson who lay patiently beside her. Never taking her lightly hooded gaze from his, she undid the last two buttons of her own ripped top and pulled it away. Billie felt empowered as she saw the darkening of his eyes as she slipped over him to straddle his waist. His erection pulsed up against her naked nether lips that were still moist and swollen. As Jackson reach his hands up to plump her breasts into his hands, she closed her eyes and moaned again. She loved his touch and wanted him to know it.

Jackson knew he would never forget how she looked at this moment. Her eyes were closed as he observed that her lacey straps were slipping down her arms from him massaging her breasts. Her skirt was hiked up around her waist, erotically showing him her bare, weeping pussy; and the thigh-high stockings displayed with her feet still encased in her four-inch heels. She was a delectable woman and he planned on feasting. Jackson reached around and unclasped her bra, throwing it somewhere across the room. He sat up and took one breast in his hand as he leaned forward to lightly kiss her nipple. The strawberry-red button puckered at his light touch, indicating her delight. She had tilted her head slightly as he began to kiss and taste her breast with gentle nips on her skin. Without warning, he suddenly latched his mouth around her breast, suckling her nipple into his wet mouth.

"Jackson, mmm. I have never felt like this," Billie managed to get out. Jackson merely hummed in response, squeezing one cheek of her ass while sucking her nipple to tight exquisiteness. Jackson had a feeling there was intense pleasure every time he nipped and sucked at her body. He switched breasts to worship the other.

"How did you keep these beauties from me, Billie? Now that they are mine, I promise you will have a permanent blush on you face, because I am going to either be thinking, looking, or touching them every chance I get. Tomorrow is Sunday dinner, prepare yourself."

With halfhearted indignation, she exclaimed, "You wouldn't!"

A devilish smile was all she received in return as he suddenly flipped them over and started grinding his pelvis into hers. He could feel her cream soaking through his jeans and decided it was time to find something new to explore. He stood by the side of the bed, ready to remove his pants when he felt her fingers.

"Please let me. I waited so long to see what I had been imagining." His button still undone from his hasty redress, she pulled his zipper down slowly. Using her fingertips, she ran them over the thick head of his cock and squeezed him through his boxers. He was so big that the bulbous, burgundy head now peaked from the top of the waistband, tempting her. She leaned and lightly ran her tongue over him, eliciting a light hiss from Jackson. Emboldened by his pleasure, she pulled his erection out and gently laid kisses up and down each side. She wrapped her hand around it, as though afraid to let it go, and made him step from his pants, boxers, and boots. Sliding off the bed, she sank to her knees and licked her lips, extracting another groan of encouragement from her cowboy. With a salacious intent, she sucked him into the warm cavern of her mouth. She ran her tongue around and around the bulging head of him, tasting a tangy mixture of herself and his cum. She was shocked as it caused her own pulse to her pussy and a flood of new arousal. She squeezed her thighs together while sucking him into her mouth over and over again. Her need began to rise as he grew even thicker as she sucked him in so far that he bumped the back of her throat. Using her discarded silk shirt, she cupped his sack and began rubbing it with the silken material.

Jackson almost lost it right there as he felt the squeezing pressure and rub of the soft silk. She was a witch tempting him to tie her to his bed and never let her go. He reached down and decided that he had let her have control for long enough. He threaded his fingers in her auburn tresses and started to pump into her hot, wet mouth. It felt like the pleasure was shooting everywhere in his body as he watched her breasts bounce with his thrusting. She looked like she was in a heavenly place, clutching one hand to his ass and the other rubbing his sack.

"Baby, lean away quickly," he panted out. She simply looked up at him and squeezed his sack hard.

"No, I waited forever to taste you. Let me."

With her confession, Jackson pumped harder into her mouth, clutching her hair, relishing his control over her movements. Blinding pleasure exploded across his body as he felt his cock blast out his release.

Jackson felt as jettisons of his cum splashed down her throat as she swallowed on him several times, much to his intense pleasure. He watched as she licked him clean and then shyly looked up at him again, as though pleased that she could put that expression of bliss on his face. Jackson unthreaded his hands from her hair and helped her to her feet.

"You are the most amazing woman, Billie. Now let me have my turn to pleasure your body. I want to taste every inch of you." His voice was rough from his orgasm.

He pulled her against his naked body and just held her for the moment, relishing the feel of her bare breasts pressed against his skin. Her perfume wafted up and teased his senses yet again into life. When was the last time he had been able to get aroused like this, over and over again? He smiled to himself. Probably never. He ran his hands down to the back of her skirt and unzipped it. She felt it slide down to the floor as he stepped away to admire her clad only in her thigh highs and heels. He wore an expression mixed with blatant possession and obvious pleasure.

Cocking his head to the side as he towered over her, he asked, "Um, have you been wearing stuff like this under your clothes every day you go to work, baby?"

Billie thought momentarily about lying to him but instead told him the truth. It was her secret pleasure and it made her feel very sensual. She almost could almost forget the reason she loved it so much because it had to do with the way Jackson was looking at her. Her husband had never looked at her like a treat to be savored. They had sex because he wanted release, not to enjoy each other or explore their physical connection. The lingerie made her feel like a sensual woman who could be desired. As Jackson leveled a very heated gaze into her eyes, she couldn't doubt that he wanted her, a lot.

"Well, then," he teased. "I see that I am going to have to keep an eye on your patient load and who gets to have an examination from my girl. I hope that these treats are for me alone now, baby."

"I almost died from sexual frustration waiting for you to come and get me, cowboy. You are going to have to suffer knowing that I may or may not be wearing unmentionables under my clothes at the office. You will have to just come into town and check it out every day!" she said with a smile in her voice.

"I just may do that, baby," he growled out. "You better wear a damned lab coat. I know Adam Taggart has excellent vision and he had better not know whether you are wearing silk or lace." With that he sat her on the edge of the bed and knelt. He slowly eased the stockings down her thighs followed by the stroke of his tongue. He gently took off her heels and placed her legs over his shoulders.

"Now I get to find out if you taste as good as you look, baby."

He kept his kisses featherlight as they roamed on the inside of her ankle, sucking softly on the skin of her calves to the back of her knees. She felt more decadent than she ever had in her life as he tasted and lapped her up with his tongue. She allowed him to part her thighs all the way, exposing her pussy completely to his gaze.

"You are exquisite, baby." He used one roughened finger to run over her swollen lips, which made her juices start running down toward her puckered rosette. She felt his hot breath just the second before he used his tongue to part her folds. She arched her back uncontrollably as a whimper escaped her mouth. Over and over again he tasted her with such obvious pleasure as he was lapping up the cream as it flowed from her.

His mind shouted in ownership as he feasted on her. He felt her quiver as he sucked on her mound while he gently inserted two fingers into her channel. She was so hot and slick with her arousal, it made him feel powerful and drunk at the same time. This woman affected him so intimately, so personally, unlike any feeling he had ever known. He placed his lips directly over her clit and sucked hard. He heard her wail as he pumped his fingers faster and deeper, curling them over her G-spot. With a shudder and a scream, she came so suddenly and with such obvious raw pleasure that he almost followed her over the edge, it was so erotic.

Thought became impossible for Billie as her entire pussy wouldn't stop spasming in delight as her orgasm rolled over and over her. Spots danced in front of her eyes as she felt faint. So overwhelmed by her pleasure, the only thing she was aware of was him, her lover. Her cowboy lover. She heard her heart thumping wildly. No one had ever made her feel like this, no one. She had wanted her husband to love her and make her feel like this, but now inwardly chuckled with the knowledge that it wouldn't have made any difference. She sadly had never felt like this for her husband. She was falling for Jackson. Perhaps already fell.

She was pulled from her feelings by the sensation of the bed dipping as a huge, hulking wall of man slowly fondled and kissed his way up from her pussy. She felt him pause at her breasts, kissing each of them almost reverently. Without warning, sharp pain and pleasure mixed as he bit down on the buds. He held them both, each in a palm of one of his hands. He pushed both together and put his face into the center while licking his tongue over the insides of the mounds. Jackson started to suck so hard, she was sure he was leaving hickeys. She wanted to say something, but the pleasure that he reignited in her was bursting into flames at his actions.

"Jackson, babe, are you marking your territory?" She giggled, glancing down at the fierce expression that she saw across his handsome features.

He paused in his suckling to answer her pointedly. "And if I was?"

With a gentle smile on her face, she said, "I am so crazy about you, sir, to be honest, I really wouldn't mind if you branded my body right now." She looked away shyly, unsure of how would he take her honesty.

She wasn't expecting his reaction. Jackson suddenly surged up her body and while leaning up on his arms, speared his cock swiftly into her dripping pussy with one thrust. Billie caught her breath as she was overcome with the sensation of being so filled and tight. She fit him like a glove. His cock felt like a long, hot iron that was melting not only her sex but her heart.

He could feel himself falling under her spell. As he slowly began to plunge in and out of her body, he held her gaze. Her beauty, intelligence, and charisma wrapped around her like a protective shell, hiding her erotic shelf. He felt like he could thrust for hours in and out of her wet pussy, drowning in the sensation. He leaned down and softly kissed her lips, still gazing deeply into her eyes. He felt and saw her breathing hitch as she shivered again from the sensations that their slow lovemaking was causing. Lovemaking. He always fucked women, but with Billie, this was something different, something he could get happily lost in. She felt amazing to him and he hoped he made her feel the same. He ran his lips over her eyelids, which closed as he kissed his way near. He nipped at her earlobes and sucked on the fleshy ends, pausing to rotate his hips and grind into her clit. He slid one hand down to cup one of her ass cheeks and run a finger over her back hole. There was so much cream over her thighs and ass, he easily slid a finger into her tight ass. He felt as she tried to launch herself up from the obvious surprise and pleasure at his brazen exploration.

Just when Jackson thought he had reached the maximum amount of pleasure possible, he felt her clench her inner walls tightly around his cock. With his head thrown back, he began pumping faster into her channel until he saw her eyes meet his again in a stunned expression. His ears rang with her screams of release as she came.

Billie felt herself start to come as he jackhammered into her pussy with a change of pace. Waves and waves of electric jolts ran over her. Just as she thought she couldn't stand it anymore, she felt his cum spray in hot pulses deep against her womb. Another orgasm caught her by surprise as it pummeled her already exhausted senses and body.

"Jackson, Jackson, oh god. Please!" she wailed as her body felt like it was splintering apart. She heard his harsh panting and reveled in the feel of his sweat-covered body mashed into hers as he collapsed into her. She kissed his cheeks and lips many times lightly as she tried to allow her brain to grab ahold of reality.

He pulled her thighs up and pushed her to wrap her legs around his waist, enfolding him into her intimate embrace. He felt like he needed the closest contact possible with her right at that moment.

"I think I have died and gone to heaven," Jackson muttered out of his mouth that was lying near her ear. "Nope, baby, I am sure that's where I am. I cannot feel my toes and I don't care. That was the most incredible thing ever, in my life, period. I am going to tattoo you, mark you, scent you, whatever. After this evening, the only word I have for you is 'mine.' Do you get that, baby? Mine."

She exhaustedly smiled up at his ruggedly handsome features. "Yes, master. I get it. However, I want it really badly, too, so if you think that I am listening to you just because you said it, well, too bad. You are now mine, too. So there! I have never felt this amazing."

"Baby, you made me feel the same. I may never move off your body because even if I could at this moment, I sure don't want to. Don't ruin my impression of controlling the situation. Let me think you are doing what I want for at least a day, okay?" He laughed. She joined in as they ran their hands lightly over each other's sweaty, satiated bodies. He lifted himself off to the side and lifted her up to the center of her bed.

"I will be right back. Just close your eyes for me darlin'." Jackson padded off toward what he thought was her bathroom. What he found was a sensual oasis that took his breath away. Her "bathroom" must have been part of the special build descriptions that Phillip and Sam had been talking about. It was an amazing combination of architectural design and sensual grotto specifically designed for invoking a certain mood. The walls were covered in roughed stacked stone, as though it was a subterranean cave with rough cut double sinks and hidden area for the commode. He could feel the radiant heat coming up through the cultured rough cut stone floor. He thought that alone was incredible until he saw the bathing area and his mouth just opened in wonder. She had a real waterfall shower with a continuing theme of the stacked stone to look natural and a tub that looked like it was a tiny pond nestled into the side of a cliff. He stood there speechless for moment. He admired her taste and design sense, something he himself loved and found yet another reason to fall for Billie. He paused at the thought of how much money she must have to have built a bathroom and house like this.

He returned to the bedroom with a damp washcloth and stopped by the side of the bed. His beautiful doctor had fallen into a deep sleep before his admiring eyes. Her breasts were exposed as the sheet only came up to her waist and he felt himself harden again. Chuckling at his appetite for her, he gently pulled the sheet down and lovingly cleaned away the evidence of their extreme and repetitious satisfaction. Placing a light, feathery kiss on her bare mound, he stood and climbed into bed with her. He gathered her into his arms so her head lay on his chest. He gazed at her beautiful feminine form pressed so trustingly against his. In the moonlight he felt his heart tighten up. As he started to fall asleep, he realized that his heart was in serious jeopardy, if not already lost to this incredible woman. His woman.

Chapter Eleven

Light had just started streaming into Billie's bedroom, highlighting Jackson's body intertwined with hers. Billie woke slowly with a smile. She was immediately aware of the hard masculinity that was spooned behind her body and the thick thigh that was wedged in between her legs. There was a hard bicep acting like a pillow while another hand was possessively cupping her breast. Even in his sleep, he was finally staking his claim. She tried not to move as she became aware of pleasant aches and soreness that she hadn't had the privilege of having in such a long time. Pleasured, she thought. Jackson had awakened her once more in the dark of night to pleasure her yet again and again. God, that man had some serious stamina. She glanced up at the heavens in thanks for the gift of ranchers. Soft kisses started moving over her hair as the sleeping hand on her breast began to awaken.

"Good morning, baby," a sexy, graveled voice belonging to Jackson murmured into her ear. She rolled over toward the voice and placed her own kisses along his pecs and neck.

"Good morning to you, too, handsome. I know I shouldn't be shy after last night but, Jackson, would it be too forward of me to ask if we can repeat it often?" Billie said without glancing up into his face, her eyes downcast. She felt a rumble of laughter as he tightened his arms around her in a steely embrace.

After abandoning her breast with some regret, he used one finger to tip her head up to meet his gaze. He lightly kissed her as he pressed her against his warm, hard body.

"I am going to make it my new life endeavor to pleasure you like that and often. I shouldn't be able to move but as you can feel, I already desire to have you yet again." He gave her a seductive look that went so well with his sleep-tousled hair and slumberous expression. She felt a rush of arousal drench her folds and rolled herself over him to straddle his cock. She evilly rocked her hips forward and back over his steely length, causing him to groan as though in pain. Feeling particularly wicked, Billie ran her finger over the tip to swipe up the drop of pre-cum and suck it off her finger and into her mouth.

The intended effect was lost as he grabbed her hips and shifted in one quick motion. He surged up into her pussy in one hard but deliciously tortuous stroke. She couldn't believe his strength as he thrust up and slammed her down in perfect rhythm. The sounds of the slapping of his cock back into her juicy pussy were echoing throughout the room, ramping up her arousal. She could smell the scent of sex and thought she would come right then and there. He was able to tilt her to grind against her clit, causing sparks of heated pleasure to shoot through her pelvis. What a way to wake, she thought. She held her breath until her orgasm started to roll over her, and she let out a lengthy series of delightful screams. He thrust up in one more hard motion and growled out his own animalistic orgasm. She could feel his erection pulsing within her and felt again some sort of primitive satisfaction that he was hers.

Lying flush along the top of Jackson's body, she sighed in satisfaction. He was perfection in so many ways to her. She quickly hoped he didn't break her heart.

As though sensing her thoughts, he started to rub his hands over her back and cheeks soothingly, as though to calm her.

"See what you do to me, baby? I cannot control my body or the direction of my thoughts around you," Jackson said with a wicked grin.

"First of all, you don't have to be a doctor to know that some of that was the morning wood stuff. Secondly, I was the one who couldn't get it under control there and threw myself onto you. You cannot take credit for this time, mister!"

Liking her saucy response, he just grinned and squeezed her cheeks apart while running a finger up and down the inner edge of the crack, causing her to pause in her speech and shiver. He pasted an innocent look on his face and just shrugged his shoulders.

He felt as Billie snuggled back over into his side and prepared to nap with him after their latest pleasure session.

"Jackson?"

"What is it, baby?" he mumbled back, already half into his napping state.

"What did your father whisper to you last night as we were leaving the bar?" she asked.

He opened one eye and chuckled. "He told me not to step foot on the ranch again until Monday morning, with the exception for Sunday dinner."

It really was nine o'clock in the morning. Jackson couldn't remember the last time he had slept that late or slept so well. He sat lazily at the island in the kitchen listening to Billie hum in blissful contentment while making them pancakes and sausage. Jackson was enjoying his own sense of satisfaction over looking at her beautiful self. She wore a simple white silk halter chemise that fell to her knees. It hugged her luscious figure without being too overt. He could practically feel himself sigh with happiness and satisfaction at this woman who had claimed his every thought. He felt more alive than he had in years with an eagerness that felt foreign to him. She smiled over at him and he gave her a huge smile back. As she turned away, he stood and sauntered over to her at the stove. Gently embracing her from behind, he leaned down and nuzzled her neck.

"Behave yourself, sir, or I won't be able to give you the nourishment you need to keep up activity like that. Now that I finally have gotten to sample some Powell love, believe me, mister, I am going to be requesting some serious repeat performances quite frequently, so eat up," Billie said with a laugh.

"You are all the nourishment I really need, baby. However, it is I who will decide when we participate in mutual pleasuring, and trust me, you are going to be sore and sleepy all the time," he said cockily as he took her lips in a hard kiss. She half turned in his arms while still brandishing the spatula as he began his heavenly assault on her mouth. He thrust his tongue into her warmth to mate with hers in an erotic caress. For several moments, they indulged in his sensual assault. She broke the kiss and leaned against him with a sigh. He turned her back toward the stove but started to rub his boxers-covered groin against her backside.

"It would be a shame to waste all that delicious food you are making. Please try to concentrate, baby. I am a hungry man! Focus!" he said with a wicked smile while running his hands over her soft mound. Billie tried to keep her attention on the cooking food, but Jackson knew that his hands were causing her to squeeze her thighs together as he fueled her new arousal.

They ate at the island with a happiness that Billie hadn't known in years. They talked about the construction of the house, her motivation to move out here after Matthew's death, and his connection to his land. As expected, he raved about the bathroom, promising of the naughty delights that were in store for her there later that day. Jackson had quickly showered before he came down with the intent of just briefly cleaning up, but as Billie had started breakfast, he got sidetracked in his idea of breaking in her tub together. Promising to be no more than a half hour, Jackson jumped into his truck to get some clothes for the weekend and feed the horses quickly.

Billie sat down on her couch and watched the dust rise as he pulled away down the lane. She laid her head back and sighed with pure happiness. Her soul felt whole for the first time in perhaps...forever. She decided that she wasn't going to try to analyze her feelings right at that moment.

She heard her cell phone ring in her purse and padded over to see who was calling. She wasn't on call so she didn't think it would be Julia calling with a patient issue. She looked at the screen but all it said was private number. As she listened to the message, she got chills. The message contained a garbled voice that was undeniably male. It threatened that she didn't know who she was dealing with and that she should weigh her choices carefully. What the heck was going on here? Who would want to threaten her at the office and now got her cell? Gwen? She saved the message and sat on the floor to hug Zeus's big, furry body to her own. Nobody was going to easily scare her. She wasn't going to allow some wacko to upset her or undermine the happiness that she felt was emanating from her pores.

Ten minutes later, a very handsome cowboy returned with a cocky grin on his face. As she opened the front door, she was pushed aside by another female desperate for Jackson's attention. Madison stood on her hind legs and planted her paws on his chest, trying determinedly to kiss his face.

"Down," he commanded in a steely voice dripping in that male strength that made women wet and weak in the knees. Madison reluctantly sat to his side as he patted her head and swept forward to his originally intended female. Billie felt herself lifted high into his arms and swung around as he planted a hot kiss on her open mouth.

"Now, that was the kiss I was hoping for! Not being licked by your lovable guardians," he groused at her with a grin.

Forming a smile of her own at her lofty perch, she said back, "Licked, kissed...whatever. Madison and Zeus cannot seem to figure out which is which." She saw that he had an overnight bag with him and a bouquet of flowers that he must have stopped quickly for on his way back over.

"I was gone less than an hour and I already missed you, woman. What have you done to me? I feel like a besotted suitor."

He placed her down so she could smell her flowers and hug him tightly. She didn't want to respond to his comment and make him question his actions. She just appreciated that he missed her. So much that she wrinkled her brow when she remembered the disturbing call on her cell.

"What's the matter, baby? You don't like the flowers?" he asked quickly.

"No, it's not that, they are just so lovely and thoughtful, Jackson. I love them. It's just that I got a weird message on my cell while you were gone and it unnerved me a bit. That's all."

Jackson immediately gave off a different energy of cold control as he asked gently, "May I listen to the message, please?"

She handed him the phone and watched his face while he listened. His features gave off no information as to his thoughts as he closed it and handed it back to her. "Save the message, baby, but I don't want you to worry. I will deal with this and no one is going to upset you. I won't allow it."

He spoke with such authority and concern that she didn't have the heart to get annoyed at his high-handed comments. She had been taking care of herself for years. It rather felt like a blanket of comfort and relief to know that she wasn't alone and this Neanderthal of a man was acting like one. Billie inwardly laughed at the thought that every now and again, a woman needed a Neanderthal for protection, comfort, and sex. Jackson appeared even more appealing the more she thought about it.

Jackson seemed to arrogantly presume that her smile was one of compliance to his command. She let him think it. It was good for him, she supposed with a laugh. The fact that he let her go up to shower alone told her volumes as to where her thoughts were. She was glad, in a way, as she didn't want him distracted over the call when they used the decadent bathroom together the first time. As she showered, memories of the morning and previous night bombarded her like the sheets of warm water running over her skin. She kept passing the soft, lathered soap over her breasts, trying to imitate Jackson's passionate touches. *Nope, not going to work.* In the past, she was able to try to imagine up a mystery man while masturbating for her pleasure, but now that she had a master of sensual pleasures waiting for her downstairs, well, nothing but the real thing would satisfy. As she stepped out from the steamy enclave of stone, she was startled by the man waiting for her. As if to watch over her, as his sexy expression indicated he had been doing, he now held a bath towel to wrap her up in. With a soft kiss, Jackson carried her into the bedroom and smacked her butt.

"Get some clothes on this fine ass, Billie. I want to go riding with you and see your land," he said with a smile. As she pulled out her bra and thong, he lay down on the bed that he must have thoughtfully made and extended his hand.

"What?" Billie asked, unsure of why he was wiggling his fingers at her.

"I want to see what is on the menu today so I know how it is going to feel in my hands later," Jackson said with a serious face.

Billie looked at him momentarily shocked and then, deciding to play along, handed him her intimates. Last night in the few moments in between the intense sexual episodes, he had remarked on how much he loved her obvious pleasure in her sexy lingerie. She had chosen a soft-rose satin bra and thong to go under her ribbed turtleneck and riding pants. She had forgone the idea of wearing a sports bra, like she ought to, instead deciding to wear something to distract him. No matter what she wore, she knew that either he would be imagining what she looked like in them all day or her breasts bouncing around so much it would distract him plenty. No matter what, she was sure of her success!

Jackson handed them back to her with an evil grin on his face. She had no idea what he had planned, but she had a feeling that she would like it, based on the look. She felt flushed and warm as he watched her dress. It was a very intimate thing to do and she felt a wash of pleasure.

* * * *

"I do know how to saddle my own horse, Jackson!" Billie grumbled as he quickly tacked up both Danny and Sheeza. *Sheesh!* Jackson moved around the inside of her tack room with a fluidity and gracefulness that indicated his expertise from a lifetime of repetition. Instead of fighting for the privilege, she leaned back to survey her surroundings. Her barn had the scent of the new wood from the build mixed with hay, almost a comforting odor. In it were two new members of her family and a man who was rapidly sucking her into his world and hopefully his heart. As if he could read her mind, he turned just then to give her a condescending smile of reassurance.

"Just because a man opens a door, puts you in a car, or saddles a horse doesn't mean that he thinks you can't, darlin'. It just might indicate that he thinks you are a lady, in this case *my lady*, and should be treated as such. Sorry, but that's just the way it's gonna be with me." Jackson didn't even turn around as he said his little speech. The man definitely didn't have any difficulty being in charge, that's for sure! She tried to feel annoyed but found herself outwardly grinning at his high-handedness. She came out west for a change. Well, this certainly qualified. It definitely would be nice to be on a pedestal for a while.

When he was finished, she walked over to Sheeza and swung herself up without so much as a step into the stirrup. She turned back to look at him up on Danny, only to see his eyebrow lift and make a smirk at her antics. With that, they both took off at a trot.

Billie took a deep breath and momentarily closed her eyes. Alive. Free. Home. She felt those words vibrating through her body. Waves of happiness surrounded her as surely as the wind that was lightly whipping her hair. Another feeling started to permeate her brain, too.

Love. What? No, it couldn't be. She had wanted all her life to feel an overwhelming love that could fulfill her, but obviously that wasn't meant to be in her first marriage. She snuck a quick glance at Jackson. He rode with as much confidence as he did everything else. He and Danny seemed to gracefully move as one unit. He exuded raw masculinity that made her wet and squirm slightly in the saddle, even as she looked at him now. He met her gaze and rewarded her with a heart-melting smile.

"What are you thinking of, baby, that has you looking so happy?" he inquired.

Billie just shrugged her shoulders and gave him a soft smile back. She rode ahead of him for the moment, not wanting him to read her thoughts as he often was so able to do. She would have to try to protect her heart a bit as she suspected Jackson was enjoying himself with her but hardly likely to fall on his knees declaring his love for her. She let out a low chuckle at the image of him on his knees in her head.

If she knew Jackson's thoughts, she might be blushing a bit more. He was at first slightly surprised at the ease she exhibited around the horses and riding, as though she, too, had done it all her life. He would have to ask her how she learned. He originally thought that she was more of a high-maintenance kind of girl, but she kept proving him wrong. It was the long work hours, cooking, cleaning, house calls, mucking out the barn, and now her riding skills that changed his perception of Billie. Yep, she was intriguing, more to him every damn day. Being the man that he was, he couldn't help but notice how fine her ass looked from behind in that saddle. He watched her use her strong thighs to glide with Sheeza and couldn't help but feel a bit of envy for her saddle as he watched it mash up into her hot pussy. He felt the stirring of his erection as he shifted his attention to watching her breasts bounce with the horse's movements. Ugh, it was going to be a long day before he could sink into her wet heat again. He should have made her wear that sports bra. Thinking about her lingerie choices had his cock pressing against his jeans painfully. He was going to have to distract himself, he thought with chagrin.

"Billie, let's walk the boundary of your property. Have you seen it all yet?

"Not yet. I have been so busy that I just take each horse for a run every other day. I have been staying to the same areas, as I am sure of the grounds there. It is so beautiful out here, Jackson. I am so happy to have moved to Wyoming," she gushed out.

He gave her another heart-stopping smile. "I hope the scenery isn't the only thing making you so pleased," he added innocently, questioningly. He was certainly pleased with his new neighbor!

She stopped Sheeza and looked at Jackson seriously for a moment. "Jackson, may I say something without you freaking out or acting all typical male on me?"

"I will try my best to control my Neanderthal," was all he said in reply while focusing all his attention on her.

Billie looked down at Sheeza's neck and decided to just say what she thought. She didn't come all the way out here to hide or be afraid. She came to get what she always wanted.

Leveling her eyes up to his, she moved her horse so close to his that their thighs lightly touched. "I mean this with every fiber of my being. I have never been this happy, in my entire life."

Jackson reached out and gently stroked his fingers over her jaw line. "Like I asked a moment ago, why?" His look was a mix of tenderness and barely controlled passion. He looked like he wanted to swoop her over to his horse and kiss her senseless. Then Billie glanced down his body and couldn't help but see his arousal straining against its confines. A ripple of awareness sent her own pulses racing and gushes of moisture to her folds. As though he could sense her own rising desire for him, he leaned a little closer to her. He leaned his hand inside her jacket and moved to stroke the back of his fingertips over the side swell of her breast, causing her to lightly gasp.

"I waited my whole life to feel alive. I think I just did what was expected of me before I got here, but now I can see I was just existing, not living. Then I moved here, to a place I only dreamed of before. To be able to ride on my own property, live in the house I helped design, and practice medicine to people who genuinely appreciate me as I appreciate them. It is amazing." She paused for a moment as his hand stilled its light exploration, gathering her courage.

"Then you showed up, literally saving me. It was surreal. I never really counted on meeting someone like you. I had hoped, but it was the silly thoughts that all women have, not a real expectation. I am not sure what this is between us, but suffice it to say, you make my pulse leap when you walk in and smile at me while my belly gets that butterfly feeling. I have never felt that. Ever. I have never felt the passion that I feel when you touch me and never felt the ecstasy that you give me when we make love. I am sorry if that is a bit much, but it's how I feel, and you asked," Billie said, ending up feeling a bit uncertain and shy after exposing her thoughts.

Jackson was quiet for a moment. Then he tilted his head and effortlessly plucked her off her horse onto Danny to sit across his lap. His erection pressed hard into her hip but didn't distract her from the intense look on his face. She was suddenly nervous, thinking that perhaps she shouldn't have expressed herself.

"Billie, you know I was married before to Gwen obviously. Before her, I was a typical young guy. I did a little roping on the rodeo circuit and riding the bunnies that come with the territory. After I settled back in on the ranch, I met Gwen and figured that she was what I needed for a ranching wife." He paused as though reflecting deeply for once. "I don't like to be reminded of how much of a mess I made by choosing what I thought I needed instead of what I wanted. Maybe I did it because I didn't know what I wanted then. However, I do know now. Never be afraid to speak plainly with me, baby. I despise games and I have had enough. What I will tell you is that I want you in a way that I have never, ever wanted a woman, and I don't just mean for a quick fuck. I can get that anytime, anywhere. You, however, do something to me every time I see you, too. I have been trying to fight it, but yesterday, I just quit. I need *you*. I am not sure I am a good boyfriend and maybe I cannot get close to a woman, but I promise I will try not to screw it up. I need you so much sometimes that I cannot think or breathe. Shit, now I sound like a girl." He ended his answer with a small laugh, looking away from her for a second.

Billie felt so many things at that moment. She wasn't going to make him any more uncomfortable, however, by saying anything else. Instead, she looked up into his eyes, giving him all the love and emotion that she was feeling at that moment. He gave her back a look of intense heat that shook her insides. Her hands stole up his muscled wall of a chest to twine behind his neck just as he crushed her to him and blasted her with the heat of his kiss as his lips met hers. He masterfully allowed no resistance as he plundered her mouth with his hot tongue over and over again. It was as though Jackson had to kiss her or die of thirsting for her just then. His hand wrapped tightly in her hair, tilting her head to a better angle for him while mashing her breast within his huge hand. His fingers ran over her pebbled nipples that were straining against her shirt. Billie could feel herself start panting into his mouth as their tongues intertwined. She felt his hands suddenly switch to rolling her nipples deliciously between his thumbs and forefingers as she submitted to his assault on her senses. She became soaked within moments of his kiss and began to shift her wet core over his jutting erection. Just as he was about to rip open her shirt, they heard more horses thundering their way.

"Shit, what the hell is this?" Jackson growled out as he cradled her face against his chest while pulling her coat closed. Billie tried to catch her breath as she burrowed her face into his neck. His arms tightened protectively around her as he saw Hunter, Troy, and Brody emerge from the woods toward them.

Jackson came immediately alert and concerned that they would come looking for either him or her today.

"What's wrong?"

Jackson noticed Troy and Brody smirking as they observed Billie clutching Jackson's coat to her face and his own very rigid posture. Jackson rolled his eyes in response, hoping that Billie kept her face hidden so she wouldn't notice their awareness of what they had interrupted.

"Nothing is wrong, cousin. Hunter found some odd horse tracks on the outskirts of his land where he hadn't been and followed them to our land. They were along the south edge. We saw him and followed them here to Billie's. Did she get lost and backtrack perhaps? It's only one set of tracks," Brody informed Jackson. Brody was the sweet, serious one since his father had passed away. He took the family's happiness and safety very personally. Jackson inwardly smiled that Brody must have started seeing Billie as family.

Hunter shifted in his saddle and just nodded, very typical communication for the hulking man. His only acknowledgment of the intimate situation that they had interrupted was his comment.

"Billie, you okay?" he heard Hunter grunt out. Jackson knew that Hunter had no misconceptions about why she was on his lap, but probably wanted to make sure that they hadn't done any permanent damage by coming up unexpectedly on them.

Billie was awash with embarrassment from being caught so aroused and about to somehow fuck the life out of Jackson in his saddle. Practically bursting with her blush, she turned her face slightly to answer Hunter without opening her eyes or removing herself from her safe position on Jackson.

"Thank you, Hunter, yes. I am just fine. Thank you for asking."

Jackson almost laughed at how polite Billie became when she was embarrassed. Her arms were tight around his waist and he gave her a reassuring squeeze. Thoughts were running through his head for the moment, though as to the broken window at the office, dead flowers, weird phone calls, and now unexplainable horse tracks. He was going to have to have a talk with the men tomorrow at dinner.

"Well, we will get ourselves going as the whole purpose of you not doing any chores was to, um, get to know Doc a bit better. See you both at dinner. Do us proud, Jackson!" Troy chortled, laughing like a loon. Troy took off pretty quickly, probably knowing that either Jackson or Hunter would have hit him in the head had they caught him.

"Idiot" was all Jackson responded. "We aren't even sure he really is a Powell," he laughingly leaned down and mentioned to Billie as though to ease her discomfort. "There could have been a mix-up in the hospital."

"Except that he looks just like all of you, just a bit shorter."

"That's why we call him Tiny," Jackson said with a smile. Light snow began falling as they watched the men ride off toward Powell land. Jackson took one finger and lifted her chin up. He held her gaze as he murmured, "Where were we before the dumbass triplets interrupted us?"

Billie lifted her eyes to melt into his heated expression. She took her hand and cupped the side of his face. She leaned up toward him and lightly kissed his mouth. He felt her tongue softly run along the seam of his, back and forth as though memorizing the taste of him. He groaned in reaction and his hands pulled her tighter against his broad chest. The snow was wet and heavy, creating a romantic picture of the two of them oblivious to the world in their loving embrace. Jackson slowly ended the kiss and looked up in surprise.

"It's a perfect day for the first real snowfall, baby. Do you like it? I never asked. It makes you look like an angel, the most beautiful woman in the world."

Billie laughed at the sweet things he said while looking around at the amazing wonderland around them, realizing it truly was hers. "Yes, Jackson, I love the snow. Always have. It was one of the big reasons that I wanted to move out here to Wyoming. Maybe I psychically knew you would be out here waiting for me and that egged me on."

"Glad to hear that you like both the snow and me, but let's get on home and get you warmed up. Perhaps from the inside out?" he said with a leer. "I think we are going to have to try out that tub together, just to warm up, you understand." He placed a hot kiss just below her earlobe and sucked lightly. With a demonstration of his amazing strength, he swung her back onto Sheeza and just grinned at her. Billie shook her head and knew he was cracking up. Maybe she would prescribe him some mood-stabilizing meds. Something. Well, he definitely didn't need Viagra. One look at his groin confirmed for her that it wasn't a med he required!

Chapter Twelve

They rode back to the barn just enjoying the weather, the ride, and each other. After they slid off the horses, Jackson went into her tack room to get a towel to rub them down. Once the horses were tacked down and munching happily in their stalls, Jackson turned to look at his woman. She was leaning against the inside of the main barn door gazing dreamily out at the sudden heavy snowfall. She appeared lost in what he guessed were pleasant thoughts, based upon the smile on her face. He quietly walked up behind her and wrapped his arms around her from behind. She leaned her body back into his and sighed in pleasure. Jackson leaned down to breathe softly into her ear and run his lips down her neck. He felt like he could never get enough of her scent and taste as he sampled his way down the column of her neck to her shoulder. She shuddered in response and tried to turn into his embrace but he wouldn't let her.

"I want to taste you, baby. No, I am going to taste you. Now." Billie felt his hands at her waist undoing her pants snap and quickly lowering her zipper. His hand slid roughly down her flat belly, causing ripples of hot anticipation to flow through her. His callused fingers easily slid into her drenched, slick folds, forcing a groan from Jackson.

"Baby, baby," he groaned out. "You are so wet. I cannot wait another second and I am not going to." With that, he spun her with her back against the door and pulled her pants down. He sat her on the bale of hay and spread her thighs with his callused palms. He was practically salivating as he took in her soaked thong and glistening juices running down her inner thighs. He hooked a finger under her rose-colored satin, pulling it to the side, and fastened his mouth directly onto her pussy. Billie let out a gasp and clutched at his head as he speared her with his tongue and lapped at her intently. He sucked and tasted her by running his tongue through her folds again and again, causing her to cream copiously.

Billie had never felt particularly sexy before, but since meeting Jackson, she felt like a different being had inhabited her body. She heard the echoes in the barn of her pleasured moans as she glanced down at him kneeling between her wet thighs. Jackson appeared to be thoroughly enjoying his task as he licked her folds from clit to rosette, making delicious sighing sounds indicating his own pleasure. The scene was surreal with the snow falling outside the barn, Jackson's lips wet with her cream, and her partially naked while her lover gave her more pleasure than she had ever had in her life. Billie knew this was a moment, a changing point, and she had no intention of ever going back to the way she was. At that moment, Jackson thrust three fingers into her and curled them to hit her sweet spot. Billie arched her back in ecstasy as she felt a fresh gush of her juices coat his hands again.

As for Jackson, he growled out his delight at her taste, a tangy sweetness, while reveling at her body's arch in obvious pleasure. With his thoughts turning possessive, he enjoyed that it was the pleasure that he was giving her. Mine, he thought. She was his and she was going to come, now. With that thought, he sucked her clit roughly into his mouth and lightly bit down. Billie let out a scream as fire burned into her pussy and forced her thighs around his head. Her hands threaded into his hair as she screamed out her incredible pleasure. She felt his lips gently soothing her down with small, soft laps of his tongue. As she began to tremble, he stood her up and pulled her pants back up into place while enfolding her in his embrace.

"Let me get you inside and warm, baby. Thank you for letting me have a taste of you," Jackson murmured into her hair. Jackson placed a soft kiss on her head and lifted her up into his arms. While carrying her into the house, she snuggled into his protective embrace. She felt almost numb, she was so overcome from his thorough pleasuring of her body. And pleasure her he did, she thought delightedly. She softly kissed him lovingly as he entered the house through the back door and could taste her own musky flavor on his lips, reigniting her passion for him.

He made his way around the dogs up to her bedroom where he gently put her down. His eyes were smoldering as he looked down on her. She turned to him and ran her hands possessively up to his shoulders to push his jacket off to the floor. She worked her hands on the buttons of his shirt, not lifting her eyes to his but rather focused on the task, licking her lips in anticipation. She heard him groan as he watched her tongue slide over her lips and bit down gently in concentration. His chest was slowly revealed inch by inch to her gaze. He was such a gorgeously fit man. Billie ran her hands over his wall of a chest as she leaned in and ran her tongue down as far as his parted shirt allowed. Jackson closed his eyes in pleasure on feeling her mouth begin to explore his body.

"Jackson, you are such a delicious man. I cannot believe a man as masculine as you wants a bookish woman like me."

His gazed burned electric pulses of arousal right to her groin, causing her thighs to clench.

"If all bookish women looked and acted like you, then I would be in serious trouble, baby. However, I have never in my life met any sort of woman like you. You are like a sweet treat that I never want to stop savoring."

With that, he lowered his head and ran his tongue over the curve of her neck while divesting her of her shirt with one loud tear from her body. She stiffened in shock that was soon replaced with her deep moans as he ran his hands up her belly to the undersides of her breasts, running them back and forth. He bent his head further to suck her nipple through the satin of the bra he had so admired earlier in the day. Billie felt the flames burst within her as her thong was soaked with fresh cream. As Jackson unfastened her bra, she watched in amazement and unbelievable pleasure as he suckled her nipple into his mouth and bit down, causing electric pleasure-pain. Her pussy spasmed again in anticipation. His hands quickly undid her pants, pushing them and her thong off to the floor. Billie clutched at Jackson's shoulders wildly, trying to melt into his body as he switched to suckle the other breast while swirling his tongue around her soft skin.

Jackson thought he had died and gone to heaven at the taste of her in the barn, but it seemed that he was never going to get enough of this woman. He felt her inquisitive hands run under the band of his jeans and one by one, agonizingly, release the buttons free with a loud pop after each. He felt as she did not waste a moment in slipping her hand erotically under the band of his boxers. He heard her sigh of pleasure that mingled with his own as she wrapped her hand around his pulsing erection. He felt as her thumb rubbed sensually back and forth over the bulging head of his cock and used his pre-cum as lubricant to run her hand up and down the focus of her pleasure.

Billie heard him groan as he straightened up and tilted his head back, obviously enjoying the feel of her exploring hand. The skin of his erection was so silky and tight, it made her mouth water to taste him again. As she leaned down to do just that, she was whisked up into his arms again. She felt him pull out of his jeans as he walked into the bathroom and put her down. Billie felt her body alive with passion as it had never been in her life. She took a glance in the mirror as she set about lighting candles and didn't recognize the woman who looked back at her. Her hair was in complete disarray, her eyes darkened with passion, and her lips moist and swollen from Jackson's kisses. The water was running, and she watched as Jackson filled the grotto tub. Billie closed her eyes momentarily in anticipation of making love to Jackson in that sensual alcove of a bathtub that she had had Sam and Phillip build.

"Baby?" she heard Jackson question as his strong arms encircled her from behind.

She leaned back into his strength to feel his huge erection pulsing into her lower back. It was so long, it just touched below his belly button. She rubbed herself against it a few times before she heard his sharply inhaled breath.

"Minx, you are going to kill me. If I don't get inside of you soon, I am going to explode. I want that ass soon but for tonight, I am just going to prepare you. You are mine and I am going to spend the rest of the evening reminding you." He looked at her with arousal blatantly evident in the tension of his stance, as if his cock wasn't reminder enough.

"Jackson, I have been yours since the moment I met you. However, feel free to remind me as much and as often as you want to."

"Thank you for your permission, Doctor, but I really wasn't asking. Come with me now so I can fuck you into oblivion," Jackson ground out.

She took his hand as he led her into the bathing area. Steam from the sunken tub cast a sensual tone to the space. Billie loved how the tub was completely hidden under stacked stone that even edged the top, like it was a hot spring. She had felt very decadent ordering it this way but must have instinctively known that there was an amazing man just waiting for her out here in Stony Creek, Wyoming.

Jackson stepped into the water first and groaned out a sigh of pleasure as he sank into the sculpted tub. She took his hand and stepped in after him. He had his hands on her hips and she watched as he just allowed his eyes to roam up and down slowly, taking in her soft curves. His lips curved into a devilish smile.

"Baby, you are perfection, from your soft, lush breasts, to this narrow little waist, to your gorgeous, fuckable ass. For now though, come here and let me pleasure you."

He pulled her forward and moved her thighs to the outside of his as he sat on the submerged ledge. She slowly sank down, inch by inch, onto his huge erection.

With her head thrown back, she sighed in raw pleasure as she felt him stretch her channel deliciously tight. It was like being speared with a scalding poker of hot fire. His face was a mask of tight control as his hands tightened around her hips as her ass met his sack. They stared into each other's eyes as she began to move sensually up and down his shaft, clenching as she got to the tip. Jackson leaned over her and roughly sucked the skin at the base of her neck into his wet mouth. As she continued to move up and down, increasing their pleasure, he bit her lightly, ensuring that there was another mark of his on her body that would brand her as his alone. His hands helped her increase the pace as one of his thumbs ran from where they were joined to the hood of her clit. He teased her by rubbing over and over it, eliciting rough cries from her throat. She felt the tip of his finger begin to run down the crack of her ass and swirl around the outside of her dark, puckered hole. She momentarily stiffened in shock.

"Easy, baby," he crooned in her ear. "I am just stretching you a bit so I will be able to sink my cock into your amazing ass soon. Just relax and let me love you."

Jackson suddenly pinched her clit with his thumb and forefinger, forcing an explosion of radiating ecstasy that pulsed from her pussy to the roots of her hair. Sensing her impending orgasm, he quickly slid his finger fully into her dark hole, pressing the sides of her soft, forbidden walls. Her pleasure raced on and on, forcing her thighs to squeeze Jackson's violently while riding him hard. Her hoarse cries and clenching had him slamming her hips into his groin, bringing on an orgasm of epic proportions that made his cock feel like it would burn away. He continued to shudder and hold her tight against him as he released long, hot streams of his cum into her channel while roaring out his pleasure.

Billie just sagged against Jackson's chest, panting uncontrollably from the bliss that he had just bestowed upon them. His harsh breathing rocked her as he caught his breath. She felt his light kisses over her head and cheeks as she rubbed her face against his wet body like a contented kitten.

"Jackson, that was…" She couldn't find the words to describe the feelings that were running through her.

"Shh. Just let me hold you. Don't try to think for once. Just be," he murmured into her hair.

She didn't know how long they lay there like that, but after a period of time, he turned on the jets and lovingly soaped up her body, worshipping her every curve. He even washed her hair, turning it into a lesson in sensual play as he used his fingers to coax every bit of pleasure not only from making love but a loving massage as well. God that man has amazing hands, she thought. Billie let out a giggle and thought that she could retire in Tahiti if she just rented this man out as a love slave.

"Are your brothers and cousins as amazing as you are when it comes to pleasuring women, Jackson?" she breathlessly asked him, practically purring in enjoyment.

He stopped his massage to roughly turn her to face him. "I wouldn't really know that sort of information, madame, but I assure you, if you ever think to test any other waters, Powell or otherwise, prepare for not being able to sit on your ass for a decade." His eyes blazed with heated jealousy.

She felt her pussy clench again in response to his possessiveness. "I wasn't interested in learning firsthand, Jackson." She tried to soothe him by running her soapy hands over his chest, placing light kisses on his sensuous lips.

"I just thought that we could make a fortune if we opened a sex ranch with the Powell men pleasuring women who need some affection both physically and psychologically. I have never been this relaxed or sexually satisfied. I think I am going to need to put this in the town's paper under services for hire." She purred into his ear. At his lopsided grin that followed, she tightened her arms around his neck in amusement.

"Just make sure my only client is one incredibly hot doctor who doesn't have enough common sense to stay off of ladders. Also please do not mention this to my mother or aunt because they have been hankering for a vacation house. They might see this as a good idea to increase revenue without them having to do a lick of work!" He laughed out loud.

Chapter Thirteen

"Good god, woman, I ought to marry you," Jackson moaned out as Billie kneaded his buttocks rhythmically with both of her hands. "I had no idea that your hands were so strong. Baby, if I knew what sort of doctoring you could do with those fingers alone, I might not have played so hard to get!"

Billie was sitting on Jackson's back but facing his feet, her naked body pressed intimately against Jackson's lower back while rubbing his butt. It turned out that he had a thing with his behind being rubbed, apparently a huge turn-on. Really, though, a soft breeze seemed to turn on Jackson. If Billie wanted to get any rest, perhaps this wasn't such a good idea. Well, it's not a bad way to go! she thought with a devilish grin. She had made them comfort food for dinner, her own gourmet version of a pot pie. Jackson was such a carnivore that she was hesitant to use only chicken, but he had devoured his own and all of her leftovers. How the heck the man had the body on him that he had, she had no idea.

Billie let her eyes wander over his taut buttocks, firm thighs, and sculpted calves. Years of ranching and life in the saddle had left him looking like a feast for the feminine eyes. It had better be only her eyes from now on, she thought suddenly. Images of Gwen's evil verbal spewings interrupted her musings. Billie decided then and there that it was time for a talk about what was going on.

"Jackson?" she whispered over the soft crackle of the fireplace.

"Mmm-hmm?" was all the reply she heard.

"I want to talk about what is going on here, if it's okay with you."

Jackson lifted his head to look over his shoulder at her bare form that was sitting on his own naked skin. She knew that he could feel her hot folds pressing warm and moistly on his cock. He sighed in pleasure. With a suddenness that startled Billie, he bucked up, almost to throw her off, and flipped over onto his back. His hands were lightning quick as he caught her just as she was going to fall to the side and locked her against his groin. He wore a naughty expression that she couldn't quite read. All she knew was that his fingertips were running lightly up and down her spine while he pressed his ever-present erection against her creamy femininity.

"I would think what was going on would be perfectly obvious to a trained doctor, such as yourself, baby. No?" Jackson quirked his lips up as though in innocent thought.

"Um, no. I was wondering what direction you see us going in. I mean, after this weekend, some things have changed." Billie was rather nervous bringing it up. What if this didn't mean as much to him as it did to her? What if it didn't mean much to him at all? After all, the Powell men had legions of women on standby to become part of their world. They traipsed through Billie's office every day talking about the Powell men, unaware of her personal vested interest. People trusted their doctors, and well, just unloaded their deepest thoughts and desires on them as though needing to vent.

"Okay, darlin'. Here is my take on what has occurred and where I think we are going. First of all, we made lots and lots of good love. Well, not entirely true. It was amazing, no, spectacular loving. Yep, that's what it was. Oh, I guess it could also be referred to in medical terminology as practicing baby making. Sure, that's it! Does that clear anything up for you, baby?" Jackson teased.

Jackson could tell from Billie's annoyed look that she didn't find his teasing very amusing. Jackson couldn't have been more pleased if he had won the lottery at that moment. Her obvious need for reassurance fired his heart and his blood like nothing ever had in his life. She must be genuinely falling for him if she needed that. No more games, he inwardly sighed in relief. His erection pulsed against her in response to his thoughts, but ironically it was his heart that took precedence at that moment.

"Baby, all teasing aside, it should be blatantly obvious what is going on here. After denying both of us for way too long, I realized that I don't think I can live without being near you. I know for sure that no other man is ever going to touch you again. Don't be afraid of me or this change. It just makes us an official 'us.'" He thought for a moment and continued with a laugh, "Now we are officially boyfriend and girlfriend."

Billie snorted at that ridiculous end to his speech. Boyfriend indeed! Men really were annoying creatures. She felt his hands still in their explorations of her back and tighten around her waist.

Jackson looked her in the eye and said, "Billie, I am so crazy about you and have been since I met you, too. You are now mine. Together we will figure out the details, but, baby, you have to feel how right this is. Mine. Yours. Ours. That's what is happening."

After several more hours of loving that took place in front of the snowy picture window, on the stairs, and finally in the waterfall shower, they fell into bed with a condition that Billie called "A pleasure coma." They woke late in the morning with their bodies curled together, his behind hers, in a tangle of sheets and limbs. She giggled not only from the light kisses he peppered on her ear and neck but the feel of his rock-hard morning arousal.

His arms tightened around her as he felt her ticklish response. Suddenly she wrenched herself out of bed and stood in the middle of her bedroom unaware of the effect of her glorious nudity. Jackson rolled over on his side and propped himself up on one hand to unabashedly observe the sway of her breasts as she jumped.

"What is the matter, baby?" he asked with a yawn.

"It's Sunday," Billie practically yelled at him. For his life, Jackson had no idea what it was about Sunday that had her crazed. He continued to look at her lasciviously. Maybe she was disturbed that he hadn't fucked her first thing and was feeling deprived. He actually thought that was hilarious and began to chuckle out loud at that thought. After settling, he looked at her and shrugged his shoulders as though to say he was confused as to what Sunday meant.

"I have to make your mom and aunt pies, you dolt! Ugh, men. Apparently all they teach in Wyoming schools is about cows, rodeo, and snow!" With that, she grabbed her robe and turned to run downstairs. Problem with that was that she hadn't looked where she was going and promptly fell right over a two hundred pound Madison.

"Ugh!" she yelled and she flew facedown onto the carpet. Jackson was by her side in a flash as was the culprit of her attack.

"Are you okay, baby? Gotta be careful of the wildlife around here. They also teach not only about the cows but also how to watch out for them!" He laughed.

Downstairs, Billie made them breakfast while rapidly whipping together two pies to bring to dinner. Jackson was quiet through the morning and she wondered to herself why. She crossed the room to wrap her arms around his shoulders while he sat on the couch.

"Why is such a good-looking man so quiet right now? Seems a shame."

He clasped her forearms in his hands and gave a gentle squeeze. "Just kinda bummed thinking that things are going to be different tonight, as I have to sleep back at my place." His voice sounded thick and held no small amount of regret.

Billie sighed and hugged him tighter. She hadn't thought about that. It was as almost though she forgot that he lived in his own house. With a pang in her heart, she kissed him on the side of his neck.

"Well, I guess we are just going to have to have a lot of phone sex and sexting. You do know how to sext, Jackson?" she teased inquisitively.

He shot her a hot look. "I think I might need some lessons, baby. We can start during dinner tonight. If I send you a text and you blush, then I guess I am doing it correctly!"

Billie moved away with a laugh and went to check on her pies. She ran her eyes over his incredible body as he unrolled from the couch to look out the window. Her eyes heatedly took in the unbuttoned jeans and his naked chest. As though on cue, her cell phone buzzed across the room. Billie didn't take her eyes from him as she moved to pick it up.

Jackson heard her gasp and quickly turned to see what had caused her obvious distress. He saw her lips tremble and was immediately concerned. He wrapped her in his arms and gently took the cell phone from her hand.

"Gonna fuck you, bitch. Gonna fuck you up real good."

Jackson engulfed her in his embrace as though to block out her very visible fear and kissed her on the top of her head. He took deep breaths in an attempt to hide his rage from her. He wanted her to see him only as calm, but what the fuck? He wanted to kill whoever was sending her these threats with his bare hands. It was going to be a very interesting dinner at the Powell ranch after he discussed this with his family.

* * * *

The Powell house was as boisterous as ever as Jackson and Billie walked up to the front door. Billie leaned forward and grabbed Jackson's hand in a death grip, effectively pulling him to a stop. He turned and looked down at his lady love with a smile. She looked anxious and pale. He was immediately concerned that she was afraid of whoever has been scaring her.

"Don't worry, baby," he quickly reassured her. He put his pie down on the railing and swept her into his embrace. He tried to block out any fear he thought she had running in her.

"How can you tell me not to worry? Everyone knows what we have been doing for two days, Jackson! How can I face you mother and aunt?"

Jackson looked at her with an impish grin, as though reliving some of the more salacious moments of their weekend in his head. Obviously enjoying his thoughts, she felt his chest rumble with laughter.

"I would think it would be my brothers and cousins that you should worry about," he teased.

"Oh god! How could I have forgotten about them? I will never be able to look them in the eyes again," she wailed.

Jackson thought the whole scenario was pretty damn funny. He had guessed incorrectly as to the nature of her upset. This was much better. He could imagine her gorgeous chest suffuse with blush as his family imagined their weekend activities. Jackson leaned over and parted the edges of her coat, leaving no question in her mind that he was ogling her cleavage. As if on cue, he ran the edge of his fingertip down the inside of one of her breasts to where the two were mashed together.

Billie felt as her G-string was immediately soaked with a rush of moisture as she sucked in her breath at his arousing caress. She observed as his eyes took on a heated look as he leaned down to take her mouth with his.

"Don't bother calling them, Mom, they are out here sucking face on the porch!" Benjamin yelled out to the rest of the house as he opened the door. "Geez, I would think that the two of you could take a break for at least a couple of hours, no?" Ben had a shit-eating grin on his face as he tormented the couple. Billie did then blush, just as Jackson had predicted, from hairline to chest.

"Looks just as arousing as I thought it would be," Jackson whispered into her ear.

He turned and looked at his over-informative brother. "Do you think you can act your age at some point in this lifetime, Ben? You are getting more and more like Troy every damn day!"

The window next to the door slid up as two male faces leaned out to join the party. "Well, that's the best compliment you have ever given me, brother!" Troy yelled from the opening. He had a huge smile on his face. If that weren't enough to cause Billie to burn up with embarrassment, Cole's face that was leaning on his hand followed a glance to the front picture window where Hunter, Brody, Bill, and Donny were observing the scene with rapt attention. Just kill me now, Billie thought.

"Excuse me, boys, but unless you want to feel the smack of my spoon against adult behinds, you had better let Doc in and stop teasing her. Once she gets over her blush, she can remind you that she knows ways to make your, um, manliness, not be so manly!" Lillian declared to her male family members.

Florence strode forward and picked up the pie that Jackson had left out with one hand and grabbed Billie's hand with the other. She stopped in her march and turned momentarily to look back at Jackson. "Your uncle would have been proud of you!" she said with a naughty smile.

"Florence!" Lillian burst out. "We are the only three women here and we are supposed to stick together."

Please kill me now and bury me! Billie thought with a groan.

As the women settled in the kitchen to talk, probably about the success of their plan at getting Jackson and Billie finally together, the men congregated in the den. Jackson was greeted with bawdy comments by his brothers and cousins. His own father slapped him on the back and squeezed his shoulder affectionately. He heard his father quietly say, "You look happy. Haven't seen that on you for a long time, son. I really like this girl."

Jackson had to smile at his father and dodge the slap to his arm that Hunter was about to deliver. Talk about emotion. Hitting him was the only way Hunter knew how to express warm sentiment.

"I hope you don't slap your girlfriend's arms when you want to turn them on, Hunter," he said with a laugh.

"Dumbass," was the only reply.

Jackson closed the door and quickly told the men about what had been happening to Billie and that he suspected Len. Curses and angry comments were flung around the room while they discussed how to keep her safe and catch whoever this sick asshole was.

* * * *

Billie was still all ablush in the kitchen with Florence and Lillian hugging her senseless. Lillian had tears in her eyes as she told Billie that she had prayed for someone to light up her eldest's life and she had received even more than she had hoped for. Her whole life, Billie had wanted to feel like she belonged to a warm, loving family. Perhaps things did work in mysterious ways. She had to remind herself that one weekend with Jackson did not a family make. However, she couldn't deny the warm wave of happiness that crested over her senses. All she had ever wanted. Love. This wonderful family seemed to have it in spades. They weren't perfect, but they were wonderful. She was ripped from her thoughts as Bill strode into the kitchen and picked up Lillian. He swung her around while loudly questioning, "Where the hell is the food, you gorgeous woman you? We men need to eat to keep fit and strong!" He let her down as she swatted his shoulder. She gave him a mischievous smile and smacked his behind.

"Get the boys in here."

"Florence, my love, I would swing you around, too, but I fear we would end up in a heap on the floor as my back is older than I care to admit to and it would damage my reputation as your new lover," Donny bellowed for everyone to hear. Raucous laughter filled the room as Florence turned to him. "I cannot mention your reputation as my sons are here, you naughty man!"

Billie smiled through the exchanges, while catching Jackson's eyes twinkling at her. Troy pulled her aside to make sure she was okay. She thought that was very sweet of him to care and told him so.

He just looked at her sideways and told her he was happy that Jackson and she had each other now. Billie couldn't get over how sweet and communicative all the men in this family were. Well, Hunter was almost family and his communications were limited to grunts, slaps, and nodding. Still, when she turned and caught him looking at her seriously, she was dumbfounded as his lips turned up into a smile and nodded again in her direction. Would wonders never cease!

Dinner was its usual fun affair. She sat next to Jackson. It consisted of him running his hand up her thigh, lightly squeezing, and her talking to three people at once while Jackson was running the pads of fingers over her soft mound, causing her to jump. She noted that Bill was asking for the potatoes while trying to compliment his sister-in-law on them. Her G-string was now so damp, she was sure that she would leave a mark on the chair.

Yep, just the usual.

"Billie, honey, is too hot in here for you? You look flushed," Lillian innocently asked. "Brody, please open up the window behind you. It needs to cool off a few degrees in here."

"It's gonna take more than a window opening to accomplish that, Aunt Lillian," Brody said while laughing himself silly. Billie was ready to crawl under the table by the time the meal was over. The men all cleared the table while the women flopped on the couches to rest. Jackson came sauntering over and gently took her hand.

"We will be back in a minute. I want to show her my old room. Gotta brag about all my rodeo buckles and show them to her." He yanked her up and pulled her determinedly behind him. They went up the back stairs to where she guessed his room was, surprised that he wanted to show her his buckles right at that moment. When they got to his room, he flung open the door and quickly slammed it shut while flicking the lock. She looked around, smiling at the floral comforter that now graced his bed.

"I was expecting Spiderman or something more boyish than the floral, Jackson," she said with a nervous laugh.

"My mom has broken the man laws and turned all our old rooms into either guest rooms or other stuff. You should see what she did to Ben's. That is now the pottery studio. I think he needs some therapy for that one." His eyes had that predatory look again as he turned off the light. Moonlight streamed into the room, casting a cozy feel to it.

"So I figure you didn't want to show me your buckles then?"

"I am going to show you one, all right. See this?" He used both hand to quickly undo his buckle and pants, not bothering to pull them all the way off. Her mouth watered as she eyed his monster erection that slapped back against his stomach as he pulled his pants down. Jackson didn't say a word of warning as he spun her around and pushed her roughly over the desk that was behind her. He lifted her slightly, and helped her simultaneously kick off her heels while deftly undoing her pants as well. He used one hand to hold her down by pressing in the center of her back. His heated gaze ran over her naked ass in the moonlight.

"My teasing game seems to have backfired on me, darlin'. I hope you don't mind, but I am going to fuck you now 'cause, well, I can. I want to. I need to." Jackson ground his steely rod against her naked ass while dipping his knees. She felt his need and answered him with a moan of her own. She couldn't move as he controlled her by pressing her into the desk. It wasn't painful at all but rather arousing to be held at his mercy. He palmed his cock in his hand and slid it from behind through her gushing folds. He began a rhythm of thrusting back and forth through her slick lips and felt a rush of primitive need. He drew back and almost violently plunged up into her pussy until he felt himself hit her womb. She cried out in sharp pleasure, causing him to growl in response. She could hear the wet, slapping sounds as he jackhammered into her wet, heated depths, almost out of control. She felt as he cupped her breast with his other hand, squeezing tightly, as though trying to not be overcome by the extreme pleasure she was giving him. His thrusts and growling had her so aroused, she knew that he could feel her cream dripping from her pussy. His hand lowered from her breast and, with one stroke of her clit, she tightened and clench down on his cock. She bit down on her lip as delicious ecstasy ripped through her body at the same time he exploded, shooting his hot cum against her womb. His pulses of seed seemed to go on and on, filling her to overflowing. When he finally stopped, he lay over her, panting onto her back. Without dislodging himself from her pussy, he lifted her up a bit and took two steps back to the bed. He sat with her on his lap, her legs dangling over the outsides of his thighs. Billie rolled her head back onto his shoulder and kissed his salty, sweaty neck.

"Oh my," was all she could say.

"Baby, any better and I think I won't be able to walk for a week."

As she got up and they both redressed, Billie looked up at him with concern. There was no way anyone downstairs was going to miss the sated expressions, wrinkled clothing, or swollen lips. Jackson, almost sensing her distressing thoughts, reached down and nuzzled her neck from behind.

"Don't stress so much, baby. We didn't lie. I did show you my buckle."

Chapter Fourteen

The week flew by with the excitement of Thanksgiving on that Thursday. Julia was singing like a lark throughout the whole office and answering the phone with, "Dr. Rothman's office, almost turkey day, can I help you?" Billie gave her another look suggesting that she was cracking up as she answered the phone again in that manner. The patients in the waiting room sat chuckling at Julia's antics. She was such a warm, special woman to work with. Billie felt like she was blessed to have met her. If only Julia had a stronger stomach. How the heck could the woman want to work in a doctor's office and not be able to stand the sight of blood, she would never know. Billie was just hugging Lizzie Carmichael good-bye and wishing her a happy Thanksgiving when Nat Winston came in practically carrying his mother, Mabel. Billie ran forward and immediately didn't like Mabel's coloring. She directed Nat into the first treatment room and yelled out the door for Julia. The only response she got was the view of Julia peeking around the doorway of the room.

"Julia, get me the defibrillator and oxygen, now!" Billie heard the odd sound of Julia actually running down the hall and no singing. She began examining Mabel's sallow coloring and hitched breathing when Mabel suddenly closed her eyes with a roll and stopped breathing. Nat stood next to his mother's head, yelling her name. Billie grabbed the defibrillator that Julia had brought into the room with her own eyes shut. Great, Billie thought quickly. No help there. She had Mabel hooked up in two seconds to see her in ventricular fibrillation.

"Clear. Nat! I said clear, now!" Nat let go of his mother as Billie gave her a zap. Nothing changed on the EKG. Damn, Billie thought.

"Clear." Zap. A regular rate and rhythm was now running across the EKG monitor. Billie let a sigh of relief as she heard a sob ripped from the normally very in-control and dominant town deputy.

"It's going to be okay Nat," she said comfortingly as she continued to tend to Mabel. "Take a deep breath. She is doing okay and I am not going allow her to change that by ruining your Thanksgiving," she said with a nervous laugh. That was a close one. Her rock-solid calm was now beginning to fracture as Mabel cracked her eyes open and slightly motioned to Nat to take her hand. Mabel kissed her son's hand lovingly while grimacing in discomfort.

"Mabel, darling, I am so sorry about the pain, but I had to zap you a couple of times. You were being difficult like everyone said you could be! Stay still, the ambulance should be here any second. Be strong and smile for your son. He is very worried about you."

She heard a hitched sob from the hallway as Julia felt free to vent her relief. The EMTs came in and quickly took over the situation. Mabel was whisked away to the hospital with Nat kissing Billie's cheeks, hugging her tightly until she thought he would break a rib. Billie smiled inwardly, so thankful that she hadn't left early for the day. She had done what she was good at and again felt so thankful.

She heard a clink of glasses and the slam of a bottle. Looking out, she was just in time to see Julia slam back her second shot of tequila. The three patients that had been waiting gave Billie a hug as she walked out to them, all in awe of what had just occurred. Julia hiccupped, promising to call all of them to reschedule for the next week. With the shutting of the door, Julia turned back to Billie and in silence poured another shot and handed this one to Billie. Billie was surprised to see her hand slightly shaking and gulped it down without comment. The burn going down her throat felt so calming. She felt the warmth of the liquor spread in her belly as another was pressed into her hand.

"I am just going to come right out and say this, young lady. I have never been so afraid one moment and so impressed by you in the next," Julia said with obvious tremors in her voice. "I thought we were going to have a holiday tragedy on our hands and be setting up a funeral for my poor friend Mabel. You were amazing. You always are, but this, I am just speechless. I am so proud of you. Thank you for saving her gossip-loving, crabby old woman life." She hugged and kissed Billie for a full minute before forcing another shot on her.

Billie was so taken aback by the love in Julia's voice that she drank the drink again without question. The move to Stony Creek was definitely proving to remind her of who she was, how strong she was, and that she in fact was worthy of all the love she was getting. She was glad she was here.

* * * *

The scent of mixed grasses and leather hit Jackson as he walked into the Braxton Feed and Seed across the street from Billie's office. It was a scent that always made him smile as he was assailed with memories of coming in here with his grandfather, Abner. His grandfather used to bring him, his brothers, and his cousins in here whenever he had to run into the store for supplies. He always bought them ice cream, no matter what time of year, and kept it a secret from his grandmother. Now he had another sweet reason to love coming into the feed and seed. His beautiful lady love's office was just across the street, and every time he came in, he would happily glance over to it, knowing she was in there. Today it not only warmed his heart but he also felt the stirring of his cock. He got a flash of her in his head on her knees in front of him, gorgeously naked, while shyly looking up to his face for permission to taste him.

His erotic thoughts were interrupted by Gus's bellow of welcome and query as to how he and everyone on Rugged Hill Ranch were doing. Exchanging pleasantries, he was informed by the very knowledgeable Gus that an ambulance had just taken Mabel Winston to the hospital and that the very beautiful Dr. Rothman had saved her life. A surge of pride rushed through Jackson and ended with a smile that he couldn't quite hide.

"That woman of yours is something else. Eh, Jackson?" Gus looked slyly at him.

With a laugh he looked at Gus. He was worse than the Ladies Guild meeting. He liked to know all the gossip and intrigue that ran through the inhabitants of Stony Creek.

"What woman?" Jackson said with a laugh.

"Don't be an ass. Your woman, Jackson! You know, the one we all saw you maul at The Pump last weekend. The one who looked like she would die if you ignored her another second. The one you looked like you would kill your brother and cousin for when they forced you to finally take action. That woman, you dope!" Gus proudly recited.

"For a man who is happily married for thirty-seven years, you have been doing a lot of noticing of a woman who isn't your wife, Gus."

"Hard not to notice a woman like that, Jackson. She's got a gorgeous body to go with her brains. Yep, very hard indeedy!" he said, and the innuendo wasn't lost on Jackson.

"Well, you had better develop an eyesight problem my friend, or I may have to pop you one for too much observing. Better yet, let's call Millie and see what she thinks of your powers of observation. Whatcha think about that idea?"

Gus shuffled his feet back and forth while muttering something about dumb kid cowboys and their big fat mouths. He shot Jackson a look saying that he would get his comeuppance soon and went off to get him the antibiotics he needed for an ailing cow.

Jackson heard the jingle of the door chime and turned to see who had come in to join him in annoying his friend Gus. Pricks of angry heat stabbed into his gut when he saw Len pause just inside of the door. Gus looked momentarily nervous and then cleared his expression. Len sauntered down the aisle straight toward where Gus and Jackson stood.

He nodded at both men. Jackson leaned casually with his hip against the counter, which belied the cold, stern stare he sent Len.

"Got a problem, Powell?"

"Yup" was the only reply from Jackson.

"So what is it, asshole?" He heard Len say with far more bluster than his body language gave off. Hell, he knew that Len had never liked him, as he had his gentleman's manner and bull riding skills. They had done some of the rodeo circuit together and he knew that Len had also resented him even then for his far superior riding skills, both in the ring and with the bunnies afterward. It was hard to be cocky when Len had to look up to Jackson's six-five frame to see his face. He knew that Len hated that he had that advantage. It was obvious that Len felt he was an arrogant asshole and was trying his best to shake his confidence a bit.

Since Jackson hadn't answered his last question, he knew that Len would be aware of his anger rise by Jackson's cold gaze.

"You couldn't even hold a wife, asshole. Gwen found her pleasure with a real man. I gave it to her good. She told me what a lousy fuck you were. Needed herself a real cock," Len said proudly.

"Well, Len. I guess it's true. She got herself a real dickhead. Seems to me that you both deserve each other," Jackson said calmly, still leaning against the counter.

"I wouldn't be so smug yet, cocksucker. I noticed a real pretty little doctor over there just dying to give me an exam, an oral one, if you know what I mean." Len laughed with a nauseating leer.

Jackson's green eyes went black as without even thinking, he lunged forward and grabbed Len by the throat. He pinned and lifted him at the same time, choking him as he growled out a warning.

"I don't ever want to hear you talk about that woman again. Don't think about her, talk about her, or look at her. If you do, I promise you, so help me, I will make you wish you were dead," he said with a snarl. Len was thrashing violently, trying to rip Jackson's hands from his throat to take a breath, when Gus intervened. Jackson threw Len to the floor with a growl and wiped his hands on his jeans, as though to get rid of the dirt. Gus looked at Jackson, almost shivering at the dark, threatening glare that he was leveling on Len.

"Get out, Len, and don't let me see your ass in here until you can talk respectfully about the doc," Gus yelled out as the door slammed shut on the retreating cowboy. "Jackson, you okay, boy?"

"Yeah. I just hate that asshole. Billie has received some threatening messages and I have to wonder if Len has anything to do with them. Keep an eye on things, will you? If anything ever looks amiss across the street, I want you to call me. No matter how small. I don't trust that fucker. He is messed up and I don't want Billie in the middle of his shit."

"You upset about what he said about Gwen?" Jackson heard Gus say. "He probably thought that he would get a rise out of you, Jackson."

"What? No. That woman is just as messed up as he is," Jackson said almost nonchalantly.

"As for the other drivel that man spouted, I guess there is a pretty medical professional across the street who could biblically confirm that you are indeedy a real man!" Gus chortled to Jackson. Jackson looked at him sideways, replacing his anger with a look of amusement. Gus really knew how to glean information out of people without even asking a direct question!

"Speaking of which, I think I will run myself across the street and congratulate the good doctor on her fine hands, er, skills. See you around, Gus, and thanks for the afternoon fireworks."

"Anytime, cowboy!" Gus said with a wave good-bye and a smirk.

* * * *

Jackson opened the front door to Billie's office to hear the most god-awful version of the Hokey Pokey. He actually cringed as Julia hit a particularly off-key note. His smile was short-lived as he heard a second voice join in to put her right knee in. He made a face as he meandered back to her office to find not only Ms. Julia singing at the top of her lungs but an obviously inebriated physician with her gorgeous butt in the air as she tried to put her right foot on green and her left hand on red in a drunken game of Twister. She did all this while singing about putting her appendix in and then appendix out doing the Hokey Pokey. Jackson knew she would fall in two seconds as not only was she drunk but couldn't multitask worth a damn. With her black suit jacket thrown over a chair and her delectable ass displayed for his viewing, he leaned against the doorjamb to take in the view.

"Jackson, darling! Come do the Hokey Pokey with a real life heroine!" Julia slurred with a smile as she noticed him standing there. Jackson pulled away from the door and bent at the waist while laughing. While upside down, he looked at his lady love who was grinning like a Cheshire cat. He felt his heart leap in his chest as he took a deep breath, inhaling her light perfume.

"Hey, sweet cheeks with the delicious buttocks, fancy to meet you here!" Billie giggled out in an upside down greeting. He unbent and helped her to stand, laughing at her antics. When she swayed once upright, he gathered her into his strong arms for support. She wore another pair of fuck-me four-inch heels that went with her silk suit. Even with the extra height, Billie had to crane her head back and up to gaze into his concerned eyes.

With a gentle, deep voice, Jackson asked both women, "Have we been drinking, ladies?" Billie swayed again against his hard body unintentionally. He felt the immediate hardening of his cock to her close proximity. He dropped a quick glance down her blouse to see the peaking edge of her lacey bra furthering his current discomfort. Her luscious breasts were within tasting distance of his hungry mouth.

"Well, Mr. Jackson Powell. I have indeed been drinking, but the darling doctor here, well, she was just being polite and holding three or six shots of tequila for me." Julia drunkenly laughed out. "Isn't she a peach? After all, she saved my old friend Mabel today. It is worth celebrating!"

Jackson smiled indulgently at both obviously very happy women, just shaking his head in pretend disgust. Julia pulled on his free arm and gave his bent head a light kiss, telling him to take care of Billie and to have a lovely Thanksgiving. Jackson watched her bang into the doorframe and trip over an invisible bump in the floor on her way out. He heard the door jingle closed and turned his attention to the other lush that he held in his arms. He scooped her up in his arms and sat on the leather couch against the back wall of her office. She rolled her head to look dreamily up into his handsome face. He not only heard but also felt her happy sigh.

"I heard you had a busy day, baby. I am very proud of you. Nat must have been beside himself. How much did you drink anyway?" he asked indulgently.

"Not sure," she slurred out. "At least one shot, cowboy. Maybe two!"

"I think there were a couple more than that, baby." Jackson laughed. He leaned down to peer into her liquid eyes and succulent lips. How could a woman be so smart and so damn fuckable? Jackson thought for the millionth time. This stunning woman was made for sex. She was made for love. Most importantly, she was his. He leaned down while cupping her soft cheeks and lightly kissed her lips. He ran his lips gently back and forth over hers, content to feel their silky texture against his own. He placed small nibbles on her full lower lip while allowing one hand the pleasure of sliding down her neck to run over her collarbone. He heard her sigh again, this time against his own mouth in obvious delight.

"Jackson, I was actually scared for a minute there that I would lose Mabel. Didn't care for it at all. When she came back to us, well, I think you can see the results of my relief. I felt so badly for Nat as he tried to hold it together." Billie hiccupped loudly into his face and laughed. Jackson cupped her breast lightly and kissed her nose.

"You did a great job, baby. I am not surprised at all. You are gonna be the talk of the town at everyone's holiday dinner. I have never seen Nat wear any other emotion than strong and calm." Just then, Jackson got distracted by the feel of something soft and warm in his palm. He gave her a playful smile and pulled her shirt opening toward him so he could see clear down to her belly. He inhaled deeply and sighed as he leaned down to kiss the tops of both of her plump globes.

"This is a very sexy bra you have on today, baby. Were you planning on showing it off to anyone special?" he asked with a wolfish grin.

"You should see the matching panties, my darling." She hiccupped. "Excuse me. They are delicious, hiccup, excuse me again." Billie's out-of-character, unladylike behavior had Jackson laughing out loud until she leaned back while erotically shimmying her skirt up to her hips. He immediately caught his breath as lust slammed into him, making him hard as a rock. He took in her soft, sensual look, partly aided by Mr. Tequila, combined with the way her gorgeous legs were slightly parted lying over his groin. He ran his hand over her lace-covered bare mound just as he scented her arousal. He closed his eyes in pain as he felt the undisguised dampness of her panties, indicating her own happiness at being near him as well. His erection pulsed against her ass as Jackson leaned over to place his lips over a nipple that was beaded through her bra and blouse. He sucked it into his mouth, wetting the materials to her delight. She ground her hips down into his cock almost desperately seeking release as he pulled the material to the side as he dipped his fingers into her moist, swollen lips.

"Poor baby. You are soaking wet down here. Doctor, this is one problem that I think I might be able to help you cure." He breathed against the shell of her ear. She shivered as the tip of his tongue lightly ran over the edge as she writhed against his hand.

"I need you, Jackson. Please…baby, please," she mewed.

"I know what you need, baby. Just let me give it to you. God, you really are so fucking wet. I feel like I could come just from touching you like this."

His magic fingers one by one slipped into her wet channel until three of them began to slide deliciously through her juices, making her moan in pleasure. She felt like molten silk on his hands. He was sure his cock was going to bore a hole into her ass all by itself. He was so aroused by her unabashed response he actually worried about ejaculating in his jeans. Jackson inwardly laughed at how embarrassing that would be. He hadn't been this close to something like that since high school! He took a deep breath and increased the tempo of his thrusts. As he curled his middle finger to hit her G-spot, Billie arched sensually in his arms, indicating her obvious approval.

"Please, Jackson, please..." she begged him like she was bordering on desperation.

He stopped his movements and looked her in the eye as he placed his fingers one at a time into his mouth. He licked her succulent juices off each as though tasting heaven. His eyes darkened in an erotic display of his own desire as he kissed her lips.

She could taste her tanginess on his tongue, further igniting her arousal. He growled into her warm mouth as his tongue twined relentlessly with hers while his thumb slipped back under her lacey panties to rotate over her clit. Lightning pulsed through Billie as she hung onto Jackson, wailing her overpowering pleasure into his mouth.

He felt her gushes of cream that now coated her thighs and his hand as she came violently, seemingly over and over again. He groaned into her mouth as he gentled his kiss into light, soft pecks. He continued kissing her gently, while murmuring loving words into her hair.

What the hell was he going to do about this amazing woman? She was his. He still wasn't sure he was what she needed, but there was no way in hell that he would allow anyone else to have her again. He glanced down at her and fervently wished she weren't so tipsy so he could slide his cock into her drenched pussy. Later, he thought. Jackson loved that he could bring her to such a state of pleasure. He was shocked to find out that he was satisfied with just holding her obviously sated limp body in his arms while he comforted her. He felt a wave of protectiveness as he recalled the earlier incident with that asshole, Len. No man was going to fucking talk about her like that and still be able to walk. Not if he had anything to say about it. He tightened her into his embrace and carried her securely in his arms. He managed to gather her purse and coat while he walked out, locking her door behind her. He placed a soft kiss on her forehead just as he looked up and caught a smiling Gus looking their way with all the Saunders men across the street. Hell, they were all grinning from ear to ear. They looked amused as though they had just learned an important piece of gossip. He imagined them sitting down with every biddy in town to take tea and share the juicy piece they had just witnessed. He had to laugh himself over the image of the masculine cowboys asking for a lump of sugar. They were worse than women!

He gave a small wave and muttered under his breath, "Idiots."

Chapter Fifteen

It was dark outside when Billie woke up with Madison curled up next to her on her bed. She had dreamed that she was lying in Jackson's arms, but a long lick of a wet tongue with distinctly nasty breath quickly identified the warm, huge body next to her. Jackson didn't wear a fur coat and always smelled of sexy man, not outside and dog. How the heck did she get home? She sat up too quickly and felt a pounding in her head. The brocade silk comforter fell away, revealing that she had slept in her usual nude state when she was with a certain man, but for a moment, she couldn't remember. Who? Oh, Jackson must have gotten her situated as there was a thoughtful glass of water on her nightstand with the very welcome painkillers just waiting for her. She got out of bed and saw a note on the other pillow.

You looked like an angel as you slept and I promise that I didn't take advantage of your impaired state, much. Rest a bit and I will be back later to remind you of how amazing I think you are.
Love, Jackson

"Love? Madison, do you think that man could ever really love me?" Madison lifted her big head to listen to her mistress's comments. An even bigger head that belonged to Zeus padded over to her and rubbed against her stomach. "I think, guys, that I am falling hard for him. Nope, I am sure of it. I love that man like I have never loved anyone. Ugh. Don't fall in love, guys, it gives you a headache." She laughed then groaned as pain pulsed through her head. Just then both hulking dogs turned and jumped to attention at the sound of steps on the wooden stairs. Billie was so startled herself that she grabbed the nearest weapon, her four-inch heel, and stood by the bed, poised and ready to throw.

Jackson stopped in his tracks by the doorway of her bedroom. It wasn't his fear of a sexy high-heeled shoe that made him pause in concern but the vision of the naked sex goddess he had obviously startled. He held his breath as he observed her standing by the side of her bed, breasts swaying from her quick movements and her weapon of choice being raised above her head in a defensive position.

"I am going to have to teach you some better self-defense, baby, if that shoe is all you got going for you," he said with a grin. She didn't look hungover but he knew she must be. He walked to her, taking the shoe from her with one hand and gently pulling her to him with the other. They both felt his shudder of pleasure as her bare form was intimately pressed against his.

"You need your rest, darlin', so please, I beg you, get some clothing on this gorgeous body before I do something to you that I will be feeling guilty about all day!"

Billie grumbled something unidentifiable but moved to tie her silky robe. "Like I can rest if you are within two feet of me. You have messed up my DNA or something. It's like my body is on autopilot when you are near. Besides, I have to get cracking on my contributions for the Thanksgiving meal and then I have to go round on Mabel. Ugh, I feel like I drank a distillery. Remind me to fire Julia. Did you do your morning chores, hon?" She leaned up to give him a light kiss and smiled at his soft nod.

As Billie went to freshen up and take a quick shower, Jackson watched her. She called him "hon." Was it said without thinking? Did she call her husband that? Or was she looking at their relationship differently? Shoot, he just sucked at figuring women out. He decided that he liked the way it made him feel and chose to believe that she knew what she was saying. He watched her shower alone under the waterfall, loving the way she apparently enjoyed the warmth sluicing over her feminine curves. Billie had her eyes closed and was lightly running her hands in circles over her wet skin with her head thrown back. Jackson felt like he wanted to rip off his own clothes and massage the soap over her luscious breasts, but he controlled himself. He didn't want her to think he had no control. It was torture for him as he had to shift his hard erection yet again or he was going to be doubled over soon from pain. She was unaware of the effect her shower was having on him and promised himself that he wouldn't touch her until she felt like herself again. He would control himself. Yep, he could do it. He hoped.

Billie glanced up from the garlic parmigiano bread rolls she was making and had to be careful not to drool. Jackson came downstairs an hour later, having showered as well for the holiday. Jackson was rubbing his hair with a hand towel while the rest of his sculpted male parts were on display as his towel dipped dangerously low. So low, her mouth became dry as her eyes ate him up, starting at the chiseled six-pack abs to the line of dark hair that led to what she knew should be a registered lethal weapon. With a silent chuckle, she admitted that it was her desire for that weapon and the man attached that was turning her from a proper professional woman to a pile of sexual mush. Oh, but what a way to go.

"Um, did you shop for your Thanksgiving outfit at Bed Bath & Beyond or Linens n Things?"

His chagrined expression was met with her laughter. "Do you like it, baby?"

"Yes, yes I do. I think you should wear it every day. Well, at least every day you do something naughty that might make me mad. Your outfit would definitely distract me!"

With a devilish grin, he threw the hand towel aside and looked down. In one swift move, he met her fascinated gaze and pulled the main towel from his hips, never faltering in his path straight for her. He was a god. There was no other possibility. Every muscle on him had definition from a life of physical labor on the ranch. Add to it his great height and gorgeous green eyes. You could easily be distracted from any conscious thought by simply watching the sway of his erection and scrotum as he strode purposefully toward his target.

"Is this any better, baby?" he asked with an innocent look on his face.

"Um, nope. Definitely not better, Jackson." Billie resorted to just covering her eyes with both of her hands. The effect, however, was ruined as she split her fingers to get one last glimpse of his naked perfection.

Jackson took pity on her and rewrapped himself as he sat in a chair at the island. "What are these that you are making, baby? They smell heavenly."

"Just rolls for your mom. It's the pies that you smell. You do know that you are a pie whore. You will eat anyone's pie. Oh, excuse me!" Billie began to blush profusely at her unintended innuendo. That was *not* what she had meant but exactly how Jackson had taken it!

"No, baby, I have had pie from here to Alaska and trust me, there is no pie in the world as delicious as yours!" He winked, licked his lips, and flashed a naughty smile.

"You are a Neanderthal, buddy! You know what I meant." She really couldn't respond with much gusto, though, because he was too darned adorable. "I must have been so knocked out. I didn't feel you leave me this morning and definitely didn't hear your truck return."

"That's because I rode Lachlan back. I didn't even want to go back for my truck because I wanted to get back to your...pie." A lump of dough slapped him right in the side of his head.

"What did I say?" Jackson asked.

* * * *

Thanksgiving at the Powell's was much like their Sunday dinners except there was even more food, football on the TV in every room, and most everyone was inebriated. Florence was in the kitchen with a distant cousin singing very off-tune to what Billie thought resembled a Frank Sinatra song. Privately, Jackson quickly updated the men on his run-in with Len and the most recent text threats against Billie while asking them not to bring it up again today, so Billie wouldn't be nervous. There was a rapid-fire discussion on the subject before the room again became the typical male haven of beer, food, and sports. The den had several men throwing napkins and plastic forks when they didn't care for a play, while in the dining room, where Billie sat with Lillian, there was serious discussion going on. That is if hearing about Ben's butt dimples when he was a baby could be considered serious. The expression on his face was. Ben sat there, red and about to explode as his mother drunkenly told the crowd that his tush was the most adorable of the bunch and everyone should give it a pinch before leaving.

"Mom! Enough! Time to put down the wine and pick up the coffee," Ben grouched.

"Lillian, leave the boy alone. You are embarrassing him. Just because he is a little klutzier than the rest doesn't mean we should put him on display," Bill drunkenly sang out.

Billie was enjoying this. Apparently, drunken Powells equaled interesting information about each of them. She liked this game and only hoped that she wouldn't have to participate in it. So far, no one had asked her why she didn't have family or friends from back East visiting for the holiday, and she was too embarrassed to tell them that there weren't very many people she would want to see. After digesting that thought, she looked around the table and realized that these people had come to mean so much to her in a very short time. Definitely more than her own family had ever meant to her. Was it sad or was it a sign that she was growing and evolving enough to recognize warmth and love when presented with it? She decided to choose the later. Hopefully the conversation would roll around to Jackson soon. She couldn't wait to hear the juicy details about him!

However, it appeared that they weren't done roasting Ben yet. At six foot six, there was a lot to roast, she supposed.

Brody yelled in from the den, "Don't forget that Ben likes cows more than he likes girls! He has never brought any women home yet!"

"Who cares if I have brought home a girl yet? I always have a date on the weekends, unlike you. Since your girlfriend, you haven't dated anyone, dummy! For someone who loves to talk to everyone, it seems you have nothing important to say." Ben returned the volley.

"I am too busy with both my hands full, cuz!" Brody boasted proudly.

Florence gave a timely interruption to where the conversation was going. "That will be enough out of you, young man! If we are going to talk about Brody, then let's be proud of him. Your father was immensely proud of you for how you handled your bronco-riding rodeo career. You kept winning and winning, yet you didn't let it overtake your love of the ranch. Martin was very proud indeed not only of all your buckles but that you knew who you were and what mattered to you. If you had to choose to continue, we would have supported you no matter what, but that you came back to something you loved even more, well, your father and I …well, you know."

"He did come home to the ranch 'cause he loves it, but let's be frank. He went through so many women that he…" A wadded up napkin was hurled at Cole's head, ending his opinion that Brody had slept with every woman in Wyoming. Billie, along with the rest of the table, was in stiches from all the laughter. Cole was normally quiet and more a listener than an instigator but Billie thought he did pretty well with that one!

"Cole cannot get his head away from learning. Never could. His father and I were always amazed how he could run bales out to the herd and come back able to tell us some new information he had learned on ancient Greece or something! Now, if only he would put that focus on a lady friend!" Florence laughed in the direction of her youngest. Cole just smiled indulgently at his mother, not quite comfortable with being the center of everyone's attention.

Suddenly Lillian's gaze shifted to her youngest. Troy looked up with his mouth full of Billie's cranberry stuffing. "What?" he said.

"My baby boy." She sniffled back her tears.

"Tiny and a baby. Now the truth comes out. Mom, are you sure he is actually yours?" Troy laughed out.

"Jackson, please behave yourself. You are next in line, buster. I would be careful what you say because there is much I want to share about you, darling boy." Lillian laughed. "Now where was I? Oh, my baby. If you hadn't gone to college and learned to be the computer wizard that you are, where would this ranch be? I cannot tell you how amazed we are that you can take care of all the ranch bills and sales on the computer. Do you have any idea how long that used to take your father to do? Or how much he hated it?"

"I did hate it, but I never took that long. I beg to differ. I could handle it all pretty well." Bill defended himself while giving Lillian a slap on her rump affectionately.

"Dad, we all know you hated it and it took you forever. Period. I don't mind doing it. I kind of like it," Troy said proudly.

Florence leaned over and whispered in Lillian's ear. They both dissolved into giggles and swung their gazes in Jackson's direction.

"Oh shoot. What? Just get it out of your systems! Ugh, someone get me another beer, please. I need liquid fortification for this! Stop laughing, Billie, or your turn may be next!" Jackson grumbled.

"Ah, but there is no one here to divulge my secrets. No one has known me since birth and can tell you my little 'isms' that I have," Billie countered with.

"I can." All eyes turned toward a quiet, masculine voice from the doorway. Cole, at six foot four inches, was hardly a slouch in the height or looks department. He loved to tease his brother and cousins but tended to be shy around others. Jackson had figured that he would be the only one to razz Billie, but then he remembered that Cole was the observant one. He wondered what he noticed about Billie.

"You came out here to belong. I suspect you have always been a brilliant woman, kind and considerate. It is why you are such a good doctor, but I wonder what your family was like back there. I think there must have been a void, one that you have just started to fill. You emanate joy and probably surprise yourself daily at how happy you are. Your beautiful home, full of detail and thought, is a reflection of you and your personality. I personally share your love of reading and plan on raiding your library of books on ancient cultures. Jackson is barely literate, so he won't mind if we have a special relationship based on old architecture."

Lillian, Florence, and the rest of the table looked back to Billie for some sort of affirmation or denial. Quickly recovering from her shock at how astute he was, she just starting to softly clap and smile. Cole returned that smile and sauntered over to the table to give her a light kiss on the top of her head.

"I am very literate, you overgrown ape. If I didn't know how shy you were, I would swear you were scheming to steal my girl. However, since you cannot take the time away from your precious reading, I know you won't be able to overcome my charming, sparkling personality!"

Billie gave Jackson a light squeeze on his thigh and leaned into him slightly to give him an unspoken moment of reassurance. Everyone laughed at the exchange, but Billie could feel Jackson's slight jealousy that his cousin had her pegged in two seconds. She leaned up and turned his face with her hand. His soft-green eyes met hers as he lowered his head to meet her lips. Billie kept her hand cupping his cheek as she gently kissed him with all the love she felt for him. She heard him groan and slant his head to deepen the kiss with gentle swipes of the tip of his tongue. Suddenly the room seemed very quiet. The two of them separated slightly to the sounds of raucous laughter as their private moment was interrupted. Sheepishly they looked at each other as he cuddled Billie into his embrace.

"See, this is why I am proud of Jackson! He can fix anything, talk anyone out of anything, and was also an amazing bull rider. However, it is this miracle, this change where his heart is full of love again that makes us so happy," Lillian said while hugging her husband a bit too tightly.

"The boy always had love, Lill, he just chose wrong," Bill said with some humorous authority. "Now he has the way of it!" he said with a wink and smile at Billie, who was blushing at the compliment.

"Now that we have run through all the Powell boys, let's get to the good stuff," yelled Brody from the other room.

"Yeah, let's talk about Hunter!" Troy volunteered with far too much enthusiasm.

"What? Why?" was all of Hunter's reply.

"It's your turn, bud! You hardly speak unless it's to all those dogs you save. You grunt, growl, and basically act like a crabby woman all the time!" Troy was treading on thin ice.

"Hey!" the women of the room yelled at Troy. Florence took it a step further and slapped her nephew in the back of his head.

"Ouch! Aunt Florence, it's true!"

"It is not." Again, Billie definitely could not see Hunter ever discussing his feelings or thoughts extensively with anyone, ever! Yet, he was one of the kindest, gentlest men she had ever met. He did love to take strays dogs in on his ranch. He obviously loved his best friends, Troy and Cole, as well as the rest of the Powell clan, but it was his surly demeanor that Billie appreciated most. It was a total smoke screen for his affections to be kept private. Billie just wanted to hug Hunter as he, too, didn't have blood family in the room.

She did the next best thing. "Hunter is a warm, wonderful, man who has no need to use flowery language or make long speeches. Women all know immediately what an amazing man he is just by his presence and smile. Besides, I have yet to see him crabby. He is wonderful!"

If it were possible for Hunter's huge, muscular chest to get any larger, it would have with how he puffed it out at Billie's compliments.

"Someone take a picture! Quick!" Cole yelled out. "I think he is going to smile!"

As if on cue, he did. Billie thought he was just charming. She could tell from the tightening of Jackson's embrace that he was again slightly jealous at her attentions to his friend. The effect was ruined, however, with Hunter stealing the show.

"Um, Lillian. Would you care to regale us with how much you love Jackson's behind? I mean, it does have that birthmark on the upper left cheek and..."

Hunter never got to finish as everyone started laughing at Jackson choking on his beer.

Chapter Sixteen

Mabel was discharged from the hospital two days after the holiday and apparently not a moment too soon. Billie heard from Julia directly that poor Nat had his hands full trying to keep his stubborn mamma in bed and from pulling out her IV lines. Billie let her go home with the promise that she would come into the office once a week until Billie was satisfied. Things were pretty uneventful for the next few weeks with the routine of work, hot monkey sex with Jackson, and taking care of the house and office work becoming set into place.

Billie sat at her desk munching on her avocado salad, thinking of how deliciously erotic Jackson was. He had ridden Lachlan over last night and crawled into bed with her while she was sleeping. Her schedule had been so exhausting for the past several weeks, even though she had tried to stay up waiting for him, she must have fallen asleep. She was awakened by the feel of his soft kisses on the back of her neck as a very naked, warm, and hard body slid into bed and pressed against her back. That wasn't all that was hard.

Billie rubbed her posterior against the hard ridge of his huge cock, which was nestled between her cheeks. Jackson continued his gentle seduction by placing his lip at the base of her throat and sucking in her soft skin. The sensations sent bolts of pleasure straight to her pussy while his hands melted her into a hot, liquid woman. He rolled her slightly to shift his mouth to suckle on her nipple while still grinding his cock into her ass. Jackson moved to glide his steely erection through her thighs, enabling him to slide against her soaked pussy lips. They both groaned in pleasure as his cock easily slipped back and forth through her engorged pussy to graze her clit erotically.

His hands circled her slim waist, almost reverently stroking her soft skin, while he gently pulled her flush against his body.

Billie thought she was going to go up in flames as he used her copious cream to lubricate her rear rosette. Small pulses of pleasure set off a firestorm of spasms in her pussy as he suddenly plunged his cock deep into her pussy only to pull out and kiss her shoulder. Without a word, he soundlessly rolled her to her belly and placed a soft pillow under her hips. Billie obediently followed his soundless directions as she felt him lean up on his knees and pull her hips back toward him. His cock felt even thicker than normal as it gently pushed against that dark, private hole. A small frisson of fear ran up her spine as he began to lightly thrust against her, slowly starting to breach her outer ring of tight muscle. He placed light kisses over her neck and shoulders, crooning loving words softly to comfort her all while continuing with his quest. Billie felt the stinging pain increase until, with his light thrusts, he suddenly slid deeply into her ass. He tightened his grip on her hips and leaned fully over her back, almost definitely in an unspoken display of dominance and possession of her.

The pain stopped and was soon replaced with sensations she had never felt before. She then felt and heard him groan as he slid his hard cock fully into her. Jackson stilled his movements at that moment to allow both him and Billie to savor the feeling of him being deep inside of her. Billie felt so full, tight, and taken in such a deliciously primitive way. He filled her as she had never been filled before, and she could barely breathe as the pleasure was indescribable. She heard Jackson let out his breath as though he was holding it, and he kissed her between her shoulders, running his tongue down her spine. It felt like he wanted to see himself planted so far within her, savor the pleasure, and taste her all at the same time.

He momentarily shuddered and then started to pull back. She felt him stroke slowly back into her again and again, his rhythm igniting nerve endings that she had no idea she even possessed to scream out electric pleasure. His thrusts began to become more aggressive as the sound of their mutual panting was mixed with the slapping of his flesh against hers. She erupted with pleasure from an orgasm so electrifying it went screaming through her body when he reached under her to stroke her clit. Soundlessly, her mouth hung open as her pleasure burned to her toes and fingers, an erotic sensation that she had never known existed until that moment. She felt him thrust deep one last time as he trembled and roared out his own incredible, trembling climax. She felt branded from the inside out as she felt his hot cum fill her as he had never before. He then cradled her body possessively into his with his cock still hard inside her ass while his hands lightly stroked her shuddering body as they both tried to catch their breath.

"Jackson." She sighed blissfully. Billie had never felt so possessed, taken, or loved in her life.

His only answer was a whispered word into her ear. "Mine."

Billie had liked it. It had been almost like love, almost like adoration as he had hugged her to him so tightly she could barely breathe. He had rolled them to their sides, still connected in that very intimate way and that was how they had slept. It was peaceful, loving, and had felt oh so right.

* * * *

"I will give you good money if you tell me what has you smiling so naughtily, Dr. Rothman," Billie heard Julia ask with a saucy look and a snicker.

Billie looked up at Julia and replied, "Not on your life, darling lady, but I will tell you it was a happy thought."

"I would think that was a given, missy! You looked a million miles away and glad to be there!" Julia laughed. "I just came back here to tell you that I am leaving a bit early today and just locked up the front door."

"Leaving early? Why and what I am supposed to do without your charm and skills to keep the natives happy?" Billie groused.

"No worries, Dr. Rothman, you will be leaving early, too. Your last two patients canceled as they had to do some serious holiday shopping. Not a very good reason, if you ask me, but there it is. I cleaned up and am going to lock up behind me. You be a good girl and go home and play with your dogs and horses, okay?"

"Um, okay. It's not like I have a choice here, do I?"

"Nope. Good night, darlin'. I will see you tomorrow." And with that, Ms. Julia was off.

With that, Billie whipped out her cell to call her best friend. "Hey, Lizzie, got the evening off as the patients felt they had better things to do than see their greenhorn East Coast doctor! I am almost proud that I was trumped by a shopping trip to the mall, if you really want to know." Billie laughed into her cell. "Would you care for a drink or dinner tonight, I mean if you don't mind being seen with me?"

"Billie, you are hysterical. Okay, I guess my reputation won't be too sullied to be seen with the gorgeous town physician who is dating Mr. Sexy Hard Body Jackson and happens to be a really, really amazing person." Lizzie laughed out. "Give me five minutes, okay?"

"Yes, madame chef, that sounds wonderful. We girls have got to stick together while the men are having poker night. I think they just left to go over to the Taggart's ranch. I saw Jackson's truck just leave. By the way, I may or may not promise not to tell Ben what you just said about Jackson! I could be persuaded if you buy the first round," Billie coaxed.

"You know very well that there is nothing going on with me and that commitment-phobe, overgrown, overdeveloped land mass of a man who cannot date a woman for longer than two or three months and barely talks," Lizzie grumbled. "I know I come off as a fun-loving woman and all, but you know the truth. I don't want to be the flavor of the month for Ben. I like him. I really like him, regardless of his baggage and bizarre dating habits. He gets me, I think, but hasn't made a move to indicate that he either wants a quickie, which I would *not* give him or that he is actually interested in me. He just always is, well, there. I turn around, and he is either looking at me, helping me, or just near. All without talking. It's weird, no?"

Billie thought for a moment before replying. "No, not really. He is such a sweet, huge, shy guy. I think he goes through women like that because he isn't sure what he wants. I know for a fact that he has never, ever brought a woman home before, never! No one can deny that he is interested in you. The way he is always trying to be near you is just adorable. Perhaps he is just trying to work up the courage to have a relationship with Ms. Stony Creek. You are the absolute opposite of his personality, but it probably would be a perfect fit, in my mind."

"Yeah, he is adorable. However, I don't think he wants me for much other than to see if I am a natural blonde!"

"Lizzie! You are awful! Ben is many things, but he definitely treats women with respect. If he found out your, um, natural state, at least he would just smile and keep it to himself!" Billie laughed. "Okay, see you in five and we can discuss the future Mr. Carmichael further."

Billie sat at her desk for another moment, savoring the peace and quiet. Odd, but when Julia wasn't in the office with her, it sure was calmer. However, she had already had a lifetime of sterile, quiet medical offices back east. This was more of what Billie liked. There was more noise, tumult, and love. Yes, it was not quite ready for the cover of professional medical office digest but her office was infinitely more welcoming. She gathered up her things and turned the lights out as she went out the back door and locked it. The light in the back alley was limited and a prickle of unease ran up Billie's spine. She looked around cautiously for a moment and pulled out her mace, just in case. Slightly encouraged that Lizzie was going to meet her out front in just two minutes, she took a deep breath and began to walk through the dim light toward the main street.

In the darkness, a hand shot out and grabbed her by her throat. Billie heard a high-pitched scream and realized it came from her. A huge, dirty hand clamped down over her mouth and she was shoved up against the side of the building. Her heart pounding in fear, she looked into the face of man accosting her.

"Don't make another sound, Doc. I just want to talk to you. Calm down and I will uncover your mouth, but if you scream again, I will have to show you how real men deal with women around here."

Billie nodded her head, as though in agreement. As the hand was lifted, she took a deep breath and was assailed with a stench as though Len had bathed in Jack Daniels. "What the heck is wrong with you? Get your hands off of me this second before I rearrange your personal anatomy! There is nothing I want to hear that could possibly come from your foul mouth!"

"Listen, Doc, it would be to your advantage to be a little nice to me, considering the position I have got you in. The Powells have gone to jerk off with the rest of the men, so there ain't nobody to come save you. So calm it on down and we can make a deal," he confidently said while running his disgusting gaze over her body. Billie felt it as though it was his hands running over her instead and shuddered in more revulsion than fear.

He mistook her reaction. "Maybe you do really want some of this," he said as he felt her shudder. He ground his groin against her, making bile rise in her throat. He put his hand over her mouth again just as she began to scream for help.

She fought like a wildcat, trying to scratch, kick, and punch him, but he was way too strong for her. He had knocked her mace from her hand and had Billie easily pinned with his ranch-strong arms. Fear started to overtake Billie as she realized she couldn't fight him and win, but she vowed that she was going to leave him marked for sure.

The tussle was making so much noise that Len didn't hear Lizzie charging down the alleyway. She jumped onto Len's back and stuck her manicured fingernails into his eyes, giving Billie a chance to free herself. Both women started screaming their heads off and viscously counterattacking the drunken sicko who dared to accost Billie. Len tried to shake off Lizzie while maintaining a one-handed hold on Billie. He howled in pain and Lizzie scoured his cheek with her nails.

In a desperate attempt to rid himself of Lizzie's interference, he suddenly bent and flipped her over his shoulder and onto the alley's pavement.

Thinking that he now had the upper hand, Len confidently stepped with one boot onto Lizzie's chest and he continued his choke hold on Billie against the wall. "Whatcha gonna do now, little bitch? Maybe I should take both of you? Might be sporting. Two feisty women make for a whole lot of fun." Len let out a loud belch and lewdly rubbed his crotch with his free hand. Both women closed their eyes in disgust instead of watching him grin with pleasure as he ran his hand up and down his obvious erection. "Old Len has enough meat for both of you to feel real good. Who should I take first? Hmm? I think I will start with Doctor Prissy Pants here for holding out on me but giving it up for the Prince of Powell. Then I will give the town's big-talking tease a ride that she won't soon forget. Yeah, I think that is a fucking great idea!"

He struggled as both women were trying desperately to scream and fight their way away from his nauseating body. It was hard for him to keep his direct focus on them. He was startled when he heard another distinctly calm, masculine voice answer his question.

"I think that would be a very, very bad idea, Len. Both of these ladies are going to have to regretfully decline your polite invitation," the barely controlled angry voice answered.

Len made a fatal mistake in his plan when he thought all the brothers had left in Jackson's truck. It had only been Jackson and Brody only who were on their way to play poker.

Len swung in the direction the voice came from right into a huge meaty fist. The women immediately broke free and held on to each other as they moved behind their saviors. Len lay crumpled and unconscious on the alleyway floor.

Ben stood like an avenging angel over the still form, eyes blazing with fury. "Are you both all right? Did he hurt either of you?" he managed to roughly ask them. Cole wrapped an arm around each of the trembling women, moving them a bit further away from their attacker. He paused only to call for the sheriff and then resumed gently rubbing both of their backs.

Lizzie looked at Ben. "We are okay, I think. When I saw him accost Billie, I ran in to try to help. I guess I need to work on my rescuer skills, huh?" She laughed. She nervously glanced at Billie who looked like she was in shock. "Billie, hon? Are you okay?"

"I think so, maybe, not sure yet," was all Billie could manage with a smile for a moment. They heard the pounding of obviously male footsteps running down toward them. Billie felt herself being ripped away from Cole and swung up into a very strong male body. *Jackson.*

She took a deep breath and exhaled slowly, allowing herself to calm down now that he was here. In the next second, she wrapped her arms in a bear hug around Jackson's waist, trying to sink into his comforting warmth. She felt the chill of her fear began to melt away as she was safe and secure in his tight embrace.

"What the fuck happened here, Ben?" Jackson tried to ask quietly.

"All I know is I heard them screaming and found this piece of shit stepping on my woman's chest so hard she could barely breathe. While he was doing that he was also choking your woman so she sure as shit couldn't breathe either. Asshole."

Jackson realized that Ben had left it at that for the moment as he didn't want the women to have to rehash the story too many times as they were going to have to tell Nat and the sheriff as well.

With Sheriff Sly Mulligan and Deputy Nat Winston's arrival, Jackson, Ben, and Cole turned the women down toward the street to wait.

"Your woman?" Lizzie took exception to Ben's reference. "You haven't yet even asked me out to dinner, dancing, or a drink, buster. Nothing! You don't even talk to me in real sentences but now, all of a sudden, I am your woman? You are out of your mind if…"

"If you all will please excuse me, I have to have a conversation with Ms. Carmichael here over her actions today. We will be back in just a minute," Ben politely murmured. Her speech was cut off as she was unexpectedly hoisted over Ben's very tall shoulder and moved out of Billie's hearing range.

"If you think you have any control what-so-ever as to whether or not I come to anyone's defense, you have got another thing coming to you mister! I can dance naked down Main Street if I chose to do so. Let me down, you overbearing, uncommunicative, can't have a relationship with a woman, too scared to commit lug!"

"We will just see who belongs to whom and who is actually the scared one in just a moment, baby." The loud, reverberating sound of a slap on her ass echoed as he walked her away.

Jackson held Billie cradled up against his chest, gently rocking her back and forth comfortingly. He and Cole passed an amused look at the slapping sound and sudden quiet that befell the retreating couple.

Jackson looked down at Billie. "Baby, are you okay?" he asked with concern.

"I am now. Where did you come from? I thought you had left?"

"I did, but Ben put out a 9-1-1 to us, so I turned right around. I am going to kill that waste of DNA." He took a deep breath and slightly tightened his hold on her as he continued. "Baby, I am sorry I about what I am going to ask, but I need to know. Did he touch you?" Jackson found himself holding his jaw clenched as he waited for an answer.

"No, Jackson. Thank goodness, no. He just scared me and roughed up Lizzie and myself. Is she okay with Ben? He looked very angry," Billie said quietly.

Both Jackson and Cole exchanged another amused look and a chuckle. "Yes, Billie. She is going to be just fine. Ben just is going to explain a few things to Lizzie, and she is going to comply with Ben's suggestions most likely," Cole answered her with an amused grin.

"Comply? Lizzie? They don't exactly go in the same sentence, Cole," Billie returned.

Cole just smiled for an answer as he sauntered off to see what was taking Sheriff Mulligan and Nat so long to haul off the trash. Jackson took the privacy gratefully as he inspected the precious woman in his arms. Precious. He kept surprising himself with these revelations. She was precious to him. Len's actions would have enraged him if it had been any woman but that it was his woman... He needed to calm down a bit more.

Billie sighed as Jackson spread light kisses over her face, trying to coax her back into her usual fighting form. She turned her lips up to his and allowed him to cover her with his affection. Billie closed her eyes and allowed herself to feel the protective security that he was trying to provide. She nuzzled her face into his neck and just breathed in the scent of his cologne. She focused on that. Delicious, familiar, comforting and as always, arousing. Not quite what she needed at that particular moment but she figured that she should permit her body to respond in whatever manner it needed to while recovering from the shock of the situation.

Jackson gently put her on her feet as Ben approached with Lizzie securely mashed up into his side. He wasn't entirely sure whether Lizzie was in heaven or was going to kill his brother but figured things would be okay if her blush was any indicator. The ladies gave their accounts of the incident to Sheriff Mulligan and then protested as the men tried to separate them.

"Ben, would you please stop being so high-handed! Billie and I were going to have a drink before we were waylaid by Mr. Asshole. We have things to discuss!" Lizzie lectured to her intended huge target of a man.

Ben looked down patiently at his beautiful charge. In a very soft but firm voice that gave even Billie the chills, Ben replied, "I thought we had just come to an understanding, Lizzie. I don't think you want me to repeat that particular discussion in front of everyone, do you?"

To Billie's surprise, Lizzie suddenly became completely docile. "Um, no Ben. You may take me home." With that, Ben excused himself and his blushing companion.

"What in the world do you think he said to her that could make her suddenly so, um, compliant?" Billie asked Jackson.

Jackson looked almost indulgently down at Billie. His eyes were warm with his feelings for her. "He probably explained that she was to never again to put herself in danger and gave her a small spanking. That's my guess," he said almost offhandedly. "Now for you, Madame Doctor. Let's get in my truck as we are going to have our own conversation about what the hell you were doing going out the back door, in minimal light and all alone at night. This may not be New York, but there are still a boat load of horny cowboys running around who find you to be pretty damn hot. I won't have it either."

Billie just looked at Jackson. "You won't have it? Just who the hell do you Powell men think you are? I am not a baby to be told what I can or cannot do! You don't own me!" Billie was furious. She went from repulsion to terror to fear and now to anger all within an hour's time. Her mind didn't know if she was coming or going. No wonder she was overreacting to Jackson's display of possessiveness.

Jackson just continued to drive as though she hadn't just had an outburst but did respond gently. He knew she was on overdrive. "We Powell Neanderthals, as you love to put it, know who we are, baby, and what matters. *You* matter. You matter a hell of a lot to me. I may not have put a ring on that finger, but more than anyone, I sure as hell own you, woman. Just as you own me. Everything is going to be all right. I am here and I am never going to allow a man like that to get to you ever again, so cooperate, please."

It was obvious to Jackson that Billie didn't feel like arguing anymore. She obviously liked hearing him confess in words that she did matter to him. It felt good. The fight was all out of her now and she just closed her eyes in exhaustion. Jackson glanced over at her as she was attempting to fight off sleep. He threaded his fingers with hers and laid them on his thigh. Realizing she had just dozed off, he allowed himself to let his guard down and unmask his facial expressions. He was enraged. That fucker dared to accost his woman! Jackson gripped the steering wheel so tight his knuckles blanched. He tried not to squeeze the hand holding hers but apparently failed. She moaned in her sleep and turned sideways so he could see her beautiful features. She was sleeping so peacefully he willed himself to calm down so he didn't disturb her further. He pulled up in front of his cabin and got out to pick her up and carry her in. She was so wiped out, she didn't stir as he undressed her and laid her gently on his bed. He undressed as well and climbed in after her a moment later. Jackson gathered her slim body against his and closed his eyes while taking a deep, calming breath. Thanking god, Lizzie, and his brother, he gazed down at the woman who dropped into his life and was creating wonderful havoc with it. Tonight could have turned out so much worse if not for their quick thinking actions. Jackson just lay there for quite a while looking down at Billie, afraid to take his eyes off of her.

Chapter Seventeen

Life returned to a somewhat normal pace during the holidays and into January. The snowstorms provided many a romantic evening for Billie and Jackson to get lost with each other as the weather raged outside. Billie sat in her comfy chair watching another few inches fall while trying to make some sense of her current state of affairs. She came out here to find herself, to find real love for the first time, and to find out what living a dream really meant. She sipped her wine and tried to digest all that had happened. She had found the man of her dreams, someone who made her feel all lit up inside every time he got near her, someone who got her and wanted her, just the way she was. She paused in thought about that fact. Jackson liked her when she was stubborn, liked her when she was submissive, liked her when she was bossy, and basically took her any way she presented herself. He just liked her from the get-go. Billie sunk deeper into her chair with a real smile on her face at that realization. The man protected her, helped her, supported her, and gave her crazy, pleasurable hot monkey sex every chance he got. Sure there were hiccups since she had gotten here. His ex-wife was a constant nuisance, there were things that she had trouble getting used to like having to shop for her naughty lingerie online as there were no stores for that within a two-hour drive, and Len had gotten out on bail while awaiting his trial for assault. However, if she was going to be truthful, she knew that she had never been happier than she was now, nor would she ever be again. Her practice was full of patients that loved and appreciated her as she did them. She had a new family that amused her every Sunday while torturing most of its immediate members, and she got to ride

Sheeza and Danny constantly as well as ride the finest man she had ever known. It was a good life.

The scrumptious scent of the spicy seafood gumbo and fresh cornbread hung in the air. Jackson loved it the first time and every time she made it for him. The look he got while eating it was similar to his look of male satisfaction on his face as he watched her orgasm from his ministrations. She was getting damp already thinking of how happy he would be when he got home tonight. Home. They spent the vast majority of their time in her house. It felt more like a home than the one she had shared with Matthew. Here there was warmth, fun, and love because of Jackson.

Oh god. That was the truth. It hit her like a sledgehammer. Holy cow. She was completely, undeniably, and utterly crazy in love with Jackson. She sat up so quickly, the big beasts masquerading as her dogs started and she almost spilled her wine. What the heck was she supposed to do with that?

She didn't have time to even ponder the thought. The silhouette of pure Wyoming cowboy rode up on Lachlan in the darkness. It was just like one of those male models posing for a cowboy calendar but for real. It was his beloved chiseled face with that huge, hulking muscled body beneath layers of warm clothes and parkas that made her rub her thighs together in anticipation of the privilege of being with this man. Already she felt the flush and cream that started to gush in her pussy from her thoughts. Her body knew who its master was long before her slow brain had ever figured it out. She watched him ride into the barn and decided to surprise him.

Jackson was stomping his feet on Billie's back porch when the tantalizing scent of his favorite meal teased his senses. Ah, what a woman, Jackson thought. After a long day rounding up stray cows, feedings, and fixing some of the equipment, there was nothing that could compare to knowing that Billie was waiting impatiently for him with a warm smile and a delicious dinner. He had never had that or the associated feelings it evoked in him with Gwen or any other woman. She had to be one of the most thoughtful, generous, and sensitive people that he had ever known. He appreciated her so much. There was never going to be another woman who could pleasure him like Billie did. Mind, body, and spirit. She took everything into account on everybody, but especially him and his needs. Today was a difficult day for him mentally. He was fighting a losing war with himself over the depth of his feelings for her. He was crazy about this woman but still a little gun-shy to tell her that he loved her. One moment, he was sure that he wanted to tell her and then the next, he was reliving his stupidity at rushing into things with Gwen. Part of him said, why rush? Let things just fall into place, but the other part of him, probably the smarter half, said to him that he should have her branded as his mentally, physically, and legally as soon as possible. Whoa! Did he just admit that he wanted to marry her? Shaking his head as though to clear the thought, he dismissed the idea quickly. Tonight wasn't the time to ponder huge decisions like that. He laughed to himself. Yeah, maybe he should get up the balls to tell her that he was head over heels in love with her first. Nah, not yet.

He shrugged out of his outer clothes and sauntered in where he knew the most amazing woman in the world would be waiting with a thoughtful meal made solely so he would be happy. She was the most perfect woman in the entire world. He stopped short in the doorway of the kitchen. The living room was lit with candles and firelight only. His love had a blanket on the floor in front of the fireplace with two dinner settings on the cocktail table. That wasn't what gave him pause, though. Billie had laid herself out on her side on that blanket wearing nothing but an ice-blue silky chemise with cut out sections that barely covered her luscious, abundant breasts and her soft, smooth pussy.

Jackson narrowed his focus as he allowed his gaze to slowly and torturously run down her body to her polished toes and back up again to her rich, shiny auburn hair. He pulled his shirt off and unbuttoned the top button of his jeans, allowing her to see not only that he went without his boxer briefs again, but the head of his very aroused cock that was peeking out over the top. He watched her lick her lips as she took notice of his state of arousal, causing a groan to softly escape his lips. She lifted herself to a kneeling position with her knees spread wide and gave him a please-come-over-here-and-show-me-more look.

"So, darlin', you remembered to make us some dinner but forgot your clothes again, huh? I may have to take you to task about that, woman. You seem to be having some serious difficulties keeping your clothes on lately. Close your eyes, now," Jackson commanded her.

"I will do as you ask, but only because I want to. I don't want you to be getting a swelled head thinking that I will do whatever you want, Mr. Powell."

"Too late, baby. My head is already all swollen," he said as he ran his hand over the bulge in his jeans to the thick, bulbous crown sticking out. He moved slowly to kneel right behind her with his knees on the outsides of hers. She could feel the heat from his chest against her back and his chin nuzzling the top of her head.

"Mmmhmm. I walked in to a veritable feast for a man's senses in this house. The food, the wine, and this body. Where should I start?" His one hand very lightly drifted over her distended nipple through the silk of her chemise while his other cupped and plumped the other breast. Billie let out a moan with the heated contact on her sensitive skin as well as the sensation of the silk rubbing her hardened nub.

"Perhaps here?" he questioned as he softly rubbed his jean-clad erection against her back, allowing her to feel its length and thickness through the soft material. "No? Then maybe this might be more toward your liking?" Billie felt the heat of his breath against her neck as he leaned down with his hot mouth to feather kisses down its column, stopping at the base to suck her skin into its depths. Jackson felt her tremble and lean into him. Her sensitive response sent a surge of arousal to his throbbing cock.

"So you aren't liking that at all, baby?" Jackson teased her. "I would hate to continue to touch you in the wrong way, baby," he whispered. "I guess this is no good either."

As Billie closed her eyes, she could only feel both of his strong hands slide over her chemise at her hips and lightly stroke her mound. He pushed the material into her folds, causing him to softly chuckle as the immediate moisture soaked the fabric, unintentionally confessing her desire for him. She pushed her rump directly backward in invitation, indicating his teasing was definitely what she enjoyed. Jackson lifted the material in front and slid his fingers through the wet, glistening folds that were revealing her pleasure.

"Keep your eyes closed, baby," he crooned to her. He removed one of his hands and pulled one of hers into his grasp. He kept his hand over hers as he ran her own fingers through her juices and around her clit. She moaned in ecstasy at the sensations that were bombarding her system. With her eyes closed, every feeling seemed magnified. She could feel, smell, and hear Jackson and his arousal, which made her own soar. Just then she felt him reach around as he pulled her hand away from her body. He took her fingers and sucked them into his mouth, one by one, licking them clean of her cream.

"Delicious. Baby, your gumbo has got nothing on you. I could eat you for the rest of my life, you taste that good." Again he could feel the tremors that his sucking and words evoked. He quickly stood and pulled off his jeans before returning to kneel this time while facing her. Jackson leaned forward and lifted her up to standing. He fastened his hot, wet mouth to one rigid nipple, causing her knees to buckle as he soaked the silk. He felt as she lost her balance and landed on one of his outstretched thighs with her pussy pressed up against his muscular thickness. He let out a hiss and slipped the chemise quickly and efficiently over her head. He laid her down and placed his body over hers, keeping his weight from overwhelming her by leaning on his forearms. He ground his cock against her smooth mound while leaning in to fuse their mouths together. He kissed and nipped his way along her jawline, running his tongue along the outer shell of her ear.

Billie gasped as he sucked in her earlobe while teasingly pushing the head of his erection against the dripping opening of her pussy.

She arched her back as she was bombarded with shooting electric sensations from the dual sucking and plunging. She bent her knees and pulled her thighs up and wide to cradle Jackson deeper into her body.

Jackson then switched his tactics and possessively thrust his tongue into her mouth while twining and stroking it along hers. The kiss turned carnal as he began thrusting it through her delicious lips while plunging to the hilt slowly over and over again into her silken depths. Jackson shifted her so the back of her thighs were resting against his muscled forearms as he opened her intimately as wide as she could go.

Billie still kept her eyes shut obediently while she savored the feel of his cock slipping deep, so deep, repetitiously into her. It made her feel so very connected to Jackson and his pleasure. She could feel the tension coiled in him as he savored what must be a silken stroking sensation as he thrust again and again.

She followed his leads so trustingly, so perfectly, it must have heightened his arousal as she allowed his control. With that, he sat up on his knees, not breaking stride with his thrusts, and she was suddenly pulled up with him. Billie sat kneeling on his lap with his lips buried against her throat.

"Jackson, I..." She stopped herself from just barely telling him that she loved him. He kept his hands on her slim waist, lifting and pulling her into his thrusts. The position forced her clit to rub provocatively against his body.

He felt and heard her heavy panting as she was on the precipice of her pleasure. Jackson narrowed his eyes and slipped one hand under her to push his finger into her rosette. Billie suddenly curled into him and screamed out as her body was rocked with the force of her explosive orgasm. Jackson had only a moment to savor her reaction in pure male arrogance as his own ecstasy raced from his cock. He roared out his pleasure as his spurts of cum streamed deeply into her body. He held her limp form against his as he allowed them both to savor the moment. He breathed in, reveling in her light perfume and the scent of sex that now permeated the room. Jackson ran his hands comfortingly over her silken skin, unsure if it was for her pleasure or his. It didn't matter really, he thought.

Billie slowly rubbed her sweaty body against his chest and groin as she placed soft kisses on his strong jaw.

"May I open my eyes yet, Mr. Powell?"

A slight rumble rocked them both as he answered. "Yes, baby." She slowly opened them up but still ended up looking like a very well-pleasured sex goddess to him.

"So what do you see, baby, now that you can?" Jackson laughed out, hugging her warm, pliant body tightly.

"Perfection, Jackson. I see you." She smiled at the look on his face. It was a mix of surprise and pleasure at her statement. "Now let me continue pleasuring you, my cowboy lover. Let's eat your favorite meal."

"Oh, darlin'. I already tasted my favorite meal." He looked lasciviously over her body still locked with his.

Billie blushed from head to toe, smiling as she was somewhat bemused that she still could still get embarrassed with him.

Chapter Eighteen

The next month and half flew by with so much going on around Stony Creek. Everywhere there was discussion of the calving season that was upon the area. This fact was made very obvious by the lack of cowboys visible in town and during the nightlife. Billie texted Jackson at night but the cell phone signal was sketchy here in the mountains and she found herself bordering on misery as she was missing him so much. How had that Neanderthal wormed his way into her life so seamlessly that the once competent and independent Dr. Rothman was now reduced a pathetic emotional bag of mush? She and the other women were just waiting for the sound of big pickups dropping off cowboys in town to see their sweethearts the moment they were freed from their respective ranch's end of calving.

Apparently, it was some sort of town tradition where the ranches drove the cowboys in so they could let off steam and relax after such a long time in the mountains with the cows. Already several ranches were done and their hands were lounging outside in various places all over Stony Creek. It seemed like every pickup that drove into town had the women pressing their faces against the glass to see if it held one of their men.

As if on cue, the roar of a big dually rolled past Billie's office. Julia called out as they all, with the patients, ran to the front window to see who the lucky ones would be. The back bed packed with happy cowboys waved as the truck rolled by her office. Just like heroes in a parade, Billie thought with a smile. Sadly, it wasn't a Powell truck. Billie glanced across the street and saw Lizzie with her face also pressed against the glass, her disappointment pretty recognizable by her facial expression. It was obvious that she was eagerly awaiting the return of "someone," and Billie didn't have to ponder too hard to figure out who it was.

"I wonder when Lizzie and Ben are just going to come out and admit that they are crazy about each other already?" Julia chirped out. "Look at that girl. She looked like she was going to cry with the passing of that last truck. They need to get it out in the open already. I am too old to be waiting around for the two of them to get it together!"

Billie, momentarily distracted from her own disappointment, looked amusingly at Julia. That woman just said whatever came into her head. Many a secret was communicated via her inability to not talk. She had to love her. Too darned talkative, gossiped about everyone and the dog, but a kinder, sweeter person never lived.

"Perhaps there is nothing more there than some flirting?" Billie offered. She didn't believe that for once second, especially after Ben's *special* care of Lizzie after the Len Drexel attack. Lizzie's blush alone said that day said that she enjoyed whatever had transpired between them, but Billie wasn't about to share that with Julia.

Billie went back to work and by 6:00 p.m., she was exhausted. As she sat in her private office, she felt rather positive about the state of things. Any day now, Jackson would come home, and there hadn't been any notes, messages, or threats since Len was arrested. She had felt rather uneasy with Jackson and the men being away while calving season was on, but luckily, Len seemed to be behaving himself. She allowed herself one quick daydream, reliving the first time she and Jackson had been intimate, if that was the description she could use for the animalistic, erotic sex they had had against her front door.

"What a nice memory," she said with a laugh. Nice really didn't cut it as a description, but nice was a four-letter word, much like what they had done in that memory! Billie gathered her things and went out the front door while locking up. Since Len's attack, she didn't go out the back way unless she had someone with her.

The drive home was peppered with naughty images of Jackson kissing her in the mirror of her bathroom, oral sex in the barn, and the close-up study of Jackson's huge penis. Billie thought to herself that she had become a sex-centered maniac because of that man. Sheesh, she had always liked sex but the way Jackson did things, it should be taught as a class or art form!

She had actually shared one of her exploits with Beth and Lizzie one evening at The Pump a few weeks ago. It had been so oddly empty in there with most of the young men out on their ranches. The Saunders men had been in attendance, as the calving season didn't affect their horse ranch, and they had done everything within their power to keep the female populace pleasured and happy. Gabe, Joe, and Preston all had a lovely lady on the dance floor, trying their best to spread themselves around. Billie laughingly thought that it must be a real hardship on the men. The girls themselves got pretty stupid on the green drinks that Billie loved and Donny very obligingly provided. He started them off with a few naughty jokes and they were up and running.

The girls had tried to outdo each other with their raunchy stories. Billie only gave them a simple memory of the time during the first snowfall when they had been intimate in the barn and how hot he could make her in ten seconds or less. She confessed somewhat shyly that he had a way about him that she couldn't resist and it made her obedient to his every erotic demand.

Billie wasn't trying to win some competition, just share, but the two had been left with mouths hanging open enough that Billie could tell if their tonsils were taken out or not. Lizzie then went on a tirade of how she was going to have to jump on Ben if she wanted to see if it was a family talent or not.

There had been a new resident there that night as well. The mayor, Elijah Carson and his wife, Thea, were eating with the town's new Veterinarian, Madelyne Daniels. She preferred to be called just Maddy. She was such a sweet quiet woman who was apparently very nervous to be the focus of so much attention. Lizzie commented on how pretty she was in such an understated way, very natural. Beth went over and asked her if she would like to join them for a girl's drink, which Maddy readily accepted. Billie found her to be a soft-spoken, gentle woman with a kind heart. Maddy was particularly interested in Billie's mastiffs, as all she figured she would get around these parts were cows and horses. Unfortunately, the conversation again disintegrated into debauchery consisting of Lizzie explaining to Maddy that she would see some cows, but it was going to be the studs that would try to occupy most of her time! The women had dissolved into hysterical giggles, which had even the new vet laughing uncontrollably, very eager to meet the men of the town.

* * * *

Billie was greeted at her front door by Madison quite enthusiastically but Zeus was nowhere to be found. Madison kept barking and trying to paw Billie in an attempt to get her attention. Billie began to search her house, becoming increasingly concerned as Zeus didn't answer her calls. Fear started to trickle down her spine as she found her sweet, gentle giant by the back door, lying on his side, panting heavily. There was blood on the floor and on his thick pelt.

"Oh, my baby! Hold on, sweetheart," Billie crooned to Zeus, trying to stop the tears from blinding her as they fell. What the heck could have happened? Billie tried to get ahold of herself but this was her baby, and she just couldn't keep herself together. She checked him over and found a chest wound that looked particularly odd and deep. How could he have gotten this? He wasn't clumsy like Madison and had never even had a fight with her. Hmm, Billie noted that there wasn't any blood around Madison's mouth so it couldn't be a bite or tooth mark. Zeus let out a whine and a moan, which sent Billie back into hysterics. She grabbed her cell and dialed in a number.

"Lillian, it's Billie! I need help! Zeus is on my floor bleeding with some sort of a wound but I cannot move him. He weighs over two hundred pounds! Are any of the men back for any reason?" she cried on her phone to Lillian. Florence as usual was with her, apparently have a nice evening hot toddy.

"Don't cry, sweetheart. Everything is going to be okay. Lucky thing, Troy just walked in to get a bottle of ibuprofen to bring back to the men. Apparently there is a spate of headaches causing the men to be excessively grouchy as they are big babies when they are in pain. I don't care for my husband's comparison that they have been acting like hormonal women, though. Anyway, so rather than continue to put up with them, Bill sent Troy back to get some meds. I am sending him right over. We will stay on the phone with you until he gets there. Do you want us to come over, sweetheart? We will have to saddle up the horses as we have been, um, medicinally 'fixing up' our hot toddy. For sore throats, you know?" Lillian said with a smile in her voice.

Billie gave a quick laugh as the darling woman comforted her. The image alone of Florence and Lillian riding horses over in the dark with doctored toddies in their systems was enough to lighten her mood and stop her tears for the moment. She could imagine them laughing and hiccupping all the way over. She shuddered at the hope that they wouldn't fall off of their horses! "Thank you, Lillian, but I don't think that you both would be able to lift Zeus either!" This sent the women into soft laughter. Lillian spoke nonchalantly for a few moments longer, trying to distract Billie while Troy raced over. She mentioned about how it should just be another few days until calving season was over and how the electricity had gone out in the line shacks, so they couldn't charge up their cell phones. Well, at least that explained why she hadn't heard from Jackson in a week. Billie just missed him and hadn't been worried about him straying or losing interest. Unless he suddenly found cattle attractive, she was probably safe.

She heard the roar of an engine outside as the lights from Troy's truck swung into her yard. She told Lillian that she would keep her updated and ran to let Troy in. Just as the door swung open, Billie flung herself into his arms sobbing incoherently.

"Whoa, sweetheart! Hold on! What's wrong, Billie? Take a deep breath. Mom and Aunt Flo babbled something about one of the dogs being sick." Troy held her while soothingly rubbing her shoulders. "Show me where they are, Billie."

Sniffling, Billie rushed Troy to the back door where Zeus lay panting. Troy sprung immediately into action, soothing the big beast while gently inspecting the obvious wound. Billie lay next to the dog's big head, kissing it lightly while her tears fell on his face. As though aware of his mistress's distress, Zeus gave a big sigh and licked her wet face lovingly. Troy made the quick summation that they should get him into town quickly to the new vet. "If only they had her number," Troy lamented to Billie.

"I already called her and she is waiting for us, Troy," Billie quickly said.

"Thank goodness for organized, smart women. How come you aren't up at the line shacks helping with the calving?" He laughed. "Things would have gone a lot more smoothly and probably a heck of a lot more pleasantly for all of us. Jackson is a bear without you. I don't know what you are doing to him but it definitely is appreciated by the rest of us!" he said with a suggestive grin. He turned his attention back to Zeus and slid his front paws and head over his one shoulder. Billie leaned her shoulder under the dog's middle as she watched in sheer amazement as Troy heaved Zeus's ridiculously heavy hindquarter onto his other shoulder, effectively carrying the dog in a fireman's hold.

"I wish I had a camera," she said in her incredulity.

Billie grabbed a towel and ran behind Troy to his truck. He gently laid the big dog into the truck and helped Billie up so she could lie next to him comfortingly.

"Just hang on, Doc, and we will get him there in just a few minutes. Okay? Everything's gonna be all right," he said soothingly.

Troy took off down the road and was at Dr. Madelyne Daniels's new office in eleven minutes flat. Maddy had a large gurney waiting outside and looked rather uncomfortable with all the cowboys gathered around her. Well, she was really attractive and shy and new in town. That would be serious catnip to the horny men circling her like buzzards. Troy jumped out of the truck, calling out greetings to the men who, thankfully for Maddy, came running over to help.

Maddy rushed over and took charge, listening as Billie sobbed out how she had found him and had no idea what had happened. Billie was suddenly enveloped into the heavily perfumed embraces of Mabel Winston, Millie Braxton, and the Mayor's wife, Thea Carson. They tried to comfort her as the men and Maddy whisked Zeus into the office. Billie noticed Gwen standing not far from the action with a weirdly smug look on her face. She looked Billie up and down confidently and then turned away. That woman was definitely some damaged goods, Billie quickly thought.

They sat with her in Maddy's waiting room while offering silly stories of how their husbands won their hands and some of the town's history. Billie found herself thankfully distracted from what Maddy was doing inside the exam room with Troy, Joe, and Gabe Saunders. Somehow she couldn't picture the feed and seed's grizzly Gus Braxton reciting poetry to Millie but she kept that thought to herself.

Just then, the door to the exam room opened and the men and Maddy came out. Maddy embraced Billie, telling her that everything would be fine and that she was going to keep Zeus here with her tonight. Billie didn't miss the look that the men exchanged and figured that she would get some answers about it from them later.

"What happened to him, Maddy?" Billie asked calmly, now that she knew her big baby would be okay.

"Not quite sure but there is an entrance and exit wound. It looks like he got shot, Billie. Weird. Whoever did it was a really lousy shot, I have to say." Billie gave a shudder at the thought.

"Who would want to shoot my dog and how did they do it? In my house! With an alarm on!" Billie watched Troy try to pry his eyes off the very attractive new vet as he answered her.

"Honey, I don't know but until we do, would you consider staying with my mom and aunt up at the main house? Please, as a favor to me? If I allowed you to go back home, alone, well Jackson just might try to string me up by some of my more delicate, important parts." She felt him gently rub her back while he was glaring at the Saunders crew as they were unabashedly trying to flirt with the woman who had also captured Troy's attention.

"Would you guys knock it off for five minutes and help me over here!" Troy snarled out.

"Excuse us, Dr. Daniels, we need to assist that large, smelly, loud animal over there. Don't go anywhere. We will be right back," Preston said with a smile.

"Okay, who is next?" Joe said jokingly. "Ah, Dr. Rothman! I don't want to seem pushy or bossy but I insist that either my brothers and I all stay at your house, with you, in very close proximity to your beautiful self, for your safety only, you understand, or you can stay with Mrs. Powell. Lovely as she is, I must suggest that you lean toward our direction in the decision making. We can keep you warm and safe." He said that with such a wicked expression on his face that it left no doubt to all assembled that he and his brothers would not find it a chore in any way to supervise her protection, both personally and intimately. "I am sure Jackson may be put out, but under the circumstances, I know he would understand."

Troy let out a snort at that last comment while Billie blushed with understanding.

"Thanks, guys, that was a real help," Troy said with sarcasm.

Billie, admittedly a bit frightened by Zeus being shot by someone, decided to end the discussion. "I will graciously take up the offer to stay at the big house. Lillian and Florence are vicious fighters and I probably couldn't be safer with anyone else." Except Jackson, she thought. "I do thank you guys for your offer, but I would hate to have to patch you up when Jackson was done with calving and found you, um, practicing your protection." She laughed. "Thank you for the thought, though."

Joe gave her a naughty grin, and she received a wink from Preston. It was Gabe however, who made her toes curl. He leaned over her and whispered in her ear that if things didn't work out with Jackson, he would personally redden her ass if she didn't come to them first as soon as she was ready to give love another shot! Redden her ass? Really? She was going to have to talk with Jackson about that. She wasn't sure it would be her thing. Since it was probably the only thing Jackson hadn't done to her body yet, maybe there was a reason.

Billie thanked Maddy for taking such good care of Zeus and promised to be in tomorrow after she got to work. While she pretended to be wishing the ladies good-night and thanking them for staying with her, Billie carefully watched as Troy tried engaging Maddy in some sort of questioning. She watched as Maddy shook her head again and again while Troy smiled patiently at her. Interesting.

In his truck on the way back, Billie was silent for the better part of the drive. When she spoke, she was surprised to hear the tremble in her voice.

"I want to thank you, Troy, for coming to help me. I shouldn't be surprised, not after all these months, but my own personal experiences have left me somewhat insecure, I suppose. You and your family have been nothing but supportive and loving neighbors since I moved in. Your brother, well, I think you know that I am crazy about him. Thank you for not leaving me alone to deal with situation. All I had up until moving out here were my puppies. This was a very unnerving night and I will never forget what you did. Never."

Troy looked sideways at Billie and gave her a soft smile. "You do not have to thank me. We all know how you feel about my brother and how the moron feels about you, even if he is having trouble verbalizing it himself. I am basically just biding my time until I can call you sister. It will be very enjoyable having a girl in the family to finally tease," Troy said with his eyes twinkling. "Besides, I know how you can pay me back."

"Anything, Troy, whatever you need." It was her only reply. She sat waiting for him to speak again as they pulled up to her house.

Troy turned on the seat to face Billie. "I know you think I am a bit of a player and all but I guess we all have personal war wounds that make us who we are. Help me get to know that pretty little vet we just left, will you? One doctor to another ought to have some influence, no?"

Billie let out a light laugh as they walked into her house. She immediately sat on the floor with a very depressed Madison and began stroking her soft head. "Not that I won't help you but, well, you always seem to go for more 'obvious' women. You know? More bunny-esque. Maddy is a natural beauty who loves to work and be with animals. You can't stand the sight of blood, for heaven's sake. She told me that she would rather read than go out. She is like me. What gives?"

"If she turns out to be half as amazing as you, Doc, then my day is made. I like, really like, more introverted women. They won't sell you out or make a fool out of you. I want a woman that I can trust and my instincts tell me that your lovely friend is a quiet firecracker. I want to be the one to make her go off, if you get my meaning," he said with a blushing grin.

"Well, that gave me more information about you than I probably should ever have known, buddy! I think this is probably the only time I will ever see you blush and I am enjoying it. I may have to share with your mom and aunt later! Okay, I lied. I would never do that to you, but I am relishing your embarrassment and it is making me feel better, so, thanks. Oh, and yes. I most certainly will assist in 'operation vet amore.'"

Troy then went out to the barn to feed the horses while Billie packed an overnight bag for her and Madison. She looked at her phone for the hundredth time. No messages from Jackson. She squeezed her eyes shut in a failing effort to stop the tears from falling. She just wanted to be in his arms. To be near him. Well, she had waited her whole life for him. She guessed she could wait a little longer to see him again. She had been strong and alone before in stressful times. She could do it again now. It's just that she had gotten so used to Jackson's commanding strength and take-charge personality. She could use it right now. She heard Troy downstairs playing with Madison and figured she had better go down.

"I have got some good news for you, Dr. Rothman. Mom just called me and told me Dad is home. Just a few more calves to drop and the big, stupid, ugly lug head will be home. I was told that I don't even have to ride back out, so dry those eyes. Everything is going to be okay. I promise."

Damn, these Powell men knew exactly how to get her. They should bottle their blood for other men to drink or something. Maddy didn't stand a chance of avoiding falling for Troy!

Chapter Nineteen

Billie spent the next part of the day feeling weary in both body and soul. First she woke to screams coming from the room down the hall from hers and then followed by peals of masculine laughter. Billie, Lillian, and Bill all descended at 5:00 a.m. on Florence, who was in another guest room, to investigate the screams. Billie arrived last to see Bill crouched down on the floor, laughing so hard that there were tears coming out of eyes. Ignoring everyone and everything else going on, she knelt next to him in order to make sure he wasn't having a heart attack or injured. Realizing he was just laughing hysterically, she stood quickly and took in the scene. Florence was yelling at Madison to get out of her bed and to stop kissing her. Lillian was trying to pull the two hundred pound dog off the bed to help her sister-in-law but was almost getting French kissed herself by a very affectionate Madison. Bill must have a warped sense of humor if he couldn't stop laughing over this nonsense. What a crazy family! Who was she kidding? She loved them and wanted to be a part of it permanently.

Since she had gotten to work and explained to Julia what had happened the night before, she spent the day alternating between seeing patients and running across the street to see Zeus.

By the end of the workday, Lizzie had noticed all the coming and goings between the other women and naturally had to be a part of it. She burst into Maddy's office and demanded to know what the heck was going on and why weren't they including her. Billie and Maddy laughed as they told her the scary story of what had transpired the night before. Billie felt herself return the strong embrace from her friend as Lizzie realized that it wasn't just fun and games that she had missed out on.

"I am so sorry that I wasn't here last night to help you! You know you can stay at my place for as long as you need, Billie," Lizzie offered. Billie was warmed with the support of her friend and surprised when she heard another offer from across the room.

"I know we don't know each other for very long Billie, but I would be glad to offer you my company as well, for as long as you might need it," Maddy volunteered softly.

"Thank you both so much. It means so much to me to have everyone's support. Let's just see how the day finishes out. Besides Lizzie, you did miss something interesting last night," Billie said with a knowing smile.

"What? What did I miss? Tell me now!" Lizzie jumped to attention.

"Yes, what did she miss?" Maddy chimed in.

"Well, if I were to actually gossip, and I rarely do, then I would report that a certain Troy Powell was quite taken with a certain new veterinarian last night. No, not the proper description. Taken is too weak of a word. Perhaps, enthralled or attracted to or charmed or fascinated or…"

"We get the idea, Billie," Maddy said with a flush. She didn't look upset, though. On the contrary, she looked rather fascinated about the subject herself.

"I am just putting it out there that there was some serious window shopping going on by a certain Mr. Troy Powell last night," Billie said smugly.

With a shake of her head, Maddy turned away slightly. "He must have just been flirting, though. He would never go for someone like me. He seems to like them, well, different from the sort of person I am, really."

Lizzie looked at Maddy and offered, "Yeah, he 'seems' to like them dumb, stacked, and loud. Maybe he doesn't want to 'like' you.

Maybe it's time for some love for Mr. Troy. That requires something different, and Maddy, you might be just what the Powell ordered!" She burst out laughing. It took the look of shock on Maddy's face to have all three women practically in tears from laughing. Zeus joined in by wagging his tail, but when a mastiff that is lying down wags, it makes a racket like someone beating on a metal drum!

Just then, the sound of several diesel engines became audible. Maddy laughed as both Lizzie and Billie banged into each other in their effort to get to the front window to see if they were the trucks that they were interested in. The joy in their gasps was heard in the office as the Powell parade of ranch hands, relatives, and neighbors all rode into town in the beds of three duallies. Lizzie got to the door first quickly followed by Billie. She tried to calm her breathing down. She reminded herself that she was in public and Jackson may not appreciate her attacking him the moment she laid eyes on him after so long apart. She lost sight of Lizzie, who had broken out into a run to find the object of her interest. Billie felt her filmy dress swirl around her calves as she made her way through the crowd of people who were congratulating the Rugged Hill Ranch family as though they were conquering heroes. All of a sudden, time stood still, and just like in the movies, the people parted and she saw him. He stood about a half a block away in the middle of the street. Billie no longer heard the voices around her and didn't see the flashing lights from Nat Winston's patrol car controlling the traffic. She just heard her heartbeat as she locked gazes with a very hungry-looking man. She felt starved herself as she took him in visually. He looked tan and tired but had a predatory look on his face that made her begin to trickle juices from her feminine parts as if on command. He wore the heavy cable-knit fisherman's sweater that she had bought him for the holidays. He stood out, not only because of his hulking height but also because he was the only man not wearing a cowboy pearl snap shirt and belt buckle. What he wore made him look like a man who wanted her to notice that he missed her. Boy, did she miss him.

With trembling knees she started for him first, willing her legs to continue to move forward. Her breathing hitched as she felt her heart pounding in her chest and her body begin to hum with arousal at the sight of his. Electric sensations started to bounce around her belly and groin from anticipation of what would happen when they reached each other. Jackson stood at the other end of Main Street like a gunfighter in an old west shoot-out.

Jackson almost couldn't believe his eyes. She was here and looking so gorgeous it took his breath away. He had finally admitted to himself by the third week away from her that he loved her. Loved her desperately. He knew the other men wanted to kill him for his ill tempers that particular realization had caused him while they were up in the line shacks. He spent his days working himself to the bone, but she was always in his thoughts.

It was the nights that had been the worst kind of torture. No matter how exhausted he was, sleep was difficult in coming. Every night he lay on his bunk, the sounds of other men's snores in his space, and there he was, hard as a rock and in pain. Every damn night. For her. He missed her laugh, her loving looks, her kisses, her cooking, and her cunt. He thought he would never make it. He felt frustrated that he had finally fallen in love, truly and desperately in love, and now couldn't be with her.

Now, as he gazed at her hungrily, it felt like all his blood had rushed to his cock. He felt himself harden with such urgency that he almost bent over from its painful surge against his clothes. He needed her, right now. He began to walk toward the most amazing woman he had ever met. He knew then that he would never want another. His gaze never left her face as he took her in. The dark-red dress she wore ignited his already-heated body to boiling. It was a V-neck but showed only a delicate hint of cleavage. It was cinched at the waist with a wide, black belt and had a flowing skirt that fluttered in the breeze as she, too, walked toward him. He read her facial expression as a mixture of excitement, longing, and lust. It was his favorite cocktail. His body tightened with further hunger as he watched her abundant breasts bounce as she made her way to him. He felt consumed by a surge of possessiveness while taking in her raw sensuality. She is mine, he thought. Forever, she will be mine. The wind blew her skirts against her legs so much that he could see the outline of the firm thighs that he knew were coated in cream just for him. His mouth began to water but it was his heart that really held his attention. He stopped walking as he felt almost faint from the rush of emotion he felt at seeing her.

He just stood still and opened his arms wide for her to come to him. Billie didn't need any other encouragement. Uncaring of who saw her or what anyone else thought, she gathered her skirts in her hand and took off in a run. The huge smile that appeared on his face warred with the obvious lust that he did nothing to hide. His huge erection was tenting his jeans and he evidently didn't care who took notice of it other than her. She stopped right in front of him and let out a sigh of pleasure as the scent of his cologne swirled around her for the first time in almost seven weeks.

Jackson was the first to break the silence. "Baby." He took one more step to her, laid his hands lightly on her shoulders, and leaned down to kiss her upturned lips gently. He felt as they both shuddered with the electricity that chaste kiss had rocketed between them. With no further preamble, Jackson bent and slipped one arm behind her back and the other under her knees, effectively swinging her high up into his arms. His lips again descended to hers but this time with much more determination. He swooped down to cover her mouth with his.

Billie felt like her blood had turned to liquid fire as his tongue swept into her dark recesses to taste and torture her. She felt him groan like a man in pain as he plundered her moist opening again and again. She felt like he was starving man and she was to be his meal. Billie returned his passion, readily mewling in her delight.

"Jackson, oh, Jackson. You are here, really here. I missed you so." Billie ripped her mouth away to cry out against his.

Jackson, ignoring the hoots and catcalls as he made his way to Billie's office, tightened his hold on her sumptuous body. He longed to throw her up against the wall of the sheriff's office and sink into her warm, wet heat. Unfortunately, he also knew that Sly Mulligan would likely throw his ass in jail for daring to deface his office unless he, too, was a part of it.

Jackson continued making his way to her office while trying to disregard the feel of her breast that was pressed up against his chest or her soft lips that were torturing him by placing soft, feathery kisses up the side of his neck. He kept hearing her sigh after she took a deep breath. She had mentioned many times to him how his scent drove her wild at the same time making her feel comfortingly safe. It made her soft sighs that much more precious to him. He felt his cock pulse at the knowledge that she felt safe in his arms. He pitched a fit when he heard from Troy and his father what had happened last night. He would take care of it, later. Much later.

He leaned down as they got to the front door of the office and opened the door. Without pausing in his movements, he shut it again and heard the locks click. He turned the lights out as he made his way silently back to her private office and shut the door. Once inside, he just shut his eyes for a moment and nuzzled her neck affectionately. Since his eyes were shut, he felt rather than saw her clasp his face in her hands and pull his sensual mouth back down to hers.

He felt as she wound her slim arms around his neck and melted into the kiss. Jackson's stomach jumped as her lips ran along the plump lower fold of his and caused him to hiss. He deepened the kiss momentarily by thrusting his tongue into her mouth, trying to devour her with his passion. He sat on the arm of her dark-brown leather couch, shifting to clasp at her buttocks. He had a look of rapture as he less than gently groped at her, wishing it were her naked skin.

Billie could sense his barely restrained arousal and decided to ignite it further. With an almost desperate intention, she ran her hands over his chest, reveling in the feel of his muscled strength. She shifted to stroke his arms, practically coming from the raw power she felt in his colossal biceps. It had her dripping from her pussy in such gushes that she was sure the back of her dress was soaked wet from it. As Jackson lifted his face from hers, she could see the dark carnality of his need. She was sure that he could smell her arousal from his position if not feel it as well. Billie felt swept away with waves of her own raw need for Jackson. Like a woman possessed, she felt herself pull the fabric of her skirts up her legs to bare her thighs to his heated gaze. She felt her body shiver with arousal as his hands roughly skimmed up and down her legs as though trying to brand her as his again, reacquainting them their softness and shape. She moaned at the sensations that his less than gentle handling evoked. She threw her head back in ecstasy as she felt him yank her skirts to her waist and her soft mound was bared to his gaze.

Jackson felt crazed with the need to bury himself in her welcoming body. He needed to remind himself that she was his and he could take her right now. Without pause, he ran two fingers through her lower lips to find her drenched with her cream, indicating her desperate need to fuck him as well. He thrust both fingers up her tight channel while consuming her mouth again with his. They were both panting with need as he ripped his mouth away from hers and swiftly stood up.

Billie felt a momentary pang of disappointment before he spun her away from him. Her dismay was immediately quelled as she felt cool air hit her bottom as he wrenched her skirts up over her back while he pressed her chest down and into the arm of the couch. There was a popping sound as he ripped his jeans open, causing Billie to close her eyes in anticipation. The only other sound in the room was their uneven, rough breathing and the moans they made as they pleasured each other. She felt the head of his mammoth cock briefly against her flooded pussy and then screamed in pleasure as he plunged roughly and deeply into her depths.

"Fuck. Oh god, baby, I'm sorry but I fucking need to take you and I am not going to be gentle about it."

"Take me, Jackson. Any way you need to, but please, just take me. I don't want to wait another second for it," Billie gasped out.

Without hesitation Jackson ran his hands up to her breasts and cupped them within his hot hands. He began a rough rhythm of plunging almost violently in and all the way out of her dripping depths. She could feel his fingers pinching her nipples painfully, twisting, and releasing. Jackson used his teeth to nip her neck as he kissed and sucked the exposed skin.

He was drowning in the taste and feel of her lush body as he slammed into her again and again. He felt her tighten and moan as he rolled over her sensitive spot. He slid one hand down and began to rub her clit with his callused fingers. His hand's skin, abrasive from weeks of outside living, brought delicious shards of pleasure to race through her body as his fingers rolled and pinched her nub. His thrusts became so hard that the couch banged into the far wall as he felt her back arch, indicating her impending orgasm.

She suddenly came so fiercely that her channel tightened around his cock like a steel cage. He heard her wail of pleasure as his body, too, fell under its own wave of ecstasy. His hand at her breast clamped down as he lifted his head and ground out his own roars of the most extreme pleasure. His body convulsed as he spurted out his seed against her womb for endless seconds.

She lay there, happily trapped beneath his gargantuan, sweaty body, feeling taken and like she couldn't catch her own breath. Jackson seemed to be having his own troubles slowing down his ragged breathing as they both descended back down to earth from the pleasurable heights they had attained. Billie felt a feminine sense of fulfillment as she felt his seed run out of her onto her thighs.

Jackson laid his cheek on her back and murmured, "I feel better."

Billie let out a laugh and answered him. "I'm glad, Jackson." She turned over her shoulder to smile at him. "I missed you so desperately, honey, but I think you might have just broken me with that hot monkey sex. That was a medically unexplainable amount of pleasure you gave me, Mr. Powell. What the heck was that?"

He felt her shiver as he slid himself out of her flooded pussy and laid the two of them down on her couch while facing each other.

"That was love, baby," he said without breaking eye contact with her. He saw her blink almost disbelievingly at him so he repeated it again. "Billie, I love you. I cannot believe that I waited this long to give voice to my feelings, but I am in crazy fucking love with you. Every single part of you."

He heard as Billie let out a gasp and then to Jackson's horror she broke down into gut-wrenching sobs. He clutched her to his body as she let out a torrent of hot tears against his chest. Not completely sure of what caused her emotional response, he tried to soothe her by running his hand over her back to her ass and then back up again.

Jackson felt Billie take several deep breaths and let out a small laugh as her body obviously reacted deliciously every time he cupped the soft skin of her behind in his grasp.

Jackson figured that he was onto something so he slid her skirts up her thigh. He proceeded to run his hand up the back of one to grasp her at her naked ass and pull her into the loving curve of his groin. They both moaned from the sensation of his still rock-hard cock pressing against her soaked lips. His hand rhythmically squeezed and caressed the soft skin of her cheeks, while his brain struggled to figure out why she was so distraught at his declaration.

"I am so–sor–sorry, Jackson," she said through her tears. "I just need a moment to calm down. You said that you loved me. I cannot believe it. Please say it again."

Jackson looked down at her tenderly and repeated it. "Baby, I am so deeply in love with you. You had better love me, too, because there is no way I am going to live this down at Sunday dinners if you don't.

My heart would be broken into a million pieces and the boys would torture me with it until the end of time or when my mother killed them."

Billie again let out a small laugh and smiled up into his adoring face. "I have to tell you the truth, Jackson." She felt him tense up momentarily. "I struggled with my feelings for a long time but not because of what you might think. We both have confessed before that we were falling for each other. I am so sorry I lied to you. I wasn't falling Jackson. When I fell from the roof the day we met, I know in the depths of my soul that I fell for you then. I was in love with you from that first day. Contrary to all my previous experiences and considering the limitation of my feelings in my marriage to Matthew, I was completely and overwhelmingly in love with you from the start. I tried to ignore it and fight it off, but you Powell men are so overpowering. I love you. I love you with all my heart."

Jackson hugged her tightly to his chest and kissed the top of her head. They lay there like that for quite a while, savoring the glow of newly exchanged love. They both were running their hands over each other's bodies with the newfound certainty of each other's feelings. Jackson whispered firmly his favorite word into Billie's ear. "Mine." As always, she felt her pussy tighten in response to blatant communication of his ownership. It might be considered sexist, archaic, or machismo but Billie didn't care. She loved the idea of belonging to Jackson. In fact, now that their personal confessions were out of the way and he didn't have to ever leave her until next calving season, she wished it were forever.

As though he read her mind, he said, "Mine, baby. You are all mine."

Billie looked up into his eyes and saw the dark, predatory mood start to emanate from his facial expression. He looked at her with a possessive gleam and a devilish grin.

Billie suddenly felt a little overly possessive herself and decided that she wanted to mark her territory in the most primitive way possible.

Jackson watched her as Billie narrowed her own gaze, allowing Jackson to watch as she slid off the couch onto the floor in front of him. On her knees, she moved in front of his rock-hard six-pack abs that were currently concealed by his sweater. She ran her gaze over him, from the top of his head to his cable-knit-covered chest. She licked her lips in anticipation as she visually took in his again hardened cock that rose deliciously from his unzipped jeans to pulse against his lower belly. Her eyes drifted down to his steely muscled thighs and calves back up again to meet his gaze.

As though he realized her intent, Jackson laid his head down, never letting his sensual gaze leave her face. With her lower lip plumped out in invitation, Billie leaned over him and blew a light breath over his erection. She watched in fascination as it responded by pulsing up for a moment in response. This time she blew on it again, following it with running the tip of her tongue around the head down to the base. She heard his soft groan as he communicated his enjoyment. Billie grew bolder and decidedly needier as she looked momentarily once more into his heated eyes before sucking him into her hot, warm mouth at the way to the root. She felt as his hips flexed up, aiding his cock's descent into heaven. She began to lick and suck him in the way that she knew drove him crazy with lust as she started to twist her soft hand up and down his shaft in a twisting motion.

Jackson felt the pleasure of her tongue and hot lips slide over him as she attended to his cock. He knew she was acknowledging his ownership of her when he said "mine." It made more blood surge to his already weeping erection and his arrogance swell. She was his and he knew that he wasn't the only one who thought that was perfect. He shut his eyes as she rolled her tongue underneath the sensitive head and felt the tightening of his sac. She must have felt the change, too, because she began a deep sucking motion, forcing the full length of his cock against the back of her throat. He threaded his fingers through her hair to hold her head in place as he took over thrusting roughly into her welcoming mouth. His body suddenly felt like it was being stabbed with a hot, pleasurable knife as electric pulses of pleasure rocketed through him as he ejaculated streams of cum down her gorgeous throat. He heard himself growl out his pleasure as it bounced off the walls of her office. He met her gaze again, this time his eyes softened in the wake of his intense satisfaction. He pulled her up to him, laying soft kisses over her face and neck.

She lay contentedly in his arms for another twenty minutes before he pulled her up, after straightening both of their clothes. He sincerely hoped no one had been near her office when he had come in her mouth. If someone was near, he knew he had been so loud, they would have assuredly heard from outside. He walked with her, arm in arm, out of the office and into her SUV. Jackson drove them out to her house, ignoring the raunchy texts that everyone was sending him that were wondering sarcastically where he was. Even Hunter and Brody were tormenting them, when they were usually the voice of reason. Well, maybe not Hunter, as he rarely used his voice at all.

Throughout the long night, Jackson pledged his love, not only in words but with his body, again and again to Billie. The shower and bathtub had been the scene of further erotic intimacies until just before dawn. Billie had passed out into another pleasure-induced coma. Jackson lay on her sumptuous bed with her clasped in his arms. He, too, was so tired from the many round of vigorous lovemaking, but couldn't stop reveling in the happiness that she loved him like he loved her. He had even let Madison sleep on the end of the bed, such a joyous mood was he in. Damn, but her dog took up a lot of the bed. He would just have to hold his love while they slept. It was a job he hoped he would be assigned for the rest of their lives and one that he would relish.

Chapter Twenty

Billie woke to beautiful streams of sunlight drifting through her windows. As she stretched and sat up, she was chagrined to realize that she was sore in places and muscles she was unaware she even had. Flashes of yesterday ran deliciously through her vision. It was mostly a blur of their twining tongues and limbs mixed with thrusts and sighs. Billie supposed she must look like the sex goddess that she felt like. Her hair was hopelessly tangled as were the sheets on her bed. Jackson had left another note on his pillow telling her that he would be home for dinner and that he probably would not be able to concentrate today seeing as how his last twelve hours had been a lesson in pleasure and stamina. Billie let out a giggle at the thought that perhaps she had worn out her cowboy. It was a very pleasant memory and one that she hoped to repeat with him again tonight. Her cell phone beeped that a message was coming in. Rolling on her side, Billie propped herself up on an elbow and looked at the screen.

Needed at the office. Got a problem patient here. Julia

Hmm. She looked up from the screen and wondered why Julia was at the office today. They were closed for the next two days. Billie had been looking forward to a relaxing hot bath and making dinner for Jackson. Oh well, she could go into the office, pick up Zeus, and still come home with enough time to make something yummy for her stud service.

That made Billie laugh. Jackson might not appreciate being compared to a huge bull, but he sure would make the sweetest babies. Where the heck the baby thought had come from, Billie had no idea but it definitely had her thinking. If he asked her to marry him, would she do it immediately and if so, would they have children? Billie loved children but with Matthews's illness and the move, she had just supposed it wasn't meant to be for her. It gave her something to think about.

A call to both the office and Julia's cell went unanswered. Billie figured that she must be taking care of office stuff or the patient, as Julia usually could multitask pretty darn well. Perhaps she might lose her award-winning composure if there was a mini Jackson running around her desk, Billie thought amusedly. After a quick shower, Billie jumped into her SUV and drove into town with a silly smile on her face. As she parked herself in front of her office, she quickly texted Maddy to let her know that she would be in to pick up her big baby after taking care of a patient. Maddy was proving herself to be true kindred spirit, quietness and all. Billie read her wiseass comeback with a chuckle. She wanted to know if Billie meant the dog or Jackson. Billie laughed to herself. That woman was showing that she was really kind of funny, once she began coming out of her shell. There was way more of Madelyne Daniels than met the eye.

After jumping out of her car, Billie walked up to her front door and was confused as to why it was locked. Did Julia just send the patient onto the hospital without calling her to let her know? That wasn't like her at all. Billie suddenly gave a start as she felt a rough hand pull her back against a hard body. It was a smelly body that was in desperate need a shower. She felt her breath catch as something very sharp was placed directly against her side as the fetid breath of whoever owned the stink assailed her senses.

"Please don't make this difficult, Doc, by making a single move or sound, okay? I am really kinda pissed off, you see, and it wouldn't really take much encouragement to slice your insides open. Please take two steps back with me and let's get in your Rover."

Billie nodded but felt the icy sensation of fear prickle up her spine. Len Drexel. Just when she thought that life would allow her some calm and peace, this waste of DNA had to keep targeting her in his crazy world. What the heck do they say about being kidnapped? Get in the car quietly or scream and kick? It isn't like they teach this stuff in medical school and the place that she lived in New York never even had a burglary, so she was at a temporary loss. Deciding that keeping her cool and not upsetting the knife-wielding, smelly lunatic was her best option, she handed him the keys. Praying that someone saw her with him and called either Sly or Nat was all that she had to go on for the moment. She dropped her purse deliberately, which set off a stream of quiet cursing from her deranged captor. The knife stabbed into her slightly, causing her to cry out in pain. Billie became really frightened now at the sick look on Len's face as his hand clenching on her arm tightened. She could feel the trickle of blood running down her belly and knew that there was enough to stain the front of her cream sweater.

"You fucking whore. Do anything stupid like that again and I will just end this here and now. I don't have nothing to lose at this point, you raggedy bitch. Gwen was right, you are more trouble than you are worth. I think making you suffer should be entertaining. Jackson is going to be a bit put out when he finds your used body. Or maybe he won't. Perhaps he is a bit tired of you already? He got bored with Gwen mighty quickly so who's to say he would even care if I 'borrowed' you for a bit? He didn't even ask you to marry him, like Gwen. She is a little bitch, too. I might even let you watch me take out Gwen first instead of the other way around. She wanted to see you writhe under my cock, but I don't need her as an audience. However, drop another fucking thing, and they will have to power wash this sidewalk to get you off of it!" Len spat out viciously as he exchanged his knife for a wicked-looking handgun.

Billie couldn't help the tremble that ran through her as he verbalized his sadistic thoughts. His hatred of Jackson must really run pretty deep to push him this far. Jackson loved her. Nothing this vile man could say would change her confidence in that. At least it all made sense now. Since that first meeting when Jackson had taken her away for lunch, this wacko probably felt it was more of the same old same old. Why would Gwen help this sicko?

"Please, Len. I will come quietly. Calm down." She was going to try to keep him talking.

* * * *

Jackson looked at his brothers and cousins. They all looked back him with unconcealed amusement. "Does anyone's ass hurt? You know like in a cramp that possibly came from a guy slapping his junk around too much?" Brody called out the question looking like he was having serious difficulties trying not to laugh.

"Nope, but I can guess that some of us are more, dehydrated, than others after losing too much body fluid since yesterday," was Troy's unhelpful reply.

Jackson couldn't even get mad at the moron saddle brigade that was made up of male family members. Instead, he continued to bait them with the same silly grin that he had been wearing all day.

Ben even joined the fray. "The way I remember it, Jackson almost got himself arrested for public lewdness at his display in front of the police station. Sly was going to have shackled him, but I think that he has a thing for watching and was enjoying the show. Or perhaps it's the shackles. Nope, probably both!" He laughed.

Now that was a distinct possibility, Jackson thought. Sly definitely had some kinks of his own, which were okay by him. He just didn't want Billie to be the star attraction in any of the good sheriff's spank bank images. He felt his phone buzz and smiled with anticipation at reading a message from his medical goddess.

"What the fuck is wrong with that woman?" Jackson blurted out. Everyone swung their heads in his direction to see why he would be so upset with Billie. "She wants me to meet her up at the hunting cabin, like I would ever meet her again in public much less in private!

Some women are just psycho guys." He looked around as all eyes looked at him questioningly.

"What is wrong with meeting her up there? She just wants more of the Powell pumping, man. No need to get mad over it. You haven't ever had a problem with giving out too much sex, Jackson. I never heard you get upset over the idea of fucking the brains out of a gorgeous woman two days in a row. Excuse the disrespectful reference to the doc, please," Brody said.

"Not Billie, you pile of cow manure, Gwen! She was the one who just texted me," Jackson yelled. Just then, Ben's phone rang. As he answered, he got a concerned look on his face and put his hand over the phone.

"Jackson, do you know where Doc is today? It's Lizzie and she is kinda concerned. She has Dr. Daniels in the café with her and Billie was supposed to pick up Zeus by now. Her office is locked up tight but they found her lipstick and some other stuff on the ground outside. Now they are beginning to get concerned," Ben said quietly.

Jackson felt unease start to spread through his system. Billie was never late for anything, ever, and she sure as hell wouldn't leave Zeus in the clinic a second longer than necessary. "Tell them to sit tight by the phone. I think I need some of you guys to come with me up to the cabin."

"We will all go," they heard Cole answer softly. "I'm gonna let Hunter and Uncle Bill know where we are going and why." The men all rode swiftly back to the barn and piled into two trucks with each man sporting a rifle, quickly letting Florence know what was going on. She surprised them by reaching into her purse and pulling out a small gun.

She handed it to Brody while quickly telling him it was loaded and to call as soon as they heard anything and that she would call Sly and Nat immediately. He looked at her perplexingly, wondering where the hell she had gotten a handgun.

As though reading his mind, she answered his unspoken question. "Donny" was all she had to say. Ah, that made sense. That man was crazy about his mother and would do anything to keep her safe. He would have to talk about this later.

* * * *

Billie was trying to hold it together as she sat in the passenger seat of her car. She tried not looking at the disgusting waste of a human life that was abducting both her and her vehicle for nefarious reasons.

Stay calm. He won't overreact if I don't. Think, Billie, don't feel, think. What would Jackson want me to do?

She struggled to think calmly as her heart beat out of her chest with the threat of not only death but sexual assault. What the heck would Jackson want her to do? Go karate kid on him? No. She didn't know any martial arts. Scream her head off? No. He didn't like when people raised their voices. Darn it. Her normally reliable brain suddenly decided that fear was the one emotion that would short it out! Suddenly, a thought did come to her. Jackson would just say, "Talk to me, baby, then I will fuck you senseless and make it feel all better."

Hey! Although the second part of that thought sounded nice, it wasn't going to be too helpful to her at the moment. However, the first part was possibly going to save her. Keeping her right hand lowered below the side of her seat and subsequently eye level, she began texting Jackson by feel of the buttons.

911. Len taking me to your cabin. Help. Armed with gun. Hurry.

That man was a one-man wrecking machine all by himself. She couldn't imagine what a whole passel of Powells could do. Please let him get to her in time. Len shot her a glance that wasn't quite as vicious as his previous mood.

"Look, Doc, I kinda feel almost badly that you have to be the one in the middle of my long-awaited revenge against Jackson.

Unfortunately for you, Doc, you are a hot piece of ass that makes my mouth water and I can't stand to fuck his other bitch, Gwen, for another second. She sucks at it. Funny, she used to tell me how lousy Jackson was with his dick. They are both unnecessary sacks of shit and I plan on doing away with both of them. Hmm, that gives me an idea. Gwen hates you and Jackson. By now, I am sure that she texted him so there is a paper trail leading to her cell. I think after I kill all of you, I should be safe after I put the gun in her hand! What do you think, Doc? Will they buy that?"

Billie had remained quiet until that point, not even meeting his eyes. She felt nauseated every time that they made contact so she looked at her driver's side door instead. What did she think? He was a psychotic wacko that she wouldn't mind castrating! That is what she thought. However, if she voiced her true opinion, it probably wouldn't aid in her attempt at keeping him from damaging her person. She had to keep him away from her until Jackson could find her.

"I hope you don't mind, Len, but I will leave all planning of this event up to you. You seem to know what you are doing and must be doing a good job, as I am your hostage in my own car at the moment." There, Billie thought. Butter up his vomitous ego. Maybe he could daydream of how amazing she thought he was and he might become distracted. Distracted enough for her to do what? She had no idea. He was too big and strong to fight and take him down, but she was sure that she could outthink him. Perhaps that was the key. He was a man after all. Maybe if she appealed to his vanity and his buffoon-like mentality, she could win. She looked in her purse for what just might become her salvation. She had dropped so many things on the sidewalk earlier, but thankfully that didn't include her cell and hopefully not what she needed. Yes! Her hand connected with what she had been searching for and suddenly she felt a bit more confident. She could do this.

"Len, um, may I ask you a question?"

He looked at her again with an annoyed expression. "What is it?" he barked.

Almost losing some of her newfound false bravado, she met his now-angry gaze. "Do you think that Gwen is an attractive woman?"

"What the fuck do you want to know that for?"

"Well, other than we both have been involved with Jackson, I was wondering if our opposite looks might, um, interest you. You know, like variety." Oh please let him continue to be an arrogant jerk and have him just think that she was a nosy, idiot woman. She was going to try to mastermind the greatest and only manipulation of her life.

Len got an odd look on him now and his body seemed less tense to Billie. "You mean, do I like that you two sluts are like night and day? Hell yeah. I got enough to go around. Why? You suddenly want some of this before I use you to devastate that asshole?"

Blech. He started to look her up and down with lust starting to enter his eyes. He let his gaze rest on her heaving bosom. She almost took a chance and jumped out of the car as he let one hand grab her breast. His fingers were painful and Billie was filled with disgust as they bit into her soft flesh. The road had begun to wind into the mountain. If Billie wasn't pretty positive that she would break a whole lot more than her arm, she would try to jump at feeling his nauseating touch. *Stay calm. Jackson will fix this. Stay calm.*

Len looked at her now with definitive interest. Billie could feel the bile rise in her throat. She pulled away and leaned against the window.

"Nice tits you got there, Doc. I am not sure if I should fuck them or your pussy first."

"Um, Len. Let me talk to Gwen, please. I might have an idea that you may enjoy. Perhaps we could work something out." Billie cringed as she choked out the words.

"I seriously doubt it but you can try. After all the trouble I went through to set this up, shooting your dog and all. You do owe me something," Len leeringly stated.

Thankfully, the cabin came into view. It was a charming small log production and under other circumstances, she would love to spend some private time here. Just not with her present revolting company. In a blink of an eye, she found herself catching her breath as the gun was once again leveled at her chest.

"Time's up, Doc. I have to say that I am really gonna enjoy fucking you raw. Get out of the car now, please." He walked to the front of the Rover and started rubbing his erection through his jeans. Billie almost retched but caught herself as Gwen opened the door cautiously at first. Anger surged through Billie like she had never known, replacing the fear that was coursing through her. She was going to make it and when she did, she was going to never let a day go by without kissing Jackson on his lips and knowing the taste of his cock on her tongue. Yes, that gave her a better visual.

"Geez, Len, it took you long enough to get here. What the fuck were you doing as it doesn't look like you did Miss Priss here yet?" Gwen gave Billie a confidently vindictive stare.

Out of nowhere, surprising both Billie and Gwen, Len quickly lunged forward and backhanded Gwen so hard, she spun and hit the ground, hard. Billie ran to Gwen. The doctor in her needed to help no matter how undeserving this icky woman was. She gently lifted Gwen's head into her lap and used her sleeve to stem the blood that was now flowing from her mouth.

"Shut up, you dumb bitch!" Len screamed at Gwen who was now trembling in Billie's arms. "You are not running the show here. In fact, I am going to fuck both of you and then kill you, too. You are such a stupid whore to think I would hold to any deal with you. You would fuck any man with a pulse and a penis. I should just kill you right here, right now."

Gwen started to cry and was gasping for breath under the weight of her terror as Len now directed the gun on her. Billie herself took a deep breath and forged ahead.

"Len, Len, wait, please. You don't need to kill either of us. Let us show you how we can calm you, together. Maybe we can please you enough that you might want to, say, keep us." She prayed his hormones would overcome his common sense. She closed her eyes in revulsion as she let go of Gwen and stood to face Len. With trembling fingers, she started to unbutton her blouse while desperately trying to look like she wanted him to be interested in her. Ugh, men really did only think carefully about one thing. Len looked like a bomb could go off on his head and it wouldn't have distracted him from eating up the vision of what she looked like as she revealed her breasts encased within a lovely lacey bra. Yuck, the first thing she would do after Jackson saved her and had sex with her was to burn this bra and thong, pronto!

"Len, let's go inside and have a drink. I think we know where this is going to go, no?" Billie tried really, really hard to give him a come-hither look but wasn't sure it was believable as she wanted to take a stick and poke out his eyes so he couldn't look at what she considered Jackson's property anymore.

Len shifted his glazed glance from the whimpering, sniffing woman who lay cringing on the ground to the pretending-to-be-confidant woman with her breasts hanging out of her shirt. Lust overtaking any sense of self preservation, Len put the gun down. He rubbed his hands against his crotch and licked his lips in anticipation.

"Why the fuck not?" he murmured.

Chapter Twenty-One

The men riding in the truck containing Jackson were solemnly silent. Jackson sat in the passenger seat with rage and tension radiating out of his body. His father leaned over from the backseat and gently rubbed his shoulder for a short moment before leaning back and sighing. Jackson felt none of the usual comfort that his dad normally provided him. He wanted to kill something, or rather, someone. How was he supposed to sit here calmly while Hunter drove at breakneck speed up the winding roads with the other truck of men in close pursuit?

"Hunter, stop driving like a fucking sissy and floor it, man!" he growled out in his intended direction.

Jackson knew that Hunter deliberately didn't even respond or make eye contact with the fire-breathing dragon that he was acting like, barking orders from the seat next to him.

Hunter had known Jackson for years and knew that his calm, controlled veneer was being mangled at this moment. Jackson never had his feathers ruffled, not when his uncle passed away, although incredibly saddened, and definitely not with his divorce from the Gweninator.

Wow, he thought, Jackson never doubted that any man in Stony Creek would give his right nut to love that woman, but knew that Hunter must be aware of how in love he really was. She was smart, beautiful, articulate, funny, and just an amazing person. Jackson knew that Hunter was very upset by the current situation, as he cared very much for not only Billie but him as well.

"Jackson, I think it might be best if you hang back and let us take the lead. You aren't in any shape to be objective here, brother," Ben tried to reason from the backseat. Jackson was unmoved by Ben's comment as he sat stonily still in his seat. Every man became tense as the trucks pulled up just short of the cabin. It had been forty-five minutes since Jackson had received the text from Billie alerting them as to her destination as well as Len being armed. Forty-five fucking minutes. No one knew what they would find and the air was so thick with the strain you could cut it with a knife. The men split up into groups of two and surrounded the small cabin. They were to wait for Sly's signal that he needed back up. Jackson wanted to storm into the cabin and kill that asshole. He didn't even care. The loss of Len's life wouldn't mean a thing to him since he had his love and obviously was terrorizing her in some fashion. He kept a clamp on his thoughts as he refused to imagine how the bastard was either hurting or frightening her. It wouldn't help her any and wouldn't serve him any good in not trying to stay calm. Both Sly and Nat had their guns drawn and were edging toward the only door. Sly indicated that he didn't hear anything from inside, causing shivers of fear to envelope Jackson's soul.

As if on cue, the front door slowly cracked open. Jackson and the others hefted their rifles onto their shoulders in sync. Jackson held his breath as his heart felt like it was going to pound out of his chest. *Please let her be all right, please god, please. I am going to marry her on the spot and never let her out of my sight again if only she could be all right.*

A small, feminine hand softly pushed the door open from the inside. Jackson let his rifle fall from his shoulder as he took off in an all-out run as Billie came into view. She flashed Sly and Nat a brilliant smile as she took notice of her Neanderthal running like a wild maniac in her direction. Jackson grabbed her up and ran off with her to safety behind one of the trucks.

She hung on to him for dear life as she prayed that she hadn't just survived one ordeal to start another as her love ran way too fast with her precariously hanging in his embrace so far from the ground. Billie just breathed in his sexy scent as he clutched her almost painfully tight to his chest.

Jackson couldn't even formulate words for a moment. It was Bill, who came to supervise the emotional release that his son was sure to have at any moment, who was the voice of reason.

"Honey, are we sure glad to see you. You have blood on you, sweetheart. Can you show me where you are hurt?"

Billie looked over in confusion. She wasn't really hurt. Before she could get any words out, Jackson gently put her down and began running his hands all over her, right in front of his father.

"Jackson, I am not hurt, baby." No verbal response.

She tried to take his hands off her rear. "Jackson, listen to me. I am not really injured honey, just a scratch, I promise." The look on his face told her that he was close to losing control. She noted that he continued to not acknowledge any of her comments. She frowned as Bill began to laugh as Jackson pulled the front of her shirt out to look down at her chest to assure himself that the blood was not coming from her gorgeous, plump breasts. She knew that Jackson would view that as a tragedy if they were damaged. Bill wisely and quickly had turned his back as Jackson had started to pull up her skirt hem to see if there were any, ah, feminine injuries.

"Jackson!" she very firmly yelled out. That got his attention.

"If you ever get in a vehicle with another man other than me, I swear that I am going to spank that sweet ass of yours for a week straight and you will never sit down again in your life! I have never been so scared in my life, baby!"

Billie nodded only in the effort to help him calm down.

"Where is all this blood coming from, baby?" he gently managed to growl out. He pulled her into his arms and began to softly rub his hands from her head down to her ass and back up again. Over and over she watched as Jackson tried to reassure himself that she was okay. Bill moved closer and put his hands on both their backs in a protective, fatherly way as he let out a sigh.

"It's mostly not my blood. It's Gwen's. She is okay, though." She figured that he would find the place that Len's knife had cut her anyway, so she didn't try to hide it from him. That was all she could manage as the intensity of the situation began to crash around her. Suddenly, Billie realized that she was safe and sagged against Jackson's strong, comfortingly hard body.

Jackson tried to suck her in as he bent over, pulling her now-sobbing body as tightly as possible against his. He saw his father reached over and took the gun he had just noticed from her shaking hand.

Sly and Nat had just walked back out of the cabin, guns holstered. "All clear. They are dead," he yelled out.

The men ran over to Billie and Jackson to see for themselves that she was okay. She barely felt that loving pats that the men gave her and Jackson. Bill cleared his throat out loud and decided to handle things from here on out to calm Billie down.

"Um, honey. You want to tell us how you managed to get his gun? I am just gonna die from waiting to hear this one!"

A loud rumble of male laughter encircled Billie and Jackson. Billie looked up at Bill and Sly with watery eyes. She knew she shouldn't care at the moment but she had to rub her eyes with a non-bloody section of her shirt. She must have had raccoon eyes with the mascara that had to be running down her face.

"I have never been so scared, but somehow I got control of myself," she began.

"Go on, baby," Jackson said, starting to rejoin the world of the living as she explained what had happened.

She looked up into his gorgeous face, one that she hadn't been totally sure that she would ever see again. "I tried to convince Len to let me go but that plan wasn't going very successfully so I moved on to plan B."

Jackson let himself move away from her a few inches so he could look directly into her eyes. He had a sneaking suspicion that she did something he was not going to love at first.

"Plan B was to buy myself more time by convincing Len that I might be willing to, you know, instead of him being, well, forcing himself on me." The men around began throwing around curses and expressing their anger. Only Sly and Bill remained calm. Sly asked her politely, if she could, to please continue.

"Well, I unbuttoned my blouse...and I convinced him to let us all have a drink together." Jackson took off verbally with a string of vocabulary that would have had his mother slapping him for a year, but Billie figured that he was allowed to say whatever he wanted to. She had been terrified and revolted at the same time while she had to bare some of her intimate self to that slimeball.

"Go ahead, honey, tell me the rest," Sly encouraged her. Sly himself was a big, muscular man, intimidating like Hunter because he was quiet more often than not. He normally had a great sense of humor and was a gentle man. It showed in how he encouraged her to proceed.

"I just tried to do what I thought Jackson would want me to do. Think and talk. So that is what I did. It saved my life."

Jackson's eyes softened and didn't even bother to hide the love and warmth that was emanating from them as he listened patiently.

"While Gwen and Len went out to argue outside for a moment, I just..."

"You just what, baby?" Jackson asked, taking her chin in his hand.

When he got that look, Billie went a little weak and felt compelled to do whatever this vital man wanted. "I took the sleeping pills that I still had in my purse from when Matthew died. I haven't needed to take them since I moved out here and met you, honey. So I just quickly crushed them up and put them in their beers. Apparently, revenge against you made them very thirsty. They aren't dead, just sound asleep."

The only sound was the wind dancing through the trees. All the men just looked at her in shocked disbelief. Nat went and confirmed that they were indeed breathing. He came back out grinning from ear to ear letting everyone know that he had slapped cuffs on the sleeping beauties.

Sly shook out of the shocked stupor first and yelled over to Jackson, "Hell, Jackson, if you act like an idiot much longer and don't marry this woman the first chance you get, well, then I am going to!"

Jackson held Billie close to him as though his life depended on it. The gaze in his eyes told her that his terror and wrath had been exchanged for undisguised love and adoration. It was so naked for everyone to see, it made her heart flutter.

"There will be zero chance of that happening, Sly. She is mine."

Chapter Twenty-Two

Jackson lay with his hands behind his head in the tangled disarray of Billie's bedsheets. After what was an endless marathon of crazy loving throughout the night and a good portion of the morning, he amazingly didn't even feel tired, just really, really relaxed. He couldn't exactly say the same for his poor bedmate. She lay curled into his side, breathing deeply against his chest where her head lay. Mine, he thought. He had almost lost the greatest thing to ever happen to him in his life. There was no way that was ever going to happen to him again. She was going to have to give up medicine and ride double with him on Lachlan every day to tend the ranch. She was never going to be more than a foot from his body ever again! He knew that she might protest a bit at his happy little utopia-like dream but he found it amusing and comforting. He inwardly shuddered at how close the psycho twins had come to taking away this remarkably intelligent, sexy, and gorgeous woman from him. He lowered his arms to wrap around her in comfort, probably more so for him than for her.

Jackson allowed himself to indulge in what he referred to as his own pity party for a moment as he reflected on that.

Suddenly he heard something that actually concerned him, ripping him from his negative recollections. His crazy nemesis and waste-of-two-years-of-his-life ex-wife were in jail, but he tensed up as he heard noises that made him more wary than a crazed man armed with a gun.

He knew he was hearing the sounds of his mother, aunt, and who knows what other women who were downstairs making enough food and noise to wake the dead. How the hell had they gotten in here? He would stand down a million Len Drexels any day, but he didn't have the nerve to go downstairs and face all those cackling women. He was pretty sure that they knew why he and Billie were still in bed at eleven a.m. and that they knew that it had nothing to do with her ordeal, directly. He had to laugh to himself.

Just then, Billie snuggled her warm, soft body against his. To his disbelief, he could feel himself getting hard yet again. He didn't think it was possible after six, no maybe seven rounds of incredibly satisfying sex since last night much less the countless number of orgasms he gave his love with his hands, mouth, and cock. It must be true, he thought. The right woman really did give you superhuman strength.

With a devilish glint in his eyes, he leaned down to kiss her forehead, her nose, and both cheeks softly before pressing them to her gorgeous lips. She smiled sleepily against his chest as he open mouth kissed her in the very sensitive spot that was just below her ear, swirling his tongue lightly over the lobe. Jackson shifted over her body as he kissed down the column of her neck, allowing his increasingly heavy breath to blow over his trail of damp kisses. His hands skimmed down her sides, the backs of his callused fingers running from her neck, to the sides of her plump breasts, down to her waist, and back up to gently cup and worship the abundant globes. He allowed his teeth to graze over one erect nipple while he gently pinched the other, both eliciting arousing moans from Billie. He felt almost light-headed as she arched her back in pleasure as he suckled at her breasts. They tasted of feminine delights that had him like a starving man as his first feast as he sucked on one then moved back to pay attention to the other.

Billie felt herself dripping her arousal yet again at his secretive wake-up attack on her body. She felt deliriously high, almost floating as he slid down her body further, kissing and adoring her the whole way. He let out a growl as his mouth brushed over her bare mound, running his tongue along the junctions of each leg to her soaking pussy. She saw his heavenly lips curl into a naughty smile of pure delight as he inhaled her feminine scent. Just then, he dipped his head and thrust his tongue up her tight channel, causing a light squeal from her. Without warning, he began to lave the outside of her wet lips, running his tongue from anus to clit while thrusting three fingers into her welcoming pussy. The rough texture of his tongue on her clit sent sharp bolts of pleasure radiating to her feet. Her back arched off the bed in delight at his attentions that were causing her to writhe in anticipation. Jackson ran his fingers from his other hand down the crack between her cheeks, pausing at her sensitive rosette. Tingles of rapture began to shoot through her as he inserted his index finger deliciously to his second knuckle. She let out a low moan as he began thrusting his finger slowly in and out of her back channel in time with the thrusts and sucking of his tongue. How did he know just how to touch and lick her to bring the maximum amount of pleasure? His reputation was so well deserved.

Jackson's cock was so hard he thought it just might crack and fall off if he didn't get inside of her soon. He sucked her clit into his mouth and furiously began to rub his fingers up into her G-spot with a singular determination. He looked up to see her mouth open in a soundless *O* as she let out a piercing scream of intense pleasure. To Jackson, it seemed to go on and on, until she lay weak and sweating under his ministrations.

Jackson had never tasted anything as sweet as his love. With a purely predatory grin, he wiped the back of his hand across his mouth as his eyes met hers. He then quickly moved up her body to slide into her warmth with one smooth stroke of his erection. He felt scalded by the wet heat of her and immediately began pumping into her dripping pussy.

Billie basked not only in the feeling of being joined intimately with Jackson but at the feel of his hard abs and chest rubbing erotically against hers. She wrapped her long legs around his muscled waist as she felt his hard buttocks clenching with effort as he pummeled into her hot depths. The bed shook with his savage thrusts as he began to groan in pleasure. It was obvious that he intended for her to join him in ecstasy again as he ground his hips in a rotating fashion against her swollen and ultrasensitive clit. His actions sent her into another sharp orgasm as shards of pure delight mixed with a small bite of decadent pain shot through her limbs.

He felt her clench around his hard cock just enough to make him explode as well. Jackson had to clench his teeth at the raw pleasure pounding through his body. He pulsed out streams of his hot cum into his love until he was wrung dry with intense satisfaction. He gently lay his considerable weight down onto her body as they both tried to slow their erratic breathing.

He was aware of the exact moment that he knew she became cognizant of the sounds that were filtering up from the kitchen downstairs. He felt her stiffen and struggle to sit up as she processed what the giggling and bawdy laughter meant.

"Jackson! Did you know that there were people downstairs this whole time? Oh my! I will never be able to show my face again! Who exactly is down there?" she asked from behind her hands, which were covering her face.

Jackson slid himself up to lean against the carved headboard, while pulling her now-rigid but just-pleasured body up into his arms. "Well, let's see. It sounds like my mother and Aunt Florence. I think that Julia is the one down there telling the really dirty jokes and maybe that is the mayor's wife talking with Mabel. See, nothing to worry about," he joked.

Billie shuddered and tried to bury her head under the blanket.

* * * *

It was some time later that Jackson was able to coax her out of the sensuous shower that they took together and forced her to have pity on his growling hunger pains. He led her down the stairs with his wet hair while wearing a shit-eating grin on his face in an effort to try to take the brunt of the attack. No such luck. They were met with hoots and off-colored remarks, however politely offered, about the late hour, the screams that rocked the house, or general air of satisfaction on Jackson's face. The ladies let out peals of laughter at the never-ending blush that graced Billie's face. After a bit, the tone became more emotional as they all took turns kissing and hugging her as they thanked god that she was able to come away from the experience relatively unscathed. Billie hadn't thought she was that upset over the ordeal, but it must have been the overwhelming cascade of love from the women that had her sobbing against Lillian with Florence and the other women crooning soft, motherly comfort to her. It helped. A lot. Jackson stood on the periphery just watching helplessly as Billie broke down and the military action of the women that immediately moved in to help her.

She lifted her watery eyes to hug each woman tightly and then walked over into Jackson's strong embrace. He stroked her back soothingly as his aunt looked at him with a warm smile. It was Julia, however, who brought Billie back to laughing again as she just had to mention that their exact positions were the reason that they were so late in coming out of the bedroom in the first place. One thing led to another, as they all sat around Billie's huge dining room table eating a lavish brunch spread, and soon talk led straight to babies.

"Lillian, you must be so overjoyed at the prospect!" Julia laughed out with glee in her voice.

"What prospect, you crazy woman?" Lillian chuckled back.

With a sideways glance at Billie and Jackson, she said, "Well, the grandchildren, of course!"

An uproar began at the table with questions of how long Billie had been pregnant being tossed around. Jackson looked just as confused as Billie, who shrugged her shoulders and looked to Lillian as she shook her head in denial.

"I think you have finally lost it, old woman," Florence said to Julia.

With a naughty gleam in her eyes she practically crowed out, "With all the noise we heard from upstairs earlier, I am sure that this house will be filled with adorable babies in no time whatsoever! They sounded like they were pros!"

Even Jackson turned a blush now.

Kill me now was all Billie could think.

* * * *

Jackson sat astride Lachlan several weeks later looking at the woman who changed his whole life and healed his heart. She sat on a blanket in the field behind her house wearing a white flowing sundress that was belted to show off her curvy figure. Contentment filled him like never before as he imagined her belly swollen with his babe. He nudged Lachlan's sides as they rode down to his destiny. She looked up to observe him with undisguised love. He climbed down and lay down next to where she sat. As she leaned in to give him a soft kiss, he heard her sigh. He had been teased all day by the other men about how distracted he had been and suffered through their usual vulgar comments. He knew it was time.

"Did you have a good day, baby?" he questioned her.

"I did actually. I baked you some fresh muffins after work and have been relaxing here ever since, waiting for my cowboy to come love me," Billie answered with a smile.

Jackson sat up and took her hand. "Baby, you do know how much I love you, right?"

At her nod, he continued. "I never expected to meet a person like you. I was expecting some man named Bill to move in over here. Little did I know that some crazy woman who fell from the sky would rock my world and capture my heart. I cannot live without you and don't want to try. I don't want to live another day without you. If I could bind you to me physically, I would. However, in lieu of that sort of joining, perhaps you will accept that I promise to adore and protect you forever. I love you with every fiber inside of this dumb cowboy and promise to take care of you until my dying day. I thank god that you were brave enough to move out here all on your own, but you aren't alone anymore."

Billie looked at him with tears starting to course down her cheeks. Jackson leaned over and cupped her face in his hands as they faced each other on their knees.

"Will you marry me, baby?" he asked softly.

Billie let out a gasp and flung herself into his waiting arms. "Yes, yes, and yes!" she cried into his mouth.

From the grove of trees, they heard loud hoots and hollering erupt. Some very loud, masculine voices yelled out, "It's about time, you dumbass" and "It took you long enough." Jackson chuckled into her mouth and held her against him as he slipped a gorgeous two-carat diamond setting onto her finger.

Billie knew she had found her love and her home. They would never be bored and probably never be alone again, judging from the comments being yelled out from the tree line. She heard the answer in her head to the question she had on her drive out to Wyoming. It took all that pain and a long road, but it had led her to her destiny. She knew how she had gotten here. She got here on her journey to find her happiness, she realized laughingly. It wasn't too hard to figure out, after all. She had been destined to find her true self, and, just as luck would have it, Jackson was the one who led the way.

THE END

Siren Publishing, Inc.
www.SirenPublishing.com

Lightning Source UK Ltd.
Milton Keynes UK
UKOW03f1906200813

215693UK00012B/327/P